The Scarlet Coat

Angela K. Couch

The Scarlet Coat

Contact Information: titleadmin@pelicanbookgroup.com

Scripture quotations, unless otherwise indicated are taken from the King James translation, public domain.

Cover Art by *Nicola Martinez*

White Rose Publishing, a division of Pelican Ventures, LLC
www.pelicanbookgroup.com PO Box 1738 *Aztec, NM * 87410

White Rose Publishing Circle and Rosebud logo is a trademark of Pelican Ventures, LLC

Publishing History
First White Rose Edition, 2017
Paperback Edition ISBN 978-1-61116-982-9
Electronic Edition ISBN 978-1-61116-983-6
Published in the United States of America

Dedication

To my father who showed me the way. To my husband
who gave me wings.

What People are Saying

"Angela K Couch brings history to life in this captivating story set during the American Revolution. I fell in love with the characters, silently rooting for them along the way." ~ Sarah Monzon

"Fast-paced historical with an unusual twist. Perfect balance between romance and action. ~ Lora Young

"The Scarlet Coat brings the American Revolutionary War to life. The characters reveal this slice of history in living colors, and you'll weave through their emotional turmoil and love right along with them." ~ Janet Ferguson

"The Scarlet Coat is a beautiful historical romance told through the eyes and hearts of a young colonist and her enemy, a British soldier. Love, heartache, and intrigue abound in their story, beautifully woven by the author. A must-read for any history lover." ~ Laura Hodges Poole

1

The last rays of sun faded into twilight, and the wind whispered through the trees, as if warning Rachel to turn back. She encouraged her pa's stallion forward, though her pulse threatened to strangle her. Somewhere, not far away, a wolf wailed into the night. The mournful song resonated within her, bespeaking tragedy. She searched the deepening shadows of the forest. What if all the British hadn't retreated? What if there were still Indians and Tories out there, waiting behind those trees?

Something unseen rustled the leaves, and a twig snapped. *Lord, what am I doing?* How would she even find them out here in the dark? Maybe she should go home or to the Reids' for another night.

Her course of action seemed so clear when General Herkimer, and what remained of his regiment and the local militia, limped their way alongside the Mohawk River from Oriskany. The general lay on a stretcher, his leg below the knee wrapped in a crimson cloth, his face pale and expressionless—like so many of the men with him. Eight hundred had marched north the day before yesterday and barely half returned.

Her pa and brother were not among them.

Stay with the Reids. That was all Pa had asked of her. Benjamin Reid's bad leg compelled him to remain behind and watch over their farms. Though the safest place for her, Rachel could no longer wait there trying to carry on a casual conversation with any of the Reid girls or hide behind her mother's Bible. She couldn't abide the confines of their snug cabin a minute longer without knowing her own family's fate. Since losing Mama to illness two years ago, Pa and Joseph were all she had. She couldn't lose them, too. But she'd ridden for hours now. Where was she?

A little farther along the trail, the wind shifted slightly, carrying on it the odor of burnt powder and blood. Battle. Rachel's hand came to her stomach in an attempt to calm the sickness churning within.

The horse whinnied, shifting as he tossed his head.

"Whoa. Easy, Hunter." She slid to the ground and surveyed her surroundings. Both sides of the road were heavily treed and thick with underbrush. Even still, she could make out the dark forms of fallen men. She stumbled over her feet but kept moving. "Joseph! Pa!" *You can't be dead.*

Dragging the horse, Rachel ran. Each step constricted her throat until she could hardly breathe. Bodies littered the road—Indian, Tory, and American alike. She maneuvered around them, searching faces in the faint glow of the remaining light. She should have brought a lantern.

The road sloped downward into a deep ravine. Her feet faltered. Hundreds of men—a patchwork of blue and homespun. All motionless. All dead. If only she could close her eyes or turn away, but every muscle held her in place.

The rasp of a voice jolted her from the trance. She yelped and spun toward the intruder.

"Rachel?" The murmur of her name accompanied the form of a man emerging from the trees. "What are you doing here?"

"Joseph." Relief at seeing her brother alive stole the strength from her legs. They trembled as she moved to him and brushed her fingers across his cheek, stained with dirt and powder. His sandy brown hair was tousled and appeared just as black. Rachel wrapped him in her arms and clung tight. "Why didn't you come back with the others? I was so worried...afraid something happened to you and..."

She glanced to his face and the strange expression that marked it. More accurately, a complete lack of expression. "Where is Pa? What happened, Joseph? Tell me."

"Tell you? You can see it, can't you? Everywhere you look."

Of course she saw it. All of it. But... "Where is Pa?"

Joseph looked back, and Rachel followed his gaze into the blackness of the timbered ridge of the ravine. She pushed away and moved stiffly in that direction. *Pa.*

"No." Joseph's cold hand seized hers. "There is nothing left in there. He's dead."

"Let me go." She wrenched away, breaking free before he was able to grab her arm and pull her back. Her vision hazed. "Let me go. I need him."

"It's too late, Rachel. He's dead. I was with him. I watched the life bleed out of him...nothing I could do to stop it. Don't go up there." His voice pleaded and his eyes glistened. Joseph wiped a sleeve across his nose and motioned to Hunter. "Please let me take you home, and I'll return for Pa's body."

Rachel stared into the trees, aching to pull away once again. She took in a jagged breath, managed a nod, and then surrendered to his firm hands. He assisted her into the saddle. Joseph retained the reins to lead the horse, but they didn't make it more than a few steps before an unusual cry wafted in the breeze.

Shivers spiked up and down Rachel's spine. "What was that?"

"It was no animal."

The mewling of human suffering perforated the night. A yapping howl followed—a wolf answering the plea.

"You stay here." Joseph forced the thin leather reins into her hands, shooting her a warning glance before he hurried off the path and into the thick foliage.

Ignoring his order, Rachel dropped to the ground, twisted the reins around a branch and ran after him. She wouldn't be left alone again. Not in this place. Not in the gathering dark. As she caught up to him, she gripped his sleeve.

Their gazes met.

Joseph's mouth opened; then, he nodded his head. Turning away, he allowed her to trail him.

Her fingers remained tangled in the fabric of his shirt.

They followed the moaning to a tiny meadow strewn with more bodies.

Rachel gaped at the shiny black patches of blood evident on almost every corpse and covered her nose and mouth against the stench saturating the air.

As they drew near, the moans ceased.

Joseph called out, but there was no reply. "He must be here somewhere." Frustration edged his voice.

"Maybe he's too weak. We've got to find him if he's still alive."

Joseph moved out, stepping over the fallen,

checking each for any sign of life.

Rachel stood back, frozen. Motionless. Numb. The man's whimpers, though now silent, resounded in her mind. What if he were still alive? What if he woke again to this dark and death, only to become as the corpses surrounding him, with no one to lend him life…to help him?

Rachel forced her feet into action as she picked her way around a dead Indian. Though she tried to keep her eyes averted, they rebelliously wandered to the large hole in the middle of his chest. Her hand flew to her mouth as she lurched away. Stumbling backward, her feet tripped over a red uniformed body. She landed hard on the ground beside him. Bile rose in her throat and she twisted, retching into the nearest bush.

"What happened?" Joseph rushed to her.

She sat upright and wiped her mouth with the back of her sleeve. Her whole body shook.

Joseph grabbed her arm and pulled her to her feet. "You shouldn't have seen this. Let's get you home. Whoever it was must already be gone." He led her away, stepping over a fallen soldier's body.

Rachel shrieked as the hem of her dress snagged on something.

"Do not leave…me." An almost voiceless plea met her ears. "Please."

She pivoted on her heel to where the soldier lay in his blood, his eyes wide, one hand extended. Rachel shivered.

Joseph also reacted, bringing his pistol to the enemy's position.

The man coughed, and closed his eyes in pain. His brilliant scarlet coat and white breeches were smudged with grit and mud, his right hip a bloodied mass of flesh, probably ripped through by a musket ball.

"Rachel, go to the road." The pistol trembled in Joseph's grip.

"You're going to kill him?" She glanced to the soldier.

His eyes remained closed. His mouth moved slightly as though speaking to someone. Perhaps he was praying.

Pushing past the nausea, Rachel swung back to her brother, reaching for him. "You can't do this."

Joseph jerked away. "This is exactly what both he and I have done since morning. How many of our neighbors do you think he's personally sent from this life?"

Silence hung between them.

Joseph lowered his head and weariness returned to his voice. "I'm so tired of this, but there's no other choice. Go back to the road and wait for me. I'll be along in a minute."

She couldn't do it. Rachel moved, but not in the direction required by her brother. Instead, she knelt beside the wounded soldier and laid a cautious hand against his cool forehead.

His eyes fluttered open and peered up with evident fear. Confusion ridged his brow. Did he know he could expect no mercy and therefore could not understand her actions? His eyes rolled back, and his head slid from the large stone on which it had been resting. His body became limp with no sign of life other than the shallow, irregular breaths which moved his chest.

"Joseph, I know he's our enemy, and I do hate him..." Rachel shook her head as she tried to swallow back the bitter taste still coating her tongue. "But we can't kill him, and we can't leave him to die out here like some dog we don't like. Can we? I…I don't know anymore."

"What are you suggesting?"

Rachel watched the soldier, her frown deepening. "Without the uniform he would appear the same as any of us." Her gaze rose to Joseph's face and the tension etched in his usually kind features. "Mama taught us to love our enemies—do good to those who hate you. That's what's written in the Bible. I see the uniform, but…"

"All that Bible talk is right and good, but it's only a book. What if this was the soldier that killed Pa…or Jarrett? There isn't hardly a family in this valley who hasn't lost someone today. They slaughtered us, Rachel." His voice faltered. "If anyone found out we had protected or saved a British soldier—an officer, no less—we could be shot. This is war."

Rachel stood, not able to look at the dying man as she stepped away. Jarrett Adler…dead? He'd only been twenty, less than a year older than her. An attractive young man with his wheat blond hair and teasing blue eyes. More than once she'd considered the possibility of a future with him, and now he was dead, too. Same as Pa.

"I'll wait by the road," Rachel whispered, too drained, heartbroken, and scared to argue further. She would never fully understand war and the insanity required for one man to kill another in such a way. She didn't want to try to understand it. Rachel hurried, almost running to put as much distance as possible between herself and the nightmare. Still, the haunted eyes of that soldier, that man, wouldn't leave her. Perhaps they never would.

Hunter waited on the road, nibbling on what grass lined the trails.

Grasping the reins, Rachel hugged the animal's neck, pressed her cheek into the soft coat and braced for what seemed inevitable—the shot of a pistol. "Let him die, Lord. Take him before Joseph has to. Please, let him be dead already." Her heart thundered. Not from fear, but with the realization that she couldn't let Joseph kill that man. She had to stop him. Pushing away, Rachel darted back into the forest, her skirts hitched high. She stumbled over her feet as the stillness of the night shattered, the sharp crack echoing. *No.*

The man had begged for his life.

And she'd left him to die.

Rachel backed away several steps before turning. When she reached the road, she laid her hand against Hunter's jaw. "I…" *I feel his death is my doing.* Was she so weak? Hundreds of men lay dead, and she wasn't sure if she could live with the death of her enemy?

Fatigue dragged Joseph's footsteps as he approached. "Rachel?"

She slipped under Hunter's neck, and then looked over his withers.

Joseph's face appeared eerie in the rising moonlight.

"Don't say anything," she begged.

"Rachel, I need you to help me get him on the horse."

Her mind could not comprehend the meaning. She moved around Hunter, her gaze drawn to the form lying at Joseph's feet. The red coat was gone, but the bloodied hip, the gash on the head, and the man's face…

"But… you said…and the shot?"

Joseph glanced away. "Wolves. I wanted to frighten them." It was said dryly. Perhaps he could find no true excuse. Wolves would be too shy to come anywhere near here tonight.

"You mean…?"

"I guess. I really don't know." A hand passed over his eyes. "We can take him home and let him die in peace."

A simple enough plan, but…

"What will we do if he recovers?" This man was a British officer—their enemy. She couldn't forget that.

"I don't reckon he will. There's not much life in him. Besides, we aren't here to save him, only give him a chance to die on his own."

~*~

Exquisite agony pulsated through his whole body with each beat of his heart. The scent of horse filled his nostrils as he attempted a breath. His lungs refused to expand, as though the full weight of the animal resided on top of them and across his stomach. They ached from the pressure. The swaying of the ground only compounded the intense pressure threatening to burst his head apart. Why did the ground sway? Was he back on a ship? That did not explain the horse sitting on him, or why he hung upside down. Nothing made sense. He opened his eyes to the blackness…and fur? The sleek coat of a horse. Hence the smell. But the animal did not lie on him as assumed. Instead, it seemed he was slung face down over the back of a horse. No wonder his stomach pinched so. He had to get off.

At first his arms refused his beckoning. Numb

from dangling above his head, they might as well have been severed from him entirely. Slowly, however, he wielded enough control to bring them to the saddle over which he was draped. Planting them against the firm leather, he pushed, writhing his body up with the same motion. As he slid from the saddle, a feminine scream pierced the air, a hammer to the spike already driven through his temples.

His feet touched the ground, but little good that did him. Like his arms, they refused to heed his will. He should have considered that before he disembarked. The frantic voice of a woman and the lingering aroma of horse sweat faded. Agony ripped through his right thigh, and he hit the ground.

"Let me help you get him back up on Hunter." The woman's words filtered through the haze residing in his mind as it resurfaced to consciousness.

"What, so he can throw himself off again?" The deeper voice rasped with anger.

Who were these people? What did they want with him?

"After bringing him this far, we can't leave him. Only a couple more miles, and we'll be home."

Home…would not that be agreeable? At least, it conjured a pleasant sensation within him. No images, though. A dim light glowed high above as he forced his eyelids open, blinking against the grit. As much as his eyes begged to remain closed, he refused to allow them such luxury. Not with the face of an angel hovering so near, shadowed but still somewhat visible in the moonlight. Young. Large eyes. A halo of gold. Who was she?

Someone yanked on his arm, heaving him upward. *Lord, not back on the horse.* Anything but that.

"No." He tried to pull away, and his body again sagged to the earth.

"He's awake." Her voice.

The man's was edged. "How is that possible when he shouldn't even be alive?"

Did they speak of him, implying he should be dead? Perhaps that explained the pain—the struggle to remain cognizant to anything around him. Dead. How far off was he from slipping away completely? What held him here? He stared at the young woman as she knelt beside him.

"We're trying to help you."

He attempted to wet his lips, but his tongue was just as dry. Blood and gunpowder tainted his senses. "What happened?"

"You were—"

The man pulled her aside. "There's no time for this. We either get him back on that horse, or leave him here."

As they dragged his body from the ground, all thoughts and awareness fled, returning in waves of oblivion and torture. Finally, he awoke on a solid surface, a floor, the only movement the flickering of a candle set upon a table across a small room. Closer, a chair held the form of a woman, her head tipped back. Asleep. He let his eyes close, allowing exhaustion and pain to take him. No use fighting it any longer. God willing, he would awaken. But if not...he only wished he could remember what he had sacrificed his life for.

2

The first rays of sun lighted upon her face, warming it. Rachel's eyes flew open as she pulled away from the nightmares. An involuntary shiver passed through her entire body, the images of death and gore slow to fade. She stretched her sore neck. A kink burned like a hot coal in her right shoulder, but that was no wonder. Joseph had told her to go to bed. Covering a yawn and trying to blink the tiredness from her eyes, Rachel leaned forward in her mother's rocking chair. With the soft glow of the sun in the small windows, she studied the man lying on the floor against the wall.

His brown hair held highlights of red, especially in the whiskers which showed on the relaxed slope of his jaw. His nose was prominent, but in an attractive way. Slight lines marked the corners of his eyes. He appeared to have several years on Joseph's twenty-two, but was probably still younger than thirty.

Rachel laid a hand across his ashen face, only to yank it back an instant later. His forehead seemed the temperature of a pot hanging over a fire. She tucked the quilt around his chin, and hurried to where a pitcher of water sat on the table. She poured some into a basin, and then grabbed a rag from the stash she'd made from an old dress.

The front door of the cabin creaked opened and

Joseph stepped in looking bedraggled, his eyes bloodshot. "He's still alive? How is that possible?"

Rachel dropped to her knees beside the man, swatting what remained of her braid out of the way. She dipped the rag into the warm water, wrung it out, and then laid it across the British officer's brow. "I don't know how much longer he'll last. He's burning up."

"What are you doing?"

She glanced at her brother. "I'm trying to help his—"

"We're not helping him, remember?" Joseph walked to the table where he deposited his tricorn hat, and poured some water. He took several long gulps before slamming the tin mug onto the table "We're only giving him a place to die, though he doesn't deserve even that much."

Rachel glanced at the man on the floor, not sure whether to retreat or go back to her ministrations. Her insides twisted. This man fought for life. He was the enemy—her mind knew it—but lying here so helpless…he was only a man. Could she sit back and do nothing while he died? Her emotional state was not up to that task.

A grunt huffed from Joseph's throat as he came to her side. He crouched, and then yanked back the blanket, baring the wounded thigh. He removed the wad of cloth they had pushed into the gaping hole to keep the injury from leaving a crimson trail.

Rachel gasped, recoiling at the mess of blood and dirt tinged with whitish-yellow pus. "How awful."

"It won't be long before the poison spreads through his body. It'll be what kills him since he hasn't already bled to death." Joseph pressed the cloth back into place and pushed to his feet, the exertion betraying his exhaustion.

"He needs a doctor." Rachel glanced to where her cap hung near the door.

Joseph followed her gaze. "What's going through that head of yours?"

"We could fetch Doctor Weber."

The man wasn't a real doctor, but the closest they had within twenty miles. He lived near what was left of Frankfort, about ten miles farther down the Mohawk.

If she rode hard, she could be back by midafternoon.

"He can't help here."

"But this man will die." Rachel stood, facing her brother.

"That's what we want, remember? He's the enemy." Joseph's voice was sharp, but hushed—almost a whisper. "There are dozens of our own men and soldiers who need the doctor's help before I would allow him to waste his time here. Even if there was only one other American man, woman, or child who needed the doctor for something as slight as a splinter in his finger, I wouldn't ask him here."

Rachel's mouth opened, then clamped shut. He was right, of course. How could she have forgotten the men who had returned with the general, or even Herkimer's own condition? Or what would happen if anyone knew this man lay here in their home? "So we sit back and let him die?"

Joseph blew out his breath. "I guess not. I reckon I didn't think this through last night. Otherwise, I would have realized that wouldn't be an option for you. Heat some water and wash this wound good and clean.

Don't be worried about hurting him, 'cause he probably won't feel anything anyways. Just scrub it out. A warm milk and bread poultice like Ma used to make will probably do the most good."

Joseph half staggered to the table to rip a large piece of bread off the stale loaf. "After I finish the chores, I'll head over to the Adlers'. I brought Jarrett's body back with Pa's." He collected his hat, staring at it for several moments before shoving it on his head and pulling it low.

"But you haven't had a wink of sleep." Rachel marveled that he still moved at all. Marching, hours of battle, fighting for his very life, staying out there with Pa until the end...and still no rest. "Why don't you lie down for a while? I'll see to the chores."

"No!" He shook his head, his eyes haunted. "I don't want you going out there. Just...stay in the cabin until I get Pa ready to bury."

No need to employ her imagination. Not after last night. "All right. I'll stay in. But you still need to rest. I tended the animals yesterday before I came for you. They can wait long enough for you to—"

"There's too much to do." He waved her suggestion away. "Besides, I dozed on the wagon. Hunter and Sorrowful didn't need any help coming home." He turned to the door.

"Joseph."

"I can't, Rachel. I can't stop, or I'll not move again. Already I can feel my body stiffening, my strength slipping away...almost like a corpse. I have to keep moving." He motioned to the British officer. "I doubt he'll wake up, but don't take chances." Joseph withdrew the pistol from his side and slid it across the table. "It's loaded. If he does wake when you're alone and causes you any trouble, shoot him."

Shoot him? Rachel glanced at the unconscious man and shuddered. Thankfully the likelihood of that was nonexistent. At least, today.

The door closed.

She raised her gaze to the window, catching a glimpse of Joseph on his way to the barn where Pa's body lay in the back of the wagon. She should be the one preparing it for burial.

Tears burned behind her eyes. *Pa.* This was as close as he would come to home. The stabbing ache in her chest threatened to consume her as she looked at the dying man. The side of his head was still caked with blood, matting the hair. They had done nothing to save him other than bring him here. And soon he would be dead, the same as the others.

Dead.

Rachel shook her head. She couldn't let it be that simple. She had to do what she could to save his life. The rest would be left to God's discretion. Her thoughts on the task at hand, Rachel stoked the fire and filled the kettle. As she gathered clean rags for bandages, a part of her screamed that she should stop and mourn the loss of her father. But she couldn't. Not now. Not yet. If she took even one minute for grief, it would be unbearable to continue, and she had to. It was her duty as a Christian, wasn't it?

With the heated water, a pile of rags, and a bowl of bread expanding in some of the milk Joseph had dropped off, Rachel again knelt beside the British officer and folded the thin blanket aside. "Oh, Lord, help me."

The side of his once white breeches had been shredded and soaked. Sooner or later they would have to be removed completely, but she would leave that task for Joseph. She took up a pair of shears and cut around the opened flesh, cringing at the jagged edges clinging to the fabric. She'd have to soak if free. A moan rumbled from the man's throat as she laid a wet cloth to the wound and let the hot water run down.

His brows pushed together, but his eyes remained closed.

Rachel relaxed the pressure. "Shhhh." Not that her soothing would have any effect on him, but she kept her touch gentle while working the section of his breeches loose. The last threads gave way and she set it aside before withdrawing the wad of cloth from the wound. Even though she'd already seen it, the torn muscle and discolored excretions turned her stomach. The bleeding had been staunched, but could she clean the dirt and strands of grass away without increasing the flow? Rachel laid a towel under his thigh and ladled warm water directly over the wound.

As the steaming liquid ran into the open flesh, the man groaned and reached down.

"No." Rachel dropped the ladle to intercept his hand.

His eyes remained closed, though his face bore the intensity of his pain.

"I'm sorry." Taking the ladle with her left hand, she intertwined her fingers with his and tightened her hold. Except for family, she'd never held a man's hand and the heat resonating from his seemed to extend through her. Not as callused as her father's hands, the man probably hadn't been a farmer or laborer. But of course he hadn't. He was a British officer. Riding his horse and shouting commands. He wouldn't know what it was to sink roots deep into the land, making a wilderness into a home…only to have an army rise against him, stealing away the people he loved most.

Rachel stared at the man's hand, wanting to walk away. She tried to ignore him as she continued to ladle water over the wound. When she'd applied the poultice, she rotated him onto his side so the soggy bread would remain in place while she covered and bound it. Finally, she folded his arms across his chest and tucked the blanket under his chin.

She gathered her leftover supplies and put them away. Her head light, she moved to wash her hands and strain the rest of the milk. Maybe the warm cream would help settle her stomach.

An anxious whinny pulled Rachel to the window, and she peered through the thin glass Pa had brought all the way from Boston for Mama. The Adlers' black mare appeared through the gap in the trees and turned off the trail toward the Garnet farm, Matthias astride. Jarrett's father.

Joseph wasn't in sight.

She glanced back at the British officer…looking little like an officer or a Brit, but a risk nonetheless. His presence in the main room had to be remedied. Immediately. Rachel hooked her hands under the man's arms and lugged him toward the bedroom door. The dead weight of his unconscious body seemed to cleave to the floor planks. With a last heave, she deposited him just within the door and pulled it closed. A large crimson stain marked his original position. She grabbed the rocking chair and swung it over the area, and then hurried to meet Matthias on the narrow porch. As she stepped out, she shut the door.

"Rachel, vhere is your Vater?"

She stared for a moment, her mind wading

through his thick German accent. The lines on his face appeared deeper. "He—he's...dead." The word sounded almost surreal, but it remained a fact, as did the fate of Adlers' youngest son.

"And Joseph?"

"Alive." Praise the Lord for that much.

"Did he say anything about Jarrett? Did he see my boy?"

The answer must have shown in her expression because Matthias took a step back and folded his arms at his chest. "He is killed. Das is vhat you mean to say. Jarrett is dead." He tipped his face from her. "Vhen I heard nothing, I knew."

"I'm so sorry." It was hard to put anything but air behind her voice, and the breeze snatched that away.

"I vill go find him." He turned to his horse.

"Wait."

The creak of hinges on the barn drew both their gazes.

Joseph stepped out, his eyes widening when he saw Matthias. He looked to Rachel.

She guessed his thoughts and replied with a subtle shake of her head. No. *That* secret hadn't yet been discovered.

A measure of relief showed on Joseph's face and he hurried across the yard. "I was about to bring Jarrett...his body...to you." He pulled the hat from his head. "I'll come with you now. If you give me but a minute with my sister..."

Matthias nodded and started toward the barn, his steps slow, no doubt dreading what awaited him there.

Catching Rachel's arm, Joseph tugged her inside the cabin. He stopped short and glanced around. "Thank goodness you had the presence of mind to move him. The Adlers are good people, but we can't take that risk."

"I know."

"Then let's be off. We'll take Jarrett home. It will mean a lot to Marta to have you there."

Rachel gave a nod and took her cap from its peg, and then wiped a hand across her forehead. When had she eaten last? A full day, at least. Her strength had been spread thin over the long ride to Oriskany and back, an almost sleepless night, and caring for the enemy. Combined with the constant ache of Pa's death, she simply had nothing left to give poor Jarrett or his family. She wasn't as strong as her brother. "Can I stay?"

Joseph's brows pulled low and together. "You don't wish to bid Jarrett farewell?"

"What am I supposed to say to him? That I wish he were still here—that he'd never left?" She let her eyes close and drew a breath into her burning lungs. "The same as I must tell Pa."

A warm hand squeezed her arm. "Marta will understand you are feeling unwell."

"Thank you, Joseph." Rachel followed him to the door but remained inside.

He disappeared into the barn. Guilt already pricked her. He'd suffered so much greater than she, yet he didn't shirk from what needed to be done.

Several minutes later, Matthias emerged and mounted his mare. Joseph led Hunter, a body wrapped in a blanket slung facedown over the saddle. Sandy hair showed on the portion of the head that remained uncovered.

Rachel slunk back and pressed the door shut.

3

Rachel leaned into the wall and peeked into the bedroom.

Though the British officer still slept, emotion played across his face as though he dreamed. Or perhaps his leg and head proved endless torture.

She turned to the basin and scrub brush. On her knees, she poured out some of the water, letting it pool over the ugly stain. The busier her hands, the easier it was to distract her thoughts from the corpses and carnage, of Jarrett being hauled away over Hunter's back, of Pa lying dead in the barn.

Rachel's hand slipped, causing her knuckles to grate against the raw floor planks. She yelped and dropped the brush, viewing the bloody scrape and more than one splinter on her fingers. But at least the floor showed only a slight discoloration now. She tended her hand, and then hauled the basin outside to pour on the garden.

Just beyond stood the grove Pa had left untouched by the ax because Mama had loved the peaceful seclusion it provided. They'd buried Mama there, and they would bury Pa at her side.

Abandoning the basin, Rachel fetched the spade from where it protruded at the edge of the potato patch, and entered the stand of trees, moving to where a stone marked Mama's final resting place. *Sarah*

Garnet, 1734-1775. Beloved wife and mother. Rachel stepped a few paces to the side and planted the edge of the spade. At least her parents would be together now.

"Rachel?"

Her fingers lost their hold on the handle. The spade tipped as she spun. The eldest of the Reids' offspring stood in his homespun clothes with one arm bandaged. "Daniel."

"I didn't see either Joseph or your Pa when we retreated yesterday. I had to know…" He looked from her to the spade and back again. "Oh, Rachel. Who?"

"Pa." She sniffled and took up the spade. "Joseph's over at the Adlers' helping to bury Jarrett."

The brown of Daniel's irises appeared black as emotion rose. "It's a miracle anybody made it out of that ravine alive."

Her thoughts went to the man hidden in the cabin. It was too early to determine if that were a miracle, or a curse. Most likely it would only be another grave.

Daniel reached for the spade with his good hand. "You shouldn't be the one digging."

"And how do you intend to do it? Were you hurt badly?"

"I was a little slow blocking a tomahawk. Took a piece out of me but should heal well enough. Any slower and I wouldn't have an arm."

Or a life. Rachel laid her hand across the course fabric. "I'm glad you're safe, Daniel." She meant every word. Their families had come to this wilderness together and a bond had been formed. Deep friendship—though both their parents had hoped for something more. Perhaps there would be…someday.

"Why don't you leave this until Joseph returns? Fannie insisted she come—she's been beside herself since you took off to Oriskany to find Joseph and your Pa. Though I half wonder if she's more concerned for Joseph's sake than for your own." He let out an empty chuckle, and took her arm. "She brought some fresh bread and—"

Rachel jerked away, stumbling back at what he was saying. "Fannie's here? Where is she?"

A deep crease etched across his forehead. "She went to put the food in to the cabin. Honestly, I didn't tell her I saw you coming into the grove. I wanted to…"

Rachel was already ducking under a branch and breaking into a full run. How would she explain a wounded British officer to Fannie Reid? Or her brother? The door to the cabin sat open, not impeding Rachel's speed. She burst into the room, and then slid to a stop. Fannie stood by the fire, a pot on the hook, a spoon in hand. The bedroom appeared undisturbed.

"Rachel. Are you all right?"

She tried to answer, but had no air. Bracing against the back of a chair, she reclaimed her breath. "I wasn't expecting you."

"I couldn't stay away not knowing. So please, tell me quickly. Is Joseph…?"

A shadow filled the door and stretched across the floor. "Fannie," Daniel said, "James Garnet was killed. Ride home and tell Pa to come. Ma, too."

The girl, one year Rachel's junior and with the characteristic Reid chestnut hair and dark eyes, nodded. "But Joseph…?"

"Joseph's fine." Rachel straightened and allowed her friend to embrace her.

"Heaven be praised," Fannie whispered. "Though it truly does pain me to hear about your Pa. I'll fetch my parents straightway to help with the burying." She laid a kiss to Rachel's cheek and was gone.

Rachel sank into the chair, unable to keep her gaze from wandering to the bedroom door.

Perhaps the British officer had already expired.

"Did you wish to lay down for a while?" Daniel's voice reminded her of his presence.

"No." She fanned her face with her hand, suddenly too warm. No surprise after a mad dash across the yard in the heat of August with the air still heavy with the memory of yestermorn's rain. "I need a moment alone, is all." She glanced to him—to the disappointment, but understanding in his eyes. "Please."

"Of course." He backed out of cabin and closed the door.

Rachel jerked to her feet and hastened to the bedroom. The British officer remained exactly where she left him, his chest continuing its slow, shallow rhythm. Alive. Why did it matter so much when it shouldn't?

~*~

"Rachel?" Fannie called from the doorway. "Joseph said to tell you they're ready to begin."

Rachel gathered her summer shawl and moved into the front yard where Abigail Reid and her oldest daughter waited. Thankfully, the younger three girls remained at home. She envied their youth and innocence. Both their parents were alive and well. They didn't need to be dragged down by her reality.

Fannie said nothing as she placed her arm around Rachel's shoulders.

The lifeless form of her father was wrapped in a woolen blanket and lowered into the grave Joseph and Benjamin Reid had dug.

Oh, Pa. He wouldn't be there to teach her the intricacies of nature, or tease her about cooking, or look at her with love-filled eyes as he spoke of Mama. Rachel clenched her teeth together to hold the tears back.

In this grove, Rachel came to talk to her mother and contemplate God. Today was the first time others accompanied her, and it seemed an intrusion. This was *her* place of seclusion. Yet, gratitude flooded her. Their friends had come to bid a final farewell and help bury her pa.

"It is times such as this, the lack of clergy in the area is especially felt," began Matthias, his voice gruff.

Rachel hardly heard the words.

After a few minutes, Matthias stepped back and patted Joseph on the shoulder.

Joseph picked up a spade and shoveled the earth to cover their Pa, his movements stiff and halting. Benjamin and Matthias joined him and within minutes the hole became a mound. Joseph leaned into the handle of the spade and bowed his head. "Lord, we ask Thee to take care of our Pa and welcome him into Thy kingdom. Amen."

Forcing herself to breathe, Rachel moved to his side, taking his arm. They still had each other. Somehow they would survive this.

"Ve vill pray for you," Marta Adler promised, taking the siblings' hands. She looked with understanding into Rachel's eyes.

Rachel lowered her gaze. She should have gone with Joseph this morning. "Thank you. I'm so sorry for your loss, as well."

"They are in a better place, ja?" Marta patted her hand. "Though I had alvays hoped…" She shook her head and moved to join Matthias.

Abigail and her husband moved forward to express their condolences.

Rachel's thoughts hung on the older woman's words. Were those killed by the British really in a better place? Was all her mother had taught her true, or merely a fairytale to bring comfort? Rachel had believed it. Otherwise, life was too bitter and tragic to face. Joseph's words returned to her.

There isn't hardly a family in this valley who hasn't lost someone today.

And what about before? Back in Topsfield, Massachusetts the Garnets had two children who hadn't lived long after birth, and one who'd died as a toddler. And now both their parents were gone. How could one survive the pain of such losses without hope that a better world did exist?

Daniel came to her side. "Your pa gave his life for a worthy cause. At least we were able to push the British and the Tories back."

General Herkimer's purpose had been to assist Colonel Gansevoort in breaking the British's siege at Fort Schuyler. Instead, they'd been massacred still ten miles from their target. Yes, their enemies had been the first to retreat, but the Continental Army and the local militia were so depleted by that point, there had been nothing for them to do but hobble home.

"You will let me know if you need anything at all?" Daniel's fingers encircled her arm.

She gave a nod.

"I could stay a while longer." He was trying so

hard to be a gallant knight.

She only wanted to be left alone. "No. Thank you, Daniel."

He managed a smile and then released her.

Fannie took his place and hugged Rachel. "Is there anything I can do for you?"

Stealing a glance at Joseph, Rachel lowered her voice. "Your mother has that salve she makes from poplar sap and other herbs, the one you keep saying can heal anything. Can you bring me some?"

"Of course." Fannie looked to Joseph. He remained oblivious to their conversation, his focus on the graves. "Who's injured?"

No lies. "Joseph doesn't want to talk about it. So please, don't say anything, even to your mother."

"Of course. I only want to help." Fannie gave her one last embrace then hurried to join her family as they left the grove.

Rachel moved to Joseph's side. They were finally alone. She ran her hand over the rough wooden cross driven into the earth. "Goodbye, Papa," she breathed. "I love you. Tell Mama I love her and miss her, too."

"They must be happy, together again."

"I hope so. Oh, I hope so."

Joseph stooped low and smoothed the moist dirt. He took a handful, squeezing it in his fist until it formed a tight ball. "There's good soil here." His voice sounded distant. "Good soil in a good land." He crumbled it between his fingers, letting it fall back to the ground, and then stood. His palm brushed in quick, jerky motions against his pant leg. "It can't be right for us to bury Pa here while the enemy lays alive in our own cabin. Why won't he go on and die like it serves him?"

The thought of the half-dead man hidden in the cabin drained the last of her strength. It would be so easy to slip to the soft ground and not move again. But Joseph's hand braced her arm.

"There's work to be done."

She took a fortifying breath. "Not for you. Go try to sleep. I'll see to everything that can't hold until tomorrow."

A nod showed his weariness.

The farm opened up before them, the cabin, barn, smokehouse, pens and chickens pecking the ground. She hadn't fed them or gathered eggs today. The little milk cow bawled, but Joseph had taken care of her earlier. The horses grazed as their tails flicked flies from their backs. The garden begged for tending...that huge stump still sitting right in the middle of the new potato patch, sapping moisture from the ground needed to be removed. It looked like a bush now, new branches sprouting from what remained of the once stately cottonwood. With it there, the vegetables didn't stand much chance. Pa talked about digging it out this spring, but there had been too much to do. Between the British's attacks, and raids by Joseph Brant, a Mohawk Indian and one of the most aggressive Tories, they were always on their guard. By the end of summer, Pa promised, he would have the stump removed. The next day he and Joseph had answered the call to march.

Joseph's feet slowed as a deep scowl crossed his face.

"What are you thinking?" Rachel asked.

"When that British pig does die, we'll bury him out on the other side of the clearing, near the slough. I don't want him anywhere near Mama and Pa."

4

As soon as he surfaced from oblivion, he wished to return. The pressure in his skull threatened to break it apart, the pain rivaling the agony burning up the side of his body. Hot and cold waves washed over him in turn, and he opened his eyes to darkness. At least, he was quite sure they were open. A moan vibrated in the back of his parched throat. Even that hurt.

A curse murmured from across the room, the deep voice strangely familiar. "How am I supposed to get any rest with him in here?"

An airy sigh sounded almost like a yawn. A feminine one. "By ignoring him."

"I can't. I couldn't last night either. He can't stay in here, Rachel."

The woman groaned.

As foggy as his brain had become, it still held her image.

"Why don't you go sleep in the loft again, then?"

"Because the cot isn't available for me out there anymore, and Pa would roll over in his grave if he knew I left you alone with this British pig."

British pig? The absence of barnyard stench seemed a clear enough answer. He clamped his eyes closed, partly against the sharp piercing in his skull, but also with the hopes of thinking clearer. *British pig.* Something rang true about the phrase. Though his dysfunctional mind could not grasp anything horrible about being British, the image of a pig was neither pretty nor flattering. The grating of wooden legs against the floor vibrated through him as someone dragged the cot across the floor. Searing pain jolted through his hip.

"What are you doing?" Her question was met by more grinding of wood.

A moment later the cot stopped—heaven be praised!

The man's breath came in gusts, but he said nothing.

"Fine." She sounded upset.

He gritted his teeth, the agony only adding to the nausea swirling in his stomach. Even after the cot came to a permanent rest, he remained paralyzed, fighting unconsciousness. A cool hand lay across his forehead. Her voice, though drawn with weariness, caressed his ears.

"I can't do this anymore. Not tonight."

"What's wrong?"

"He's not as hot, but he's soaked now. He's drenched in sweat."

"Leave him. We can deal with it in the morning."

"He'll chill. That's hardly what his fever needs."

A fever. That explained the shivers. And the inexplicable fluctuation between overheated and freezing.

The man's voice mumbled. "A lot less than if I dragged him out to the barn right now. That's where we should have thrown him to begin with, Rachel."

Rachel. He didn't try to open his eyes. He focused on the single spec of light in the darkness that had swallowed his world, the memory of her pretty face, as all else slipped away.

~*~

Another day passed. The British officer was still alive. Rachel went about her chores, her thoughts detached.

Joseph slammed the door closed, cutting off the evening breeze. "Can't you shut him up? I could hear him from the barn."

"I'm trying, but he's still unconscious. The fever's worse again." Rachel dropped her cloth back into the water basin and pushed it aside. She stepped away from the cot, and then wiped her palms across her apron. If only he'd die and leave her in peace. Yet something deeper within still hoped for his life.

He moaned again, his head tossing from side to side. "How do you not fathom what you have done," he shouted, and then lowered his voice. "Why can you not see it...?" He continued speaking random sentences and words, many incoherent.

Joseph slapped his hat on the chest beside the door. "Course' he has to talk as if he's directly from London. Listen to him. If anyone was passing by close enough to hear that, we'd have a fine time explaining."

Joseph was right, of course. Most of this area had been settled by Germans. The others, like the Garnets and the Reids, had lived in New England for at least one generation.

"What do we do?" They should have left him where they'd found him.

"I figure we have two options. We can put him out of his misery, or find some way to stop up his mouth." Joseph grabbed the sweat-stained handkerchief from his back pocket and moved to the occupied cot.

Rachel caught his arm. "What will you do?"

"Don't worry," he growled. "I'm only making him quiet." He wrapped the cloth taut through the man's mouth, tying it at the side of his head. "That'll hopefully fix it." Joseph moved back to the table where Rachel had left his supper.

The British officer flung his head from one side to the other, as though in an attempt to escape the handkerchief.

Rachel placed her palms on either side of his head to hold him still, but only succeeded in making him more violent as he struggled for freedom. He groaned, loosening his arms from the blankets. "This isn't working." Rachel grabbed his hands as they tore at both the gag and the bandage. "He'll hurt himself."

"What else do you have in mind? Perhaps we should open the door and let the world know we're harboring a Redcoat? Do you think they'd help him?"

"I don't know. I just...I can't watch him like this." She pulled the handkerchief away and threw it on the floor.

"Rachel!" Joseph bolted to his feet, slamming a fist against the table. The dishes vibrated against it and a cup tipped, spilling water onto the floor.

She ignored him, something melting within her as she folded the man's arms across his chest. "Hush," Rachel soothed, moving her hands to cradle the wounded soldier's head. "You're all right, but you must be quiet."

"Don't go. Don't go," he pleaded, over and over.

"Rachel," Joseph warned.

"I'm here," she comforted, disregarding her brother. "I won't go. It's fine."

"I did not want you to go." The British officer moaned. "Why? Why must you do this?"

"It's all right. I'm here. I won't go. Hush."

Slowly the man quieted.

Rachel sank to her knees beside the cot, running her fingers across his forehead and hairline, moving carefully around the bandage. It was hard to hate him right now. He was a helpless soul whose pitiable existence demanded compassion. She couldn't withhold it.

Joseph rewarded her with a disapproving glare. "Don't forget who he is." He opened his mouth to say something more, but a knock cut him short.

Both startled.

"You keep him quiet," Joseph mouthed, aiming a finger at her. He twisted away.

"Hello, Joseph," Fannie's voice came as the door creaked open. "How are you this evening?"

"Fine."

"Did you get any hay brought in today?"

"Some."

A long pause followed.

Poor Fannie was probably trying to figure out what else to say to the scowling man standing in the doorway. "Is Rachel at home?" she squeaked.

"She's busy right now."

"I understand, but I brought her salve like I promised. It'll heal most anything. I'm sorry I didn't have a chance to bring it over sooner."

"I'll give it to her. Anything else?" The last words came as a growl from his throat.

Fannie made a silent retreat.

As the door slapped closed, Rachel's gaze fixed on the man in the cot, not daring to meet Joseph's eyes.

Her brother's anger filled the room, sending a chill down her spine.

"Don't you realize how dangerous this is?" His voice sounded hoarse from the tension. "Don't you have any clue what people would do if they knew we had him here? Did you tell the whole country that we have a friend from our king staying with us for a while? What were you thinking? That she would help? That she wouldn't tell anyone?"

"I didn't say anything. I only asked for the salve. She doesn't know what it's for." Rachel stole a glance at the man.

"Well, let's hope she doesn't." Joseph breathed hard, his jaw working. He eyed the small leather bag with the salve and flung it against the far wall. "I honestly hope he doesn't make it through another night." He dropped into a chair, bracing his elbows against the table and pressing his palms into his eyes. He wasn't eating well, and he worked just as hard—no, harder—than when Pa had been with them.

Rachel had never seen him looking so worn out. If only he would let her help more, but he insisted she keep to the chores that had already been hers.

The British officer mumbled something she could have sworn was a line from the Bible, and she laid a finger to his lips. They stilled. He had a shapely mouth, though pale and chapped. "I didn't want him to die." The words were scarcely spoken than she regretted them. But she wouldn't take them back now. "That's why I asked Fannie for the salve. If it helps him heal…"

"And when he heals? Then what are we supposed to do with him?"

"I don't know." She was tired of death.

Joseph groaned. "Why us? Why did we have to find him? Why couldn't he have died on his own that first night?"

The British officer lay silent on the cot, as though he had finally fallen into a real sleep.

Rachel could only imagine what he'd endured, and yet he hung so stubbornly to life. "Perhaps he has something worth living for."

"Like what? Crushing Continental rebels?"

"Maybe he has a family back in England. People he cares for." Perhaps he was a father with a half-dozen offspring dependent on him. And a wife. Rachel withdrew. "I don't know. Maybe it's not him. Perhaps it's the Lord who wants him alive."

Joseph shook his head, wiping his hands down his face. "Why ever would He want that?"

"To try our patience?" Rachel almost chuckled, but it caught in her throat. "It's working well enough."

Joseph's gaze fell steady on the man, and he released a long breath. "We should burn his clothes—any evidence of who he is. I'll bury his boots in the morning."

A twinge of a smile tugged at her mouth though she didn't feel it any deeper. "On the other side of the clearing near the slough?"

Joseph turned his focus on his dinner. He ran the spoon along the inner circumference of the bowl. "Let's just say I'm not over the urge to bury something there." His words lingered in the air.

She stood and moved to fetch the salve from where it landed. She would apply it immediately. Anything to keep her hands busy and her thoughts still.

5

Letting the Bible fall back to her lap, Rachel closed it. The first time in almost a week she'd picked it up to study, but she might as well have left it sitting beside her bed. Nothing diminished the numbness that continued to expand within her.

Resting her head on the back of her mother's rocking chair, Rachel found some comfort in the swaying motion. Only four days the British officer had been lying there, hanging on to life. It seemed longer since the night they'd brought him home...and Pa was killed. A lifetime ago.

Rachel set aside the book and stood, omitting her prayer at the end of her study. She simply wasn't in the mood for pouring her heart out to the Lord. Besides, He didn't seem to be listening to her. Else why would He have let Pa die like that? Hadn't He heard her prayers all that day? She hadn't stopped until she'd found Joseph. Not ready to confront her thoughts about God, Rachel crossed the room. She placed a hand on her patient's forehead. The fever had dropped again, ever so slightly. It was a step in the right direction.

"I suppose we should redress that wound of yours," Rachel said out loud, despite the fact the man was incapable of responding—or hearing, for that matter. "You sit tight, and I'll have everything ready in a minute." She released a mirthless chuckle. "Or lay there, if that be more comfortable."

As she gathered clean rags and put the kettle over the fire, Rachel continued the one-sided conversation with the unconscious man. "You know," she stated after several minutes, "you definitely seem a better listener than most men around here. Better than Joseph, for sure."

A sharp knock cracked against the door.

Before she had a moment to react, Daniel erupted into the cabin. His eyes scanned the room before his gaze came to rest on the British officer's sleeping form.

"Isn't it customary to wait for someone to answer?" Rachel snapped, her heart leaping to her throat. Why hadn't they thought to move the cot back into the bedroom? "If you want Joseph, he's probably in the east field. I was about to join him."

"You know I didn't come to see him." Daniel crossed the floor. "Who is this man supposed to be? It's strange you didn't mention him earlier."

"Should we have?" Rachel masked her fear with annoyance. "As for who he is, I don't know his name. He was wounded at Oriskany, and we brought him back with us. He's been unconscious since." No lies. "Honestly, Daniel, everyone has enough of their own problems—especially right now—why should we burden you, or anyone?" She brought her hands to her hips, and raised her chin a degree. Hopefully, he wouldn't hear how loud the pounding in her chest was becoming. "Why are you really here, Daniel?"

A slight smile lightened his brown eyes as he studied her. "You sure are pretty when you get upset like this."

Heat rushed into her cheeks, and she reached up

to tuck a loose strand of hair behind her ear.

Daniel's smile faded as quickly as it had come. "I can't allow you to carry on so foolishly, Rachel. What are you and Joseph thinking, bringing a Redcoat into your home like this?"

"Wha—"

"Fannie overheard you and Joseph talking. She's been beside herself with worry. Understand, I promised I'd not breathe a word to anyone, but you know how I feel about you." Uncertainty flashed across his face and he rushed on. "And your brother. Tell me the truth. Is this man a British soldier?"

"No," Joseph answered from the open doorway. "What would we be doing with one of those?" His droll smile was taut. "The mere thought is lunacy."

"On that point, I agree. But then, who is this?"

"Hopefully not what you say or—"

"Stop it, Joseph." Rachel calmed her voice as she waved toward the British officer. "He is recovering. We can't hide it forever if he lives, and then what good will lying do? We can trust Daniel."

"Rachel," Joseph warned, his voice edged. He held her gaze for several moments, challenging.

She refused to back down this time. They needed an ally.

Joseph was the first to glance away. "Fine."

Rachel took a breath and turned back to Daniel. "Fannie was correct. He is British."

"Then what is he doing here? Why would you bring him into your own home? Are you both crazy?"

"Please listen. The night the British and Tories pulled back, I went looking for Pa and Joseph. When I found Joseph, we heard a man crying out for help. Then we stumbled upon *him*. It would have been wrong to kill him or leave him to such a miserable end out there." Rachel lifted her shoulders an inch. "So we brought him home, thinking he would die and we could simply bury him. No one would know the better. The only snag is that he wants to live, and, as of this morning, I would guess he has a chance."

"Rachel…" Daniel glanced at the man in question and then returned his searching gaze to her. "I don't understand why you couldn't have left him there to rot, for your own sakes."

"How could we when the Bible clearly teaches us to do good to our enemies? Sure there are wars, and we'll fight and die, but must we forget Christian love and compassion?" The words came with a fervency Rachel didn't expect, and she twisted her hands in her apron.

"I love my family and that's why I risked my life fighting Redcoats. That was why your pa gave his life."

Her ribs pinched as they constricted. Everything was such a mess. Still, could she have done differently? Could she step back as Joseph had suggested time and time again, and let the man die? "I know what my pa died for. But the fighting is over."

"I think I understand what you are trying to say. But, Rachel, the war's still far from over." His voice rose with conviction as he continued. "We don't know how long before they're back. I mean, there's battles raging all over New England."

"I know, but I can't help but take pity on this man. He has no protection save us. What would you have us do? Put him out of his misery?"

A laugh broke from Joseph's chest. He had closed the door, but continued to linger near it.

Daniel took Rachel's arm. "You know I would do

anything to help you, and so I give you and Joseph this advice: Let's take him as a prisoner to Fort Schuyler and turn him over to Colonel Gansevoort. We can claim we found him. We could even change him back into a British uniform. Nobody would ever be the wiser."

Rachel shook her head. "He's barely starting to improve. If you take him all the way to Fort Schuyler, just the traveling will kill him. And even if he did survive the journey, the care given a prisoner would be next to nothing if they even remembered to feed him. No." She folded her arms. After all the time she'd dedicated to the man's life, she wouldn't see it thrown away. "I won't let him go. Not until he's recovered enough to survive."

"Never mind we don't know if the siege has been lifted from the fort yet." Joseph blew out his breath. "I'm afraid the only immediate way to resolve this is to shoot him as Rachel just suggested. Put him out of his misery. That was always my favorite option."

Despite the hint of sarcasm, Rachel's stomach knotted. How close he had already come to that. "Joseph, you couldn't. That would be cold-blooded murder now."

Daniel threw his arms up and then winced as he brought the bandaged one back to his side. "Rachel, you keep forgetting this is war. Your pa was killed by one of this soldier's comrades. Most likely we even know someone who was killed by this one. You owe him nothing. He deserves nothing."

"He deserves a chance at life. My pa did, and we all do. I won't let anyone take that from him while he can't help himself. You can't haul him out of here until he can support himself."

Daniel squared off to her, his broad shoulders settling back. "And then we may do with him as we see fit?"

"Yes, short of murder. You may turn him over to the army as a prisoner." Rachel held his gaze with her own, sealing the contract.

Daniel glanced to Joseph who shrugged. They seemed equally weary of this fight. "I guess that will be the plan then," Daniel said. "We'll be as cautious as possible to keep this from getting out. Fannie and I will be safe with it. You just be careful with that Redcoat here. I'd definitely never trust one under my roof, even if he was half dead."

Rachel smoothed her apron to keep her hands from taking Daniel by the shoulders and shaking some compassion into him. She didn't want to hurt his injured arm. "Then it's a good thing he's not in your care."

"Only a good thing for him."

The two men left the cabin.

Their conversation had tied Rachel's stomach into knots and fortified her need to keep this man alive. "Lord, I can't help but ask Thee for this man's life. He doesn't deserve to die no more than anyone, I don't think." Rachel gritted her teeth, but she couldn't hold the images from her nightmares at bay. "Nobody deserves to die like the men in that ravine...and my pa."

She took the kettle from the fire and returned to the gathered cloths needed for cleaning and redressing the wound. Rachel held her breath as she pulled back the quilt and removed the bandages to reveal the side of the man's hip. The cream colored cloth was soaked red, yellow, and green from the salve and the poison it had drawn from the broken flesh. The smell was strong, but not as putrid as yesterday. He stirred, moaning as she set a clean bandage over the wound.

"Hush. You're actually starting to heal now. Praise the Lord Fannie brought this salve. I don't think you could beat this infection without it." She pulled the blanket into place and tidied the mess she'd created. About to turn away, Rachel stole a glance to the British officer's face.

Two eyes, green as young pine needles, studied her every move.

6

He could not remove his gaze from the girl, much more youthful than he had thought, seeing her for the first time in daylight—though his vision was anything but clear. Or perhaps his vision was clear and his brain remained hazy. Either way, she was the only reason sufficient to endure the piercing throb the light inflicted.

After gaping for a moment or two, she leaned forward and laid her warm wrist across his forehead. "Glory be. The fever's broke."

"Where…" His voice rasped, forcing him to cough. If he had not known better, he would have suspected someone of feeding him sand.

"Somewhere safe." Uncertainty flickered in the girl's expression, as though she did not fully believe her own words. "I'll get you some water." She hurried to a rudely crafted table at the far side of the small room where a tin pitcher sat, poured some water, and then moved back to his side. "Here, drink this." She lifted his head and pressed the cup to his sore lips.

The tepid liquid eased its way down. Relaxing, he let the moisture sooth his raw throat.

A single word rose from his shadowed thoughts. He coughed in an attempt to clear his voice. "Rachel." The name rang in his own ears, stark—naked, as it were, in its simplicity. Intimate.

She released his head back to the pillow and drew back. "Yes. My name is Rachel Garnet. I've been looking after you since the…since you were hurt."

How long had he been laying helpless? What was the cause of his injuries?

"And you? What's your name?"

*My name…*he searched the recesses of his mind, fully expecting to find it there. Instead the spike already extending between his temples gave a mighty twist. He waited until the pain subsided before acknowledging the panic. He tried to move.

She planted a hand on his chest, holding him down.

His lack of strength did not allow a struggle.

"Stay still."

"What happened?" Questions bombarded but were greeted by a lack of answers inside his brain. "Why…?" But he was helpless against the wave of blackness washing her from his view.

~*~

Rachel pulled away from the British officer as he sagged into the pillow, unconscious. The alarm that had risen in those green irises at the questioning of his identity gave her pause. Could he honestly not remember? Was it a momentary lapse due to his weakened condition, or had the blow to his head caused more lasting damage?

The slamming of the barn door drew Rachel to the window.

Joseph swung onto Hunter's back and spurred him toward the road.

She threw open the door. "Joseph! Where are you

going?" Her voice went unheeded.

Daniel left shortly after their conversation. Could Joseph have had something more to say to him?

Moving to the fireplace, Rachel stoked the fire enough to boil the bone remaining from their supper. A hearty broth would be in order when her patient woke again, to build his strength as he healed.

She poured water into the pot and swung it over the flames. Her neck ached from the building tension. Joseph never rode off without telling her, and yet there was no sign of his return when she walked to the garden for some vegetables to add to the broth. Back in the cabin, she washed the small potatoes and took up a knife.

"Is there more water?" The deep tones resonated across the room.

Startled by the intensity of the man's eyes, Rachel cleared her throat, setting the knife aside. "There's some broth you can try." It had been boiling for a while now.

His gaze followed her.

She turned toward the cast iron pot. His piercing stare traced her every move. He was a British officer, and she was far from a Loyalist. What if he knew—had overheard them talking? He'd already been aware of her name. Rachel glanced to the oak chest where Joseph had hidden the pistol. She mentally shook her head. The man could barely remain conscious, never mind pose a threat.

After propping his head up with a wild goose down pillow, Rachel dragged a chair to his side.

He reached for the spoon, but his hand shook and he put it back to his chest. He chuckled, his brow crinkling as one corner of his mouth twitched. "It does not *look* that difficult." The tones of England touched each syllable.

"It's fine." Her lips pressed together as she steadied her own hands. "That's why I'm here." With care she spooned some of the steaming broth into his mouth and waited for him to swallow.

They continued this way until he shook his head, silently informing her that he'd had his fill.

"How are you feeling?" Rachel touched her wrist to his forehead.

"I was about to ask you that same question." A small dimple appeared high on one of his cheeks. "How am I feeling?"

"You..." Rachel raised an eyebrow at his attempt at humor. "Your fever hasn't returned, but you're still a little warm. Now perhaps you'll answer my question."

"To be honest, I am not sure—other than the constant stabbing pain down my leg and the throbbing in my head. I have no recollection of anything that has happened, or the extent of my injuries, hence it is difficult to understand what I feel."

"You don't remember anything?"

"Only several peculiar dreams, but I would have great difficulty explaining them, since they are all I know."

"What about your name?"

He gave a soft groan. "I have been lying here trying to remember exactly that. Unfortunately, it also remains elusive. Can you not tell me?"

"I don't know your name."

His brow furrowed. "How is that possible? May I inquire how I came to be in your care?"

Rachel sat back in the chair, her hands clasping the bowl. "You're certain you don't remember anything at all?"

"Not a thing. It is as though everything before I woke is obscured behind a dense fog. At least for my mind, that is." Something seemed to occur to him, and he reached up to gingerly touch the cloth binding his head. "Have I struck my head on something?"

"As far as I know you must have hit it against a stone when you fell."

The man closed his eyes for several moments, a pained expression distorting his features. "This head of mine fails to do me any good whatsoever. Could you please tell everything you know about me? What exactly occurred?"

It was easier to organize her thoughts without looking at him. She stared down at the bowl. "You're from England—a soldier...an officer." Even as the words were formed, they felt strange on her lips. "There was a battle not far from here and you were wounded. Your leg was. That was four days ago."

He glanced up. Shades of brown circled his pupils, merging with and darkening the green of his irises. "How did I come to be here?"

Rachel struggled to keep her thoughts from returning to that day—the gruesome images which hadn't ceased haunting her. "We found you."

"The American Colonies," he stated absently, rubbing the back of his knuckles against his short whiskers. He paused as his gaze sought hers. "Is that where we are?"

"No. These are the United States of America."

"United States of America." He squinted at her. "I have the most peculiar feeling, a little unsettling...but my mind is completely absent of details. Who are you in connection to me?"

"I am..." She blew out her breath. "To put it bluntly, you attacked this valley."

"*I* did?"

"You and other British officers led hundreds of Tories and almost a thousand Iroquois against us. Thankfully, the Lord preserved us." Thoughts of Pa ached in her chest. "Most of us."

"Then I am your enemy?" The man swallowed, the cleft between his eyes deepening. "If that be so, why am I here?"

"My mother raised me a Christian. We couldn't leave you there to die when you were no longer a threat." She stood, smoothing out her skirts with her free hand. "If you want the truth, we didn't expect you to live through the night. Unfortunately, you did."

"Unfortunately?" Then he nodded. "I understand." Drained from the effort of speaking, his eyes grew heavy, as did his voice. A muscle danced in his cheek. "I apologize I could not have been more cooperative."

Rachel returned to the potatoes that still needed to be chopped. Something in his last comment refused to leave her. There had been a depth to his voice—almost as though he'd meant every word.

7

Rachel finished the evening chores and pulled the barn door closed. The sun continued its downward course, sinking below the tops of the trees to the west. It was already well past supper and still no sign of Joseph. She wasn't sure what to think, but the longer his absence, the more she feared the reasons for it.

She detoured to the well to draw water. The pail hung heavy in her hand as she pushed through the door, glancing at the British officer just long enough to know he was still awake. After hefting the pail onto the table, Rachel tested the soup she'd removed from the fire before she'd left. Lukewarm. She dished a bowl for herself and sat at the table with some fresh bread.

The British officer's reflective gaze never deviated from her.

She turned away from him. What she wouldn't give for some privacy. She ate quickly, and then continued the mending she'd started earlier. Joseph needed the tear in these breeches stitched, and she wanted to get it done so she could begin other required projects.

There was wool to spin for stockings, mitts, and a warmer shawl for herself, as her last one was beyond repair. A growing pile of other mending also awaited her, as well as gardening, curing meat, and helping Joseph. The list was endless. After several minutes her stitches faltered, The sensation of constantly being watched was grating. Rachel dropped the breeches and retreated to the bedroom.

It was too much to resist sinking into the comfort her bed offered. She closed her eyes and folded her arms. Just a few minutes of sleep and she'd feel better. Would it be so wrong to push everything else from her mind for a little while? No worries, no cares to trouble her…thoughts began to drift.

A loud crash and pained cry echoed within the cabin's thick walls.

Springing from the bed, Rachel ran into the main room.

The wounded man lay face down on the floor, the blanket wrapped snugly about his torso and legs, his hands working to pull himself to the chair she had abandoned.

"What happened?"

He looked up, his face pale, eyes stricken with the agony inflicted upon his hip. He slammed his fist against the floor.

"You were trying to get to Joseph's breeches, weren't you?" Did this man have no sense? "You have been on death's doorstep the past four days, and you tried to get up on your first day of progress? With that stupidity, it's no wonder the British will lose this war."

He glared at her, his jaw clenching. "Indeed. And perhaps it would have been better for you if your mother had taught less Christian goodness and more common sense." He rolled onto his side, protecting his right hip. His eyes clamped shut, his teeth ground together. A short laugh escaped him only to merge into a moan.

Rachel restrained from assisting him. "Would you

have preferred we left you with the rest of your dead, to join them?"

"I don't know," he groaned. "But you would have preferred it."

"And what if I would have? At the moment it's too late for turning back. If you don't die of your own foolishness, you'll probably recover well enough."

"And then what?"

"Then you'll be turned over to our army as a prisoner. You'll neither be our concern nor a threat."

"A threat? How could I possibly threaten you?" His gaze again found hers. "Look at me, I cannot...I cannot even function as...as a human, never mind the soldier you claim me to be." He cried out as he rolled to his back. "I only wish that if I had to lose my memory, it would be of this part of my life and not the earlier." He began to chuckle, pained and pitiable.

Rachel knelt beside him and laid a hand on his shoulder. It really wasn't fair of her to badger him. "Do you think you can get back onto the bed with my help?"

With a glance at the cot, he shook his head, causing several reddish-brown locks to fall into his eyes. "I think I would rather stay here if it is all the same to you."

On impulse, Rachel brushed the hair back from his forehead, wet with sweat and deeply ridged. She reached for a pillow and placed it under his head, then rolled a blanket and slipped it under his right side to protect his thigh. In several minutes she had him situated relatively comfortably on the floor. "You've done a fine work on your hip." A scarlet stain saturated the side of the blanket. "I'll change the bandaging as soon as Joseph returns and we can get you back on the cot." Rachel softened her voice. "Is there anything else I can do for you now?"

He hesitated.

"You can ask."

"Well, I suppose since I have fallen this far..." He almost smiled as his eyes did a slight roll. Then he shook his head, color rushing to his face.

"What is it?"

He looked away, his expression somber. He pinched his eyes closed and set his jaw. "You would not by chance have..."—he released the air from his lungs,—"a chamber pot."

Flames lit Rachel's cheeks, as well. "We don't." She stood. "But I'll find you something."

A grunt rose in his throat. "No need to hurry." Again his pale face flushed with red. "I am truly sorry."

"Don't be sorry."

"But I am..." He glanced at her. "Ardently. I apologize for the trouble I have caused you, and I do...I do appreciate you sparing my life."

Her chest tightened, and she opened her mouth. But what was she supposed to say to that? *"You're welcome,"* didn't quite seem appropriate.

The pounding of hooves as a rider neared the cabin pulled Rachel from his penetrating gaze.

A horse whinnied and was greeted by the gelding in the pasture.

She turned and rushed to the front yard in time to catch a glimpse of Joseph as he led Hunter into the barn. Hitching her skirts high, she darted across the yard. "Where were you? Why did you ride off without telling me? Do you know how worried I've been? Dinner's cold."

Without a word Joseph pulled something red from his saddlebags and thrust it to her, then turned back to heave the saddle from the horse.

A gasp escaped as she grabbed the soiled British uniform. "What...? Where did you get this?" She stared at it, heart pounding. "Joseph, you didn't..." Her hands lowered as her gaze rose. "It's his, isn't it?"

"Yes." His voice lacked emotion. Instead of returning the horse to its stall, Joseph gave him some oats and started gathering harnesses for the wagon.

She clung to the red coat, fighting back the sudden rush of feeling as she followed after him. "What are you doing? Why don't you come in for something to eat? There's soup. I can put it back on the fire."

He wouldn't look at her.

"Stop walking away and talk to me!"

He turned, his face granite, the harnesses draped over his shoulder. "All right, I'll talk to you. I'll tell you about riding into that ravine full of rotting corpses. The stench. The turkey vultures." His hand crossed over his eyes. "I've thought this through, and Daniel's right. We can't risk keeping that man here. I'm taking the wagon to Fort Schuyler tonight while everyone is in their homes. That coat and its owner are coming with me."

"But we agreed to wait. It's twenty miles. If you take him now, he could die."

"Better him than us." The fear in his words glowed vivid in his eyes. He hurried back to Hunter and worked to fasten the harness. "Rachel." His voice softened. "We can't hide him anymore. We can't risk it. He isn't our problem."

"Why can't we wait a little longer? Only Fannie and Daniel know, and they wouldn't tell."

"No one else knows?"

"Of course not."

"Do we know that? How could we? Anyone else could have overheard us that night from the road. We could never be sure. And even if nobody else knows right now, how long do you really believe it'll stay that way?" Joseph moved the horse to the wagon, connecting the straps and buckles. "Rachel, surely you remember the way it was at the beginning of the war. The Cunninghams and others who professed their continuing loyalties to King George and Britain—they were considered a threat. They were persecuted, their homes burned, crops ruined and livestock run off. People got hurt. Everything that could be done short of murder, until the Tories were driven out. That's who we were fighting a few days ago—the ones we used to call neighbors. We were face to face. I even recognized some of them. Bayonets, the butts of our rifles, even our bare hands. That's how we killed each other." He released the last of his breath. "We would be considered the same if we were discovered to be hiding this man." Joseph took a rope to get the other horse from the pasture. He returned several minutes later with Sorrowful, the lanky gelding, and hitched him beside Hunter. Joseph climbed onto the wagon seat.

"What about the siege at Fort Schuyler? You said that we don't know if it's been broken."

"Then I'll head down the Mohawk instead. I don't care if I have to take him all the way to Albany, he's not staying here another night."

She took hold of the strap that ran across Hunter's shoulder. "Don't do this. Please."

"Rachel, haven't you listened to a word I've said?

Don't you understand we don't have a choice any longer?"

"He woke up today."

"What?"

"He's awake now." She ran a hand down the horse's neck.

Joseph lowered the reins. "Why should that change anything? It appears he'll probably live. That's what you wanted."

She looked up at him and shrugged one shoulder. "He doesn't remember anything—not even who he is."

His eyebrows pressed together as he frowned. "That changes nothing." Joseph clicked the reins against the back of the horses, encouraging them forward.

"But—" Rachel grabbed the hook of the bit and jerked Hunter to a stop. "I'm won't let you do this. Not tonight. Not like this."

"Let go!"

"Not yet, Joseph. He needs more time. Give him a couple more days. Give him a chance to—"

"A chance to what? Get us hung?" He slammed his fist with the reins to the wagon seat. Both horses flinched, but remained in place. "Can't you see it, Rachel? I'm scared. Yeah, and I'm even pathetic enough to admit it. It's like some awful dread welling up in me, telling me we've got to get rid of that man before he becomes the death of us." Joseph yanked off his hat and raked his fingers through his thick locks. "Why must we risk our lives for him?"

Rachel walked to her brother, draping the coat over the side of the wagon as her hands stole to his closest knee. "A couple more days, Joseph, please." She leaned her head against his leg, a sob welling within her. She refused to release it despite the growing ache, even as his hand smoothed over her hair like Pa's often did when she was a child. She missed Pa so fiercely the effect was suffocating. If only he were here now and they didn't have to figure this out on their own.

Joseph sagged into the seat. "Fine. A couple of days. But no more."

8

He stared at the roughhewn rafters above, not really seeing them. His mind instead rehearsed the few things he could remember—mostly since he had woken up in this...shack. Even some of those memories were obscured by the dense fog clinging to every thought. Frustrated, he pushed up, maneuvering the downy pillow so he could see more of the room. Pain jolted from his thigh in every direction. He breathed deeply as he waited for it to subside to a throbbing ache. The four or five days since he'd awakened had seen little improvement of his hip, though the gash on his head seemed to be mending quickly enough. If only his mind would heal. If only he could remember.

Locking his jaw against the heavy weight sitting on his chest and the tightness in his throat, he focused his gaze on the girl seated on a stool across the room. No, *girl* wasn't quite right. A woman. Old enough to be out in society. *Society?* Several faded images of elegance flickered in his mind, but not enough to understand its meaning to him...or his place in it.

Rachel. The name fit her well. The beloved wife of Jacob, a virtuous woman. A kind, compassionate, lovely creature...who was married. But then, how awkward would her care of him be, as she attended to his needs and nursed him to health, if she were unmarried? Unimaginably.

He dropped his gaze to the tall, wooden, barrel-like contraption on the floor, held in place between her knees. A long, thin pole stuck out of the top. She pumped it upward and down, her mouth moving slightly, and her head swaying as though she were...was she singing? Silently?

"What is that you are doing?"

She glanced up, her movements halting. "Making butter. Have you never seen a churn and dasher before?"

"No, I am quite sure I have seen something similar in the past, only, I was unsure of how to employ it. I thought perhaps a laundress may put clothes in there and then..." He winced at the profound disbelief in her brown eyes. "Never mind."

She returned to her work as though he had never spoken.

He allowed several minutes to pass. "What is that you are singing?"

Rachel didn't look up. "A song my mother taught me. It helps me maintain rhythm with the dasher."

The room again lapsed into silence.

How weary he was of silence. "Are you opposed to conversation?"

She didn't pause or look up this time. Her face remained unreadable.

"If you would rather not, I understand." They had not spoken much since the day he'd first regained consciousness—at least, not more than necessary. She seemed to prefer it that way, but the need for some human interaction gnawed at him.

"No, I suppose it's all right," she said, still maneuvering the stick. "What did you have in mind?"

"I am not sure. Perhaps you could tell me about

this farm?"

"Like what?" She plunged the dasher downwards. The cadence of her motions faltered.

"I hardly know. I am unacquainted with general farming practices. At least, that I remember. I have glimpses of memories of the streets of a large town, or city, perhaps. Strange, I cannot remember anything more. Nothing of my family, or what I did before the army. I suppose I may always have been a soldier."

That brought a reaction. Her lips thinned and her movements quickened.

He grimaced. "What of your family?"

"My parents came here from Boston about four years ago for a new beginning. This was their homestead. They've both since passed on."

"My condolences." That made sense as to her age. She had come with her parents, and then when illness or accident took them, she had married. Though she seemed to care for the man who shared her room, deeper affection appeared to be lacking. It was probably a marriage of necessity. A knot formed in his stomach. A marriage of convenience. No love. No feeling. But why should he be so affected at the thought of such? It didn't concern him, and thinking about it only hurt his brain. He cleared his throat. "I apologize for so greatly imposing upon you and your husband. He appears to strongly disapprove of my recovery."

The dasher stalled and she looked up. "What?"

"Your husband understandably resents my presence here. I am—"

Her gaze never left him as she released the pole and wiped her hands across her apron. "First of all, Joseph fought against your troops more than once.

Secondly, my father was killed in that last battle. And thirdly..." Her mouth hung open for a moment before she closed it with a tight smile.

"And thirdly?"

"It's not important. The other reasons are plenty to excuse his behavior." Her knuckles showed white as she sent the dasher down with force.

But what was 'thirdly'? He glanced back to the rafters. So her father had been killed by the British and her husband had fought them. Was it any wonder they attempted to ignore him? What made no sense was that they had kept him alive in the first place and were still sheltering him and nursing him back to health.

"I am sorry for your loss." The apology was meager at best. He search for something more he could offer her. Words flowed from the darkened recesses of his mind, forming on his tongue. "'I am the resurrection and the life, he that believeth in Me, though he were dead...yet shall he live.'"

Lashes flickered over deep pools of brown as her gaze met his.

"'And whosoever liveth and believe in Me shall never die.'" He let his eyes close. There was so much clarity with the words—surely he could remember more than them.

"Christ said that, didn't He?"

He nodded.

Rachel pulled hard on the stick. It smashed against the lid, dislodging it and spilling buttermilk and chunks of yellow curd onto the floor.

He pushed himself up a little more, wincing as he did so. Pressure built within his skull. "I have upset you."

"You've not upset me." Rachel jerked to her feet.

"It's the way you speak and the red coat that is now hidden under a pile of hay in the barn."

He dropped back. Pain spiked through his lower body. "Then for that I am sorry."

"And for that I will allow you to apologize," She said as she snatched a rag from the table, "though at this time I cannot accept it." She hurried to sop up the mess on the floor, then tossed the rag onto the table and fled the house, leaving the half-churned butter behind.

~*~

Rachel stumbled as her feet touched the hard-packed ground. She recovered and took a few more steps, her hands coming to her face. What was wrong with her? She'd left the butter, and it would spoil if not attended to soon. And yet she didn't care. Her insides seemed turned upside-down. Lifting the hem of her dress, she ran across the yard toward the grove where her father lay buried beside her mother. She made it only as far as the tilled earth of the garden. The large stump remained in its place, new branches turning it into a round bush, thick roots reaching unseen beneath her feet.

The spade stuck out of the ground where she'd left it at the edge of the potato patch. Rachel wrapped her fingers around the handle as she moved past. The dirt was hardest near the base of the stump, but she started there anyway, hacking away at the tops of the roots, her motions too unfocused to make any real progress as she tried to push the image of the man from her head. He was a British officer. They had killed her father, and now he was disarming her. She wasn't supposed to feel this much compassion. She wasn't supposed to worry so greatly for his wellbeing, his health. He was the enemy.

Why would God torture her like this? Had He no consideration for what He'd done—was doing—to her?

"Oh, Papa." Her chest heaved as she paused, her gaze nailed to the stump and the life it boasted, the life it stole from the vegetables. The spade slipped from her fingers as she dropped to her knees. Tears flowed down her face, no longer able to be contained.

9

Faces, hazed but familiar. Images of a room, its walls polished wood—so different from the ones surrounding him now—and a chair, dark leather. Memories. But what was this room...and where? Who were the people?

He clamped his eyes closed against the agony piercing his temples—his reward for thought. This was the way it always was. The harder he tried to climb through the mist, the thicker it became, adding to the constant pressure at the front of his skull until it became unbearable and he was forced to stop. He pressed the heel of his palm against his forehead. After a while the pain subsided, and he relaxed. Taking deep breaths, he allowed his mind to empty, succumbing to the numbing silence of the vacant house. The part he hated most this past week was the hours and days of nothingness—a vast void encasing him.

Surely there were household chores. Ones that took more than minutes to perform before the woman—Mrs. Garnet—escaped the cabin. *Escaped.* That was probably all too apt. It was so easy to forget his position when he had no memories of his past. And his feelings were far from war-like. He wanted words.

But there were none.

He lived for the few minutes before the young couple retired to their room. They would sit at the table while they ate their dinner, and talk. No conversation was directed to him, only a plate of food and turned backs, but he savored the sounds of their voices.

He eyed the handle of a broom leaning near the door. If he pushed down the straw bristles, it would probably be tall enough to fit under his arm like a crutch. But leaving in his condition was lunacy. Still, how much longer could he inflict himself upon them?

"God, help me."

His voice cut the silence, but not the loneliness.

~*~

"Excuse me, ma'am?"

Rachel refused to look at him. The quicker she washed the dishes that had piled up, the sooner she'd be free of his presence. "What do you need?" Her words came harsher than intended. With a sigh, she glanced up. The man's gaze did not waver from her face, his own stringent. Rachel released her rag into the basin. "What's wrong now?"

"Do not concern yourself, madam. It is obvious you are occupied and do not wish to be disturbed."

"It's too late for that, so you might as well speak your mind."

"Speak my mind?" He released a tight laugh. "Indeed, you say that, but you have no desire to listen to me, or anything I might say. I shall not torture you."

"I..." Rachel planted her hands on the table. She had done everything humanly possible to keep him alive and comfortable, catering to every foreseeable need. Was he angry because she hadn't rushed to his side when he was in want of something? She let her eyes close, though it was impossible to tell if they burned from want of sleep, or frustration. "What do you expect from me?"

He turned his head enough to avert her gaze as the rigidity drained from his face. "Nothing. It would be wrong of me to expect anything more than you have given. My words were said in haste."

Rachel dried her hands. Did this man have any idea how greatly he manipulated her emotions? "What is it you wanted? Just...tell me this time."

"You have informed me of the whereabouts of my coat, but I was wondering what became of the remainder of my garments."

"We burned them."

He gave little reaction to the news.

"We thought it better not to leave evidence of your identity."

"Just my coat."

"Yes."

The creases at the corners of his eyes deepened. "What of my boots, or shoes, or whatever I wore?"

"We buried them."

"Indeed. Of course you did. What could possibly be more logical?"

"You don't seem to realize the risk we are taking having you here." She shoved her hands into the lukewarm water to find her rag.

"I apologize, I did fail to grasp that. I would think your army to be grateful for another prisoner. An officer, no less. Though I do not suppose interrogation will get them very far."

"What were we thinking? Why did we bother keeping you alive if you'll be of no real use to them?" Rachel landed her hands on her hips, the wet rag soaking her dress. She tossed it to the table. Perhaps she'd talk to him when he was acting more rational. Or she could simply avoid him. The latter held most appeal. She would finish washing the dishes in the evening. There was enough work to do elsewhere.

The wind that morning had been a bit gusty, so Rachel made sure her white lawn cap embraced her head properly as she stalked to the door. The British officer's voice caught her hand on the latch.

"You shall leave at that?"

"Joseph is probably finished hitching the wagon and will be waiting for me."

"Except he said that he would come for you."

She turned to face him fully. "What do you want?"

"While I am very grateful for this shirt you have given for my use, and I am equally aware of my position in this..." his eyes focused past her to the door, "prison, and that I have no rights to ask anything of you—"

"It's so British of you to make the full speech." Rachel shook her head. "Can't you simply tell me what you want?"

His gaze momentarily dropped and a muscle tightened in his jaw. "Clothes, Madam. That is all I ask."

"Clothes."

He gave a nod.

She pursed her lips. Clothes. Fine, then. Rachel spun toward the bedroom, skirting past the table and pushing the door halfway closed. Clothes. Pa's oak trunk sat against the far wall, Joseph's limited wardrobe piled on top. Her brother would have to forgive her later. There was no way she was giving a British soldier her father's attire.

She couldn't let herself forget that fact, as easy as

forgetting would be when he turned those green eyes her way, flecks of brown changing their depth with the flow of his emotions. Rachel fought a smile. She hadn't seen him this angry before today, but did it ever make his eyes vibrant. *You can't think like that. He's the enemy. He's the enemy.* And it was only a matter of time before he remembered that as well. If he didn't already.

Rachel chose the recently mended breeches and a pair of long socks, her motion slowing. What if the loss of memory and identity was all a ruse, a ploy to keep their guard down? No. There had been too much sincerity in his confusion when he'd first regained consciousness. But what about after that? His memory may have returned quicker than he let on. That would explain his change in attitude over the past few days. Did it make him dangerous?

"Rachel?" Joseph's call jerked her upright and caught her breath. She hurried, depositing the clothes on the foot of the cot with hardly a sideways glance at the British officer. She stepped outside into the sun.

"We need to hurry," Joseph said. He pointed to the north where a black haze cradled the tree lined horizon. Storm clouds filled with moisture. How many hours did they have to get the cut wheat from the field and into the loft? Probably not enough.

~*~

The mumble of their voices faded, and silence again seeped through the walls, enveloping him. He stared at the breeches and socks resting over his left leg. Still no boots. Or coat. He breathed out, but the feeling of someone sitting on his chest remained.

Lord, what am I doing?

Sun streamed through the window, warming the room beyond the point of comfort. He pushed up on one elbow and caught his fingers in the folds of the clothes, ignoring the pinch in his thigh as he dragged the material close. One of the socks showed a snagged thread threatening the start of a hole. Maybe he needed to wait longer. How far would he get without proper footwear? A chuckle tightened his throat as a spike of pain greeted his attempt to sit up a little more. The lack of boots was the least of his problems.

Unfortunately, he had already determined his course of action.

10

Rachel tightened the ties of her cap to keep it from being snatched away by the wind that howled through the valley. What had been neat stacks of wheat were being flattened and spread out, and the branches of the tall trees lining the field whipped violently. Another gust stole her breath. It was cold—almost frigid—despite the fact that there was still more than a week until the start of September.

Between blasts of wind, Joseph forked the last of one pile onto the back of the wagon and signaled Rachel to move it forward. She clicked her tongue, more out of habit than necessity, and jiggled the reins to encourage the horses. They seemed as anxious as she and bolted forward. Rachel jerked on the reins, but they still overshot the next stack.

"Back it up, boys," she mumbled, giving the reins short pulls. With the wagon finally where it needed to be, Rachel rubbed her arms vigorously. She should have dressed warmer, but there had been no reason for it a couple hours ago.

Joseph caught up to the wagon. "Why don't you slip up to the cabin and grab your cloak. It will take me a little while to load this pile. Actually, you might as well stay where it's warm. I'll bring the load around to the barn after this one."

The thought of warmth was truly tempting,

regardless of the British officer's presence in the house. Still, she hesitated. It wouldn't be fair to leave Joseph alone to battle this weather. "I can wait," she said as a shiver worked its way through her body. "You might need me."

"Not as much as you need to warm up," he shouted over the howl of the wind. "You're wasting time arguing. Tie off the reins. The horses will stay put. It'll do no one any good if you catch your death of cold."

"But—"

One look silenced her, and she did as directed, notwithstanding the heavy feeling dragging her steps.

The storm was on its way, and there was still too much to do.

Rachel paused at the barn first. Upon stepping out of the wind, warmth began to return to her body. Her extremities remained chilled. As much as she wanted to bask in the relief of shelter, she needed to fetch her cloak from the cabin if she was to help unload the wagon. But *he* was there. She slipped deeper into the protection of the barn.

The milk cow greeted her with a prolonged melancholy bawl.

Rachel stopped to scratch the wiry brownish-red hair between its ears. "Have you missed me that much?"

Two large dark eyes seemed to answer, and Rachel rubbed a little harder.

"Don't worry. I've missed you as well. All right, not really." She sighed. "Not after you kept trying to step in my pail this morning." She lowered her hand to scratch the jawbone. "But don't worry—you're preferred company."

With a final pat on the cow's neck, Rachel reached for the wooden pail hanging from a beam, and searched out where the chickens had laid their eggs that morning. Thankfully, their favorite spots rarely changed. Within a few minutes she'd gathered almost a dozen.

"Why does it have to be so cold today?" She moved back toward the doors.

They couldn't afford heavy rain until they'd gathered in the last of the cut wheat.

There were a couple acres Joseph hadn't touched yet, but the moisture would do them little harm at this point.

Rachel slumped against the door, out of reach of the wind. She took a breath, but her chest remained tight, weighed down with the enormity of keeping their farm from failing—of surviving this wilderness without Pa. She glanced to the skies, but there was only gathering darkness—no sign of God. He had abandoned them.

Her red, icy fingers still held the handle of the pail, and she shivered. She needed to go to the house but was frozen in place, so weary in every form of the word. She couldn't feel like a stranger in her own home. The thought of facing another day, catering to the every need of that man..."I can't do this anymore. I just can't." She'd put off Joseph's insistence that they needed to turn the British officer over to the army too long already. He would no doubt survive the trip now, so why hesitate? If the rain delayed harvest, now would be the best time. No more excuses.

Another tremor coursed the entirety of her body. She exhaled. There was no time to stand here moaning. The barn groaned from the wind, and the temperature continued to drop. The clouds approaching looked even darker than the ones overhead.

As she entered the cabin, Rachel glanced to where the British officer lay, and then moved to add fuel to the last of the glowing coals. The room wasn't very warm anymore. She halted mid-motion. The cot was empty.

Her heart leapt as she bolted across the room, barely aware of the eggs as they cracked against each other in the pail. Without thought, Rachel tossed them and the bucket on the bed and tore into the bedroom. It was empty. She couldn't even call his name because she didn't know it.

"Joseph!" Running from the cabin, Rachel hollered even though it would be impossible for him to hear her over the wind. "Joseph!" Rachel raced past the barn. She climbed the rail fence, almost falling to the ground. The wind whipped, snatching away her breath and stinging her eyes. They watered, hazing her vision. "Joseph!"

Joseph worked to fasten down the high load even as the wind tried to scatter it over the field. "What's happened?"

Rachel braced against the high walled box as she caught her breath. "He's...he's gone."

"Who's gone?"

"The...the man. The British...officer."

"Where?"

"I don't know. He's just...gone."

Joseph's smoky blue eyes showed the depth of his pondering. He started toward the front of the wagon. "Perhaps it is just as well. We needed to get rid of him somehow. It's better for us that he accomplish it himself."

Rachel stared at her brother. "But—but what'll happen to him?"

"What does it matter to us?" Joseph climbed onto the seat and loosed the reins. "We have at least one more load before it begins to pour. And you still haven't put on something warmer. Are you coming?"

Rachel's mouth opened as her mind churned. Maybe he was right. Maybe they should let the man go and be done with it. "Joseph, he can't make it very far on that leg, and in this weather? He'll die. And what if someone finds him? He's wearing your clothes. What if someone recognizes them?"

He shot her a look of disbelief. "No one will suspect us of helping a Redcoat."

"What if he tells them?"

"That's not what you're concerned about, is it? I bet you don't even believe that he would tell someone. Now, do you want a ride back or are you walking?"

Rachel scanned the area. "I know he wouldn't tell anyone. I can't let him..." The sentence broke off as she raced back toward the cabin.

Reins jingled as leather cracked over the horses' backs, encouraging them to a run.

She cut through the fence, and they arrived back at the barn at the same time.

Throwing the reins to the seat, Joseph jumped to the ground.

Rachel reached the cabin, pulled on her cloak, and shoved past him.

Joseph stood in the doorway. "What are you doing?" He grabbed her arm, jerking her back.

Rachel yanked away. "I'll go look for him, and don't expect me back alone."

"Since when did you worry so much for a British

officer? Have you forgotten who he is?"

How could she forget? But...Joseph was right. Why couldn't she leave him out there? "He is not a bad man, Joseph. I know he fought with them, but he's not evil and doesn't deserve this. He doesn't even remember who he is."

Joseph's jaw flexed. "A lot of men die who don't deserve to. Pa didn't deserve it either, but some Redcoat Brit shot him dead without a second thought."

She turned back to the growing dusk. The scent of rain saturated the air. "We're running out of time."

"Don't be a fool, it's already too late."

Clutching the cloak, Rachel hurried into the chill wind toward the more heavily treed portion of the farm. It seemed logical that the fugitive would want to remain out of sight. Directly west.

11

The rain was light at first, but now it fell with increased fervor.

He stumbled toward the nearest tree, letting the makeshift crutch drop as he slid down the trunk. He muffled a cry with his sleeve as he met the ground. Agony lanced through his thigh and down his leg. His eyes watered from the pain. What had he been thinking, leaving the comfort of the cot and the cabin? Pride? No...it had to be something more.

The pain in his hip was slow to ebb, only to be combined with the throbbing in his chest. He had taken matters into his own hands and removed himself from their home and their lives, but now what? The wind had turned surprisingly cold and his clothes were soaking through. Would he simply die here, a stranger even to himself?

"That's peculiar." The deep resonance of the voice pulled his gaze toward the road where Joseph Garnet stood, peering down at the ground, his hat pulled low, and his chin nestled into the collar of his coat. He was probably wondering where he had lost the trail—the broom handle left an obvious mark for anyone looking for it.

"I'm such a fool," Joseph mumbled. "I need to find that girl and give her a good talking to." With one final glance at the horizon, he turned back in the direction of the cabin.

If Joseph was out looking for him, they obviously still considered him a threat to them and their settlement, though he couldn't understand why. He'd be the death of himself long before he caused them any harm. He buried his face in his hands. Moisture filled his eyes, pressing against closed lids.

Joseph's footsteps drew near.

He'd been discovered. Wiping his hands down his face, he set his view into the distance. He flexed the muscles in his jaw, blinking. Hopefully the rain disguised his tears.

Joseph stopped only a couple of feet away. "Did you really think you'd get far on that leg and in this weather?" The hand holding a pistol slipped from the coat.

"I had no such plans." His chin rose. He held his voice even. "But I am not returning."

"Do you think you have much choice in the matter?" A gust of wind made both men shiver. "You don't play the part of a prisoner very well, do you?"

"Why do you delay in turning me over to your army?"

"Don't worry, that's still the plan. But until then, you'd better not cause us any more trouble."

He held Joseph's gaze. "That is not what you really want. You do not want to turn me over to be eventually traded back to Britain, and Mrs. Garnet is no longer here."

"*Mrs.* Garnet?"

"Yes. So why hesitate? You came with that pistol for a reason." He lowered his head, the taunting in his voice diminishing. "At this moment, I would not hold anything against you if you were to do as you like."

"Perhaps." A long pause followed as Joseph shook his head. "But I'd sure hold it against myself. Shooting an unarmed man, who by rights shouldn't even be able to walk, seems a little too close to murder." There was the breath of a chuckle. "That's why we need to give you a while longer to heal."

He swallowed the lump forming in his throat. He was the enemy and could not forget that.

Joseph sat on the soggy ground.

They remained silent as the heavens poured.

A shiver worked its way through his injured body. The light, homespun shirt was already soaked through and hugged his skin. Soon he shook violently, his body no longer up to the task of shutting out the cold on its own.

"Sure you don't want to come back in out of the storm?"

Go back? To warmth, comfort...and the insufferable silence of the cabin.

He shook his head.

"How long do you figure you'll make it out here?" Joseph questioned. "It's bound to get mighty cold tonight. I knew a man once, someone new to the area. He went hunting and didn't make it home before supper. That night it turned fearsome cold, and the rain poured like it is now. Next morning they found him—caught in a bear trap and dead as could be. Bear trap hurt him some, but not enough to kill. It was the weather that did him in. Sometimes a man's pride can be just like that there trap. It won't kill a man, but it sure as fire don't help him none."

Again silence.

"I'm wasting my breath, aren't I? You British are too pompous to ask for help."

"Pompous?" he choked out as a spasm of pain eased. "What have I to be proud of? I do not know who I am, nor does there remain with me any sure memory of my past." He stared at the murky puddles forming on the ground. "I cannot remember whether I have place for pride."

"Then will you stay out here and die?"

The question haunted him. "I hardly know."

"You don't know much, do you?"

A laugh sounded, but he didn't feel it. He wiped a hand across his forehead and through his soaked hair, pushing it away from his face. Words, strange, yet understood, echoed in the back of his mind. *"Hen oida hoti ouden oida."*

"I thought you were supposed to be English. I don't even know what that was."

"It is Greek. 'I know one thing: that I know nothing.' Socrates."

"Greek?" Joseph shook his head. "I may have to take back my comment about you not knowing much."

"But you were not mistaken. I cannot manage to make sense of anything right now." He glanced over. "Least of all you."

To his surprise, Joseph laughed. "Don't feel bad for that. Not a person I know has been able to make sense of me—myself included."

"At least you know who you are." He gritted his teeth against the pain in his leg, and to keep his teeth from chattering. "All I have are glimpses of images. Emotions...but nothing to secure them together." He sniffed back the moisture threatening to escape. He looked at his hands. What a mess he was. His memory was faulty, his pant leg was soaked with blood where his wound had reopened, and he didn't even have a handkerchief. "Are you sure you do not wish to put that pistol to use? It could solve both our problems."

With a sigh, Joseph withdrew the gun. He held it in his hands as they both stared at it. Then he raised it and squeezed back on the trigger. The air was split with the sound of thunder. Joseph lowered the pistol. "There, that leaves us with one less option. I didn't bring another ball."

"What options does that leave us? I suppose you can go home and I shall..." He shook his head. A mistake. It throbbed from the motion. "I guess that is the question, is it not?"

"Here's an answer. You let me take you back to the cabin before you catch your death."

"And then what? It always brings us to the same place. It makes as much sense for me to stay out here."

"There are always options."

"There were until you spent that last shot." Derision filled his tone. "Now look where that leaves us."

"I could always drag you back with me, or carry you."

"You would have to." He bit down hard, but still his eyes watered. "I cannot walk. I cannot even move."

Joseph slipped the pistol into the pocket of his coat. "You staying out here isn't an option. It never was. So what's the easiest way to get you back to the cabin?"

He had no answer. Both legs were numb with pain.

"Then let's simply give it a try." Joseph slipped an arm around his torso and pulled him up.

He groaned, the stabbing torment of his thigh sharp. His fingers clung to Joseph's coat as he leaned against the stronger man, balancing on his left leg. "I cannot do this," he moaned.

"You have no choice unless you want me to carry you over my shoulder."

A cry escaped his throat as Joseph maneuvered forward a step, forcing him to do likewise.

"It may yet come to that." He let his head drop forward, and clamped his eyes closed. The world spun. Clinging to Joseph, he did his best to focus his thoughts past the pain, to the movement required by his good leg.

~*~

Wet, weary and with no light left by which to search, Rachel trudged back to the cabin. Mud coated her dress from the times she'd fallen over large roots or slipped in puddles. It seemed to weigh more than her body as she fought for each step.

The flicker of a lantern shining through the window became visible through the trees.

Joseph most likely sat with his feet up by the fire, chuckling at her foolishness.

Holding back her emotions had already caused a mountain of pressure behind her temples, but she continued to fight them—and the desire to pray. She wouldn't be foolish enough to ask for help this time; though, without the help of God or her brother, no wonder she'd failed.

A branch breaking nearby jerked Rachel around. Her heart hammered as she peered through the darkness. "Who's there?"

The only answer was the movement of a dark form pushing through the bushes—the shadow of a large man, but not Joseph. Who would be wandering the woods in this storm? An Indian? No, he wore a hat. A Tory?

She dropped low, her hands searching the brush for protection. Her fingers closed around a branch about the thickness and length of a musket. It would have to do. Rachel straightened, bringing one end to her shoulder as she cleared the fear from her voice, deepening it. "I'm armed. I suggest you tell me who you are and what you want."

The reply was a deep chuckle.

She tightened her grip on the branch. "I'm giving you fair warning. I won't hurt you if you speak up quickly."

"With you, getting shot by a branch is the least of my worries—even if it was a real musket."

"Daniel? Daniel Reid, so help me, is that you?"

"It is." As he walked to her, a large boyish grin spread from one ear to the other. "Sorry if I startled you." Daniel took the branch. "I'm just glad it's not loaded."

Rachel scowled. "What are you doing here?"

"That's what I wanted to ask you." An amused expression played on his features. "I've known women to do strange things, but this takes the prize."

She rotated but slipped on the soggy ground and fell backward into his arms. He held her, not seeming in a hurry to release her. Only when she tried to right herself did he move. "I'm sorry, Rachel." The apology came as he assisted her to stand. "I was trying to find you. Joseph came by the farm a half hour ago and explained what happened. He's looking for you, too. You were foolish to come out here on your own."

"I don't want to hear it, Daniel. I get it enough

from Joseph, I don't need it from you." She moved toward the faint light glowing from the cabin. "You men always seem to have it figured out. Everything is simple—black and white.   No questioning,   no wondering...no feeling."

"Rachel." Something in his voice made her turn to face him. "You're wrong, you know. We see plenty of gray. Maybe too much. We do question and wonder. And we have feelings the same as anyone. Only we don't show it so much. We have to put life into order. Get the work done—keep shelter over our families' heads, food coming to the table, and enemies off our land. That is how the good Lord made men, and I—" Daniel's speech ended abruptly.

Joseph reined Hunter into the yard, pulling to a halt several feet away.

"Goodnight, Daniel." Rachel hurried to the door. She slapped it shut and leaned back as a sob rose.

Her brother's voice shouted over the howl of the wind. "Thanks, Daniel. I'm obliged for your help." The sound of a palm slapping against the horse's wet coat followed his words. Joseph was probably letting Hunter make his own way to the barn.

"I'd best be getting home 'fore this storm gets much worse." Daniel's voice faded. "I'll be over sometime tomorrow. It's far past time that things get settled."

Rachel pulled away from the door. The heavy cloak clung so she removed it and draped it over the back of a chair. The inviting fire beckoned. Where was that British fool? Out there somewhere, probably collapsed in the forest, soaked to the bone and freezing to death. The poor man. He'd die alone without even remembering who he was.

His face appeared in her mind. The corners of his eyes wrinkled with the hint of smile as he'd tried to coax her into conversation. A crease in his cheek suggested a dimple. His penetrating pine-green gaze made her heart throb.

Rebellious, Rachel's gaze stole to where the empty cot stood. She hugged herself against the chill. Then she stopped, peering through the shadows that created the appearance of a sleeping form.

12

Joseph came through the door, shaking off rainwater, an apologetic grin on his face.

With a gasp, Rachel stumbled to the cot. Her knees met the floor and her muddied hands hid her face. Her shoulders trembled as her insides untangled. She was helpless against the tears, unable to dam them any longer.

"It was as you said. He could tell who it was who helped him." There was a soft chuckle. "Besides, imagine the information breach if he happened to get back to the British lines. They wouldn't be afraid of our guns anymore. They'd know that if they happen to get wounded, all they'd have to do is find a good Christian woman."

Rachel wiped her damp cheeks. Still, fresh tears fell. "What will we do when he does recover?"

"We'll discuss it later. First thing is to get you cleaned up and then get that leg redressed. I hope you have more of that salve, 'cause he needs it."

"There's still some." She braced against the cot as she pushed to her feet, the saturated skirts heavy. "Did he do much damage?"

It wasn't Joseph's voice that answered. "It definitely feels like it."

Rachel's gaze flashed to the man's face and those piercing eyes. Humiliation and anger seared her cheeks. She pushed the embarrassment aside, savoring the frustration. "What were you thinking? Why would you try to leave with your leg still needing to heal and the storm on the verge of drowning the valley? Are you trying to kill yourself, or did hitting your head on that stone knock *all* the sense out of you?"

His eyes darkened. "I no longer wished to burden you."

She ignored him as she lifted the blanket away from his leg and the blood-soaked breeches. Joseph would need to get them off of him so she could freshen his bandaging before it dried, though that would take some time. His clothes were every bit as wet as hers.

"I know how much you hate me. You don't have to do this anymore."

Joseph headed to the bedroom, probably for a change of clothes.

She brushed her tangled tresses from her face and leaned over her patient. "If I hated you, tell me why I spent all evening searching in the rain and cold." Even with her voice lowered, it retained the essence of feminine rage. "Maybe you can explain why I couldn't leave you to the fate of your British stupidity?"

His reply came too quickly, as though it had been rehearsed. "Because you are a good woman who would scarce let an ornery dog go hungry. But admit it, you would be happier, and you would sleep better at night if I were no longer here."

"Of course I'd sleep better." Rachel flipped her braid over her shoulder and out of the way. Her teeth clamped together as she scowled at him, too tired to keep up pretenses. "I *would* sleep better without worrying that you might not be alive by morning. Not wondering what will become of you—hoping that you'll continue to heal." The truth slipped from her with a will of its own. Rachel spun away, tears again escaping their confinement. She cupped a trembling hand over her mouth, hushing a cry welling up in the back of her throat and the words that she couldn't tell him. *I wouldn't have been able to sleep tonight if Joseph hadn't brought you back.*

Her brother pulled a woolen sweater over his head as he reentered the room. "Rachel, you need to get out of those clothes before you freeze to death."

"I'm fine." She sniffled and swiped a hand across her cheeks. "Let's take care of him first. He's been wet longer."

Joseph took her by the shoulders and directed her toward the bedroom door. "That's my job. I'll put the kettle on and get his leg so you can doctor it. You have time to get changed out of your clothes. And take those boots off before you track muck everywhere. You'll have a hard enough time getting the floor clean, as it is."

Rachel scanned the mess on the floor, and the rude appearance of her garments hanging damply about her frame. "Fine." She hastened from the room, still trailing mud. She'd worry about that later.

~*~

His mind still failed to grasp a reason for the passion behind her words. How could the woman be so compassionate to her enemy? She was even more perplexing than her husband, who worked to remove the soaked clothes that clung to him, tossing them and the now damp blanket in a pile on the floor.

"Cold?" Joseph chuckled as he tucked a dry quilt

around his shivering body.

"A little," he growled.

"Serves you right." After throwing more logs on the fire, Joseph returned with another blanket, arranging it so his damaged thigh would be accessible.

A yelp escaped as pain stabbed through his leg.

"Sorry. Looks like you tied this on so it wouldn't ever come off. I might have to cut the bandage."

He took a breath as the agony ebbed. "Admit it, you only brought me back here so you could practice your techniques for torture."

"Have to find out somehow what will break the British." Joseph slid a knife from the sheath at his hip and slit the ties of the bandage.

He eyed the six-inch blade. "Could you not have listed that among our options? Another ball for your pistol would not have been required, after all."

"Just don't try that again. I don't think I'd waste my powder a second time. I'd have to shoot you in the other leg. We don't take kindly to patients leaving without permission."

"I shall consider myself warned."

Rachel reappeared in dry clothes. She went to the fire to pour what had to be now scalding water into a pan.

"It still remains unclear why you are helping me."

"I admit to not knowing myself until an hour or so ago." Joseph glanced at Rachel and then back again. "But now I realize it's because somewhere in a place I've never been, in a time I've only heard of, a man said to love your enemies. If it had been an ordinary man, I could have shrugged it off without a second thought— I almost did—but it was the Son of God, so it seems the thing to do."

Even though his eyes remained on Joseph, letters and pages of a book flashed across his mind, growing bold. He could see the words. He knew them so well. "'Love your enemies, bless them that curse you, do good to them that hate you, pray for them which despitefully use you and persecute you...that ye may be the children of your Father which is in heaven.'" He looked to his benefactors. "There are people who actually live Christianity, and not merely profess it?"

"Don't look at me." Joseph motioned toward his wife as she gathered clean cloths. "If you want a true Christian, Rachel is the one representing this family. Her goodness sort of rubs off on the people around her." Joseph stood and moved away as she approached. "Hunter will be waiting for oats and a good currying."

Rachel remained silent as she set the basin near the cot. She finished removing the bandage, her hands much kinder then Joseph's had been. Still, a groan couldn't be contained as she cleaned where the scab had opened.

"I'm sorry." She winced as though she were the one in pain.

"What have you to be sorry for? I am sure we can blame everything quite easily on my British stupidity." The humor he'd tried for didn't make it past his clenched teeth. "I should be apologizing for causing you more trouble."

Her hands paused as her gaze found his. "Just give yourself time to heal, all right?" She spread a dark salve across the fresh bandage, and pressed it gently against the wound. "If you try to kill yourself again, I'll shoot you myself."

He grunted in acknowledgment, the side of his

mouth pulling up against his will. "You and Joseph both."

She straightened the blankets around him, her countenance grave. "Any of our friends and neighbors would gladly come with loaded muskets and do just that if they knew you were here. Don't you understand that? You put us at risk, too."

"Forgive me." He covered his eyes with his hand. How could he have been so foolish? He did not want to hurt the Garnets in any way. That was all the more reason to leave...as soon as he was well enough.

13

He jerked awake to the dimly lit room. Images, faces, flashed across his foggy mind. Everything abstract. Clouded. Even his surroundings. The small rustic room. The hard bed making his body ache. He didn't feel overheated and yet perspiration trickled from his face.

The creaking of a door pulled his gaze to a young man as he stepped into the room and stifled a yawn. Recognition pushed back several layers of the haze.

And then *she* appeared, stepping around Joseph, moving directly toward the cot.

"How did you sleep?" Rachel crouched over him. "You don't look well." She placed her palm on his forehead. "That's strange. You're soaked but you feel chill." A spark ignited in her eyes. "You fool. Your fever probably returned last night thanks to your escapade yesterday."

He pushed her hand away. "Do not concern yourself. I believe I have learned my lesson."

"I hope so." She sighed. "I'll get you fresh blankets."

With a glance down at his bare arms and chest, he grimaced. "Could I disturb you for clothes, as well?"

She pursed her lips, as though deeply contemplating his request. "I don't know if I trust you with them now."

Joseph chuckled from across the room. "The man did say he's learned his lesson. The least you can give him is a clean shirt."

"Fine, but anything else he has to earn by behaving himself and staying where he belongs." She moved toward the bedroom.

He nodded his thanks to Joseph, who held his gaze, all joviality draining from his face. "Rachel, give him some of Pa's clothes. They'll fit him better than mine."

She twisted back to Joseph. "But..."

"It's all right. Just do it. I'll get all the stock looked after this morning so you can see to our friend here. I'll stop for breakfast when I bring the milk." Joseph pulled a tricorn hat onto his head and disappeared out the door.

Rachel didn't move, still staring after her husband, her cheeks white. No doubt the thought of seeing her father's garments on the likes of him turned her stomach.

"You do not have to."

She glanced at him before dropping her gaze. "It's fine. Joseph is right. It's impractical to leave them sitting in the trunk when Pa has no more use for them." Her eyes shone, and she turned toward the bedroom.

"I am sorry."

"Apology accepted." Her hands came to her face as she slipped from sight.

He massaged the dull ache behind his temples.

Rachel returned within a few minutes, setting the clothes on the rocking chair and then laying a new quilt over him. "Can you hold this one in place while I withdraw the damp ones?"

He nodded, doing as directed. A moment later she hung the used quilts over the back of two chairs to dry. "Do you need the pot?" she asked, her back still to him.

"I can wait until Joseph gets back." He would probably never get used to needing help with that. Even now, his face heated discussing it with a beautiful young woman—even if she was married. "Would you help me with the shirt?"

Stepping to the rocker, she took the garment in her hands and shook it out. Moisture again brimmed in her eyes, making them appear larger. With the shirt draped over her arm, she moved to his side and pulled the blanket from his chest. Her gaze lingered a moment too long, and he fought the urge to squirm.

It wasn't as though she were a beautiful, unmarried lady with whom there could be any attachment. She had a husband and was only serving in the capacity of a nurse.

Still, warmth crept up his neck as Rachel rotated him slightly onto his good side, sliding his arm into one sleeve and tucking the shirt behind him. She moved to the other side and helped him with the second sleeve, knelt beside the cot and put her hands on his chest as her fingers worked to button the front. While worn, the shirt was actual linen, not homespun.

"I can do that." He cleared his throat. "I am sure you have more than me to attend to."

Her hands paused then she nodded, her eyes flickering briefly to his. "I'll fix breakfast."

After he finished with the buttons, he looked to the ceiling.

Rachel's presence was marked by the clanking of pans, the gurgling of water being poured, the cracking of eggs—she commented at least a couple had survived yesterday's misadventure, whatever that was—and the scrape of smooth wood against wood. The rafters remained silent and unchanging, just as they had for the past week and a half. He moved his gaze to her, folding the pillow in half to hold his head higher as he watched everything she did.

"You know, I won't poison your food or anything of the sort," Rachel said after a few minutes, her voice terse.

He raised a brow. "I am hardly concerned about that."

"I wasn't sure, the way you watch me—as if you're scrutinizing my every action."

No wonder she had avoided the house in the past. "I did not intend to appear so audacious. There is not much for me to do except stare at the ceiling. I fear I have become rather bored with that."

"I imagine so." Regret touched her face and softened her features. "I'm sorry I purposefully stayed away. I never gave much thought to how you would spend those hours."

"You had your reasons."

"Though very poor ones. It was wrong of me. Perhaps we could find you something to do." Her lips gained fullness with the suggestion of a smile. "I don't suppose you knit."

He chuckled. "I do not." He raised his hands. "I am afraid these are not so useful."

"Would you like something to read? I assume from the manner of your speech, that you are capable."

"You have books?" Why did that surprise him?

Her chin lifted. "Perhaps we are not the peasants you assume us to be. My mother brought volumes of poetry and other books to teach us to read by. Even several novels. And we have the Bible, of course. Though I don't suppose you need it."

"Why would I not need the Bible? Is it not written, 'man shall not live by bread alone, but by every word that proceedeth out of the mouth of God'?"

"That's why. You probably don't need it because it seems you already have every verse stored in your head. Tell me, how is it you can't remember your own name, but can quote scripture as if you wrote it?"

He relaxed into the pillow, the hazy rafters no longer his focus. Still his mind could not grasp the answer. Either the human brain was a finicky thing, or the words of that book meant more to him than even his own identity.

Rachel came from the bedroom a moment later and handed him a thick, leather-bound volume. He took it, wiping his sleeve across the dusty cover.

"I got to thinking last night," she said on her way back to the table, "maybe it would help your memory if we listed some names. If you heard your own, perhaps you'd recognize it."

"I suppose it is worth the attempt if you are willing to assist me." He opened the book and glanced at the words. The prophecies of Isaiah. "I have spent hours searching my mind, yet it continues to evade me."

She picked up the bowl and moved to the fireplace where the table blocked most of her actions. She stirred the coals and set something over them on a rack. "What are some fine English names? How about Thomas?" she asked.

He shook his head.

"James, Andrew, Simon, John?"

"Are you listing common British names or the

Apostles of Christ?" He smiled at her.

"Well, you do seem to be Christian, and they are quite common names here. I'm not British—at least, not anymore—so you tell me which names are popular in England."

"No, let us continue with this." He flipped through the pages of the Bible. "You are correct. I am Christian. I do not remember it, exactly, I simply...I know it. My belief in Christ seems to run deeper than memories or thoughts. It is the core of who I am, as though I would cease to exist without that sense of faith in the Lord. For 'who shall separate us from the love of Christ? Shall tribulation or distress or...'" He looked to her with a sheepish smile. Pulling himself up a little more, he redirected his attention back to the Bible. "Shall we continue? What are some of the other names?"

The sizzle of batter meeting a hot skillet was followed by a mouthwatering aroma.

His stomach pinched and churned. Had it been most of a day since he had eaten last? The pain in his thigh had been distracting enough until now.

"Do you want them from the Old Testament? There's Adam, Jacob, Ezekiel, or, perhaps," she flashed him a grin, "Nebuchadnezzar?"

"Nebuchadnezzar? Do you really think that fits?" He shook his head. "Perhaps we should start with the New Testament. I am sure you agree I look more like a Herod or Pilate?"

"I wasn't planning to say anything, but I think you're right." She shot him a disapproving glare. "We're wasting time. Let's be serious."

"I thought we were."

He was rewarded with another scowl, but, so far

as he could remember, he had never seen one as pretty. He chuckled and turned his focus to the Bible. "What other names are there?"

"What would a mother call her little redheaded boy? I know your hair is dark now—browner—but I am guessing you were quite fiery as a child. How about Peter, or Thomas...oh, I said that one already. There's also Stephen."

"Stephen." There was something about that name.

"Is that it? Is that your name?"

He searched his mind, ignoring the pressure mounting there. "I think not."

"Oh, no." Her cry was accompanied by the scent of something charring. "You distracted me, and they started to burn." She flipped the flat cakes onto a plate and poured more batter into the skillet.

He continued his trek through the pages until he came to a list of the disciples' names. "You did not mention Philip yet, did you?"

"No. I didn't list even half of them."

"Nathaniel, Matthew, and of course there is always Judas."

"Your mother would have been a cruel woman to name you after Judas."

A laugh formed in his chest, tendrils of pleasure spreading through him as it released from his throat. What a relief after days of tension. "There were two of them."

"Yes, but only Iscariot is remembered." Rachel placed the batch of hot cakes on a plate under an overturned pot. "I think I like the name Thomas for a redhead. That, or Andrew. But I already said that one, too. I guess we will have to move on to names not in the Bible, or back to the Old Testament. Are you sure it's not Nebuchadnezzar?"

He closed the Bible, but continued to stare at it. "Say that name again."

"What name—Nebuchadnezzar?"

"No. Before that one. Andrew." What was it about that name? Almost a familiarity.

"What about it?"

He met her gaze, but remained somber as he willed the fog to lift. "Say it to me again."

"Why?"

"Please, repeat it once more."

"Andrew?" she asked, her voice unsure.

"Again. Speak it as though you were addressing me."

"Andrew."

Something in her voice, a gentleness, brought his gaze back to her.

Rachel's hair was pulled into a tight braid, yet already fine strands of gold had escaped to frame her olive-toned face. With the lamp dim at her side and the morning light pouring from the window, she seemed encircled as if by a heavenly aureole.

He fought down the lump in his throat and again looked away. Not only was he an enemy soldier—she was another man's wife.

~*~

Rachel struggled to catch her breath. His gaze had become so intense; it was as though he had reached out and touched her. His abrupt withdrawal tugged at her heart. She turned back to the skillet. "What's wrong?"

"Nothing. I recognize that name, is all."

"Do you think it could be yours?"

"I could hardly be sure."

"It's a good enough name." She cleared her voice, but it still sounded strange to her ears. "Would you mind if we called you Andrew? It seems odd having nothing at all."

"You mean nothing that would not rally the Continental soldiers."

She glanced over her shoulder.

His dimples showed, then deepened, extending down his cheeks as he smiled. It transformed his face and lit his eyes. Her heart did a little skip. "I suppose."

Rachel quickly directed her attention back to the fire and stirred down the coals. "I wonder." What of his coat under the pile of hay—had Joseph ever checked it for anything that would identify their patient? Strangely, such had never occurred to her.

"What was that you said?"

Rachel dropped the poker back to its place and hurried through the door into the rain. Darting into the barn, she went directly to the stack of hay. Joseph was nowhere in sight, which was good. She didn't want to explain. She'd wait until her search proved fruitful—if it proved so.

The coat was well buried, literally in the heart of the stack. Joseph definitely wanted to take no chance of it being discovered. Sprigs of dried grass clung to her dress and head by the time she pulled the red uniform out. Rachel sat back, reality turning her empty stomach. She couldn't think about that now. She had one purpose—to find out who that man really was, and to help him remember. But what if that was a mistake? Right now he was a harmless nobody with no alliances or duty. What would become of that man when his memory returned?

A paper crinkled under the pressure of her fingers as they gripped the coarse fabric. Rachel reached into the pocket and withdrew a letter. The blue waxen seal already broken, she unfolded it, flattening the parchment over the scarlet coat.

Captain Andrew Wyndham,

I have written to inform you that the request for Lieutenant Stephen Wyndham's transfer to the Eighth Regiment has hereby been approved. Though this is highly irregular, I have been made aware of your family's situation. I trust you shall continue to put your duty to your country and the uniform you wear above that which you owe to your kin.

Lieutenant-colonel Barry St. Leger

Rachel stared at the words. Andrew Wyndham. The name of a gentleman...and a captain in His Majesty's army. She folded the letter into the coat and shoved it again under the haystack, burying it well. Then she dusted her skirts clean. At the sound of heavy boots plodding their way toward the barn doors, Rachel scurried back to the cabin.

"Where did you go?"

She finished stirring the coals and placed another split log over them. "I remembered that...that there was something I needed to take care of in the barn."

"Something involving hay?"

Rachel glanced toward his raised brow. Andrew. She knew his name now. She should tell him. But how? "What makes you say that?"

"Your hair is quite lovely ornamented with it."

"My hair?" She caught coarse strands of pale green between her damp fingers. Returning to the door, she discarded the bits outside and then dried her hands on her apron. "I was thinking, you've been here for two weeks in our home; you may as well know me by my Christian name."

"Rachel?"

"Yes." She remembered how shocked she'd been the first time her name had crossed those lips. She'd been afraid of what he knew. If he would become a hazard to them. If only she could trust him enough to tell him everything she'd discovered.

"Begging your pardon, but perhaps it would be more appropriate if I called you by your husband's name."

14

Rachel stared at him. "My husband?" Did he honestly think her married?

The door opened and Joseph stamped his way in. "Is breakfast ready?"

"I only need to get the plates down." Rachel rotated to the shelves behind her. "We've come up with something to call our patient." She glanced at her brother as another man entered the house. "Oh...Daniel."

"Good morning." He reached for his hat and a stream of water trickled to the floor.

"Set out another plate, Rachel." Joseph hung his soaked coat on a peg. "I invited Daniel to join us."

"If that's all right with you," Daniel was quick to add.

"Of course. You are always welcome at our table." Rachel turned her back. She replaced the rack over the fire and started a second batch of batter. Pins and needles prickled her spine from the tension building in the room.

Joseph set the pail of fresh milk on the table and brushed past for a clean container and cheesecloth for straining. "It's a good a time as any to discuss what needs discussing."

"Must we? Now?" After the skillet heated, she filled it with batter and laid the bowl aside. Plates and cutlery clattered as she set the table, pausing every few moments to flip or remove the cakes, piling them with the others.

"We are only talking, Rachel." Joseph poured the milk through the cloth, and then placed the emptied pail on the floor. "Nothing happens today."

Rachel piled several of the nicest cakes on a plate and spread a generous amount of butter and strawberry preserves over them. She took the plate and a cup of the warm milk, and started toward their guest…Andrew.

Daniel caught her gaze and his eyes narrowed.

"With how well you're feeding that Redcoat, it's no wonder he was up to taking off as he did yesterday. That should be ample sign that it's time."

Rachel set aside the food long enough to aid Andrew in sitting up by sliding a straw pillow behind the down one.

"Thank you," he replied.

She placed his breakfast on his stomach and the cup on the edge of a chair before shifting it close enough for him to reach.

"At least you've taught him how to be polite," Daniel said.

The muscles danced under Andrew's whiskers.

Daniel crossed to the table and jerked out a chair. "Though that's how the Brits are, aren't they? Fancy words and pleasing manners. They needed all the taxes from us colonists to pay for that book learning."

"At least he has book learning." Rachel hurried back to the fireplace. She tossed several steaming cakes on a plate and shoved it in front of Daniel.

"Now look here, I can read and write as well as the next man. I am not ignorant, and you know it."

"That may be, Daniel Reid, but—"

"That's enough, you two." Joseph slapped his hand against the table. "Sit yourselves down and listen for a change. We will be civil and work this thing out so everyone can agree."

Daniel sat back with a huff and folded his arms. "Must we do it here with that bloody Redcoat watching us?"

"This concerns him more than any of us. Andrew has the right to be part of this conversation." Rachel let the plate in her hands clang to the table. She hadn't meant to use his name—not with Daniel in the room. The odor of scorching cakes again assaulted her nose. She jerked the skillet off the flame, then yelped and dropped it to the floor as pain seared her hand.

"Are you all right?" Joseph started to stand, but she waved him back.

"I'm fine." Rachel wrapped her hand in the wet cheesecloth and dropped into a chair. She would worry about the mess later. "Let's talk."

"Let's." The anger in Daniel's tone faltered, but quickly returned. "It seems things have changed quite a lot in this house. Andrew, is it? And now he has rights? We're going to discuss everything with him—make sure he agrees with it?"

"You're right. Things have changed a little." Joseph took a bite his food. "I agree with Rachel that he be able to participate as we decide what's best."

"Fine," Daniel growled. "Last time I was here everything was decided. As soon as the British pig is not in danger of dropping dead, we turn him over to Colonel Gansevoort. He's off our hands."

"We can't do that," Rachel said, unable to keep the frustration from her voice.

"Why? Because he's caught your fancy? The British and their gentlemanly ways always turn the ladies' heads."

"You jealous ox!"

"Jealous of what? His fake smile and lying words—like fat King George himself?"

"If both of you would quiet down." Joseph shook his head. "This has little to do with our personal feelings, but with what is right. As long as we keep this quiet, it's reasonable to give him a tolerable place to finish recovering."

"And then?"

Joseph eyed the double prongs of his fork. "I don't know yet."

"Perhaps we could give him a musket and enough powder and shot for him finish what he came here to do." Daniel stood and snatched his hat off the corner of the table. "I think I should go. I haven't the stomach for dining with Loyalists."

Andrew's voice rumbled from the back of the room. "If they are Loyalists, it is a wonder the King continues to reign even in England." He pushed himself up a little more. "As for me, I was a soldier following his country's commands."

"And are you not that same soldier?"

"No." He winced as he shifted. "I tendered my resignation. The British army believes me to be dead, and as far as I am concerned at this juncture, the person I was has ceased to exist. Even his memories have fled with his life."

Daniel was momentarily silent before turning to Joseph. "It isn't safe to have him here. If anyone found out..."

"I wholly agree." Andrew set his plate aside on the

chair, his food hardly prodded. "It is not safe for anyone if I am here. It would be better to turn me over to your army as planned. That way you would be considered heroes and not traitors."

"How can you say that?" Rachel surged to her feet. "Don't you understand you'd be a prisoner? They'd lock you up in some cold hole and give you little more than scraps to eat. Your leg's healing, but it still has a long ways yet, especially after yesterday. Who could guess what would happen if you're not cared for properly?"

Andrew's mouth formed a straight line. "At least I would be able to sleep better."

Daniel found his seat. "For once I've heard some common sense come out of a British mouth. It's the only way, Joseph."

Her brother shook his head. "I don't believe that it is. Nobody else knows he's here and we asked you to keep our secret. It's not your problem anymore, Daniel. If you could pretend nothing has happened, that he's not here. For now we'll let things be, and after he heals...we'll have to see." Joseph glanced around the room, meeting each pair of eyes and holding their gazes for several seconds. "Is that acceptable to everyone?"

Daniel pushed up from the table once again. "I guess it will have to be." He pulled his hat on and exited the cabin. The door slammed.

"Do not assume your generosity goes unappreciated, but he is correct." Andrew ran his fingers over the whiskers darkening his jaw. "It is not safe for either of you if someone discovers me here. You have been more than patient already—I cannot ask for, or expect, additional favors at your risk. Please reconsider. Give me up to that colonel he spoke of, or at least let me go."

"How far do you think you would get?" Joseph arched an eyebrow, and chewed down another bite. "Yesterday you didn't even make it off our property. And where would you go? Not many Americans in this area are willing to help British spies. Even wounded ones. Most Tories have resettled up north, and your army is probably back to Lake Ontario by now—almost a hundred miles."

"Then give me up."

"I'm afraid that is also out of the question. But I'll tell you what we should do." Joseph ate his last forkful and downed it with milk. "You lay there and finish eating, I'll go spread the wheat to dry, and Rachel can do whatever it is she has planned to do next." He pulled on the light buckskin coat and moved out into the rain.

"I agree with Joseph," Rachel said as she put her hand into the basin of cold water. Though not burnt badly, it stung.

"That hardly makes it safe."

"Safer for you than any other idea so far."

"I am not so concerned with my own welfare at the moment." He sounded almost as upset as Daniel.

Rachel cleared the table. Joseph was the only one who had emptied his plate. She hadn't even fixed one for herself, but her stomach clenched too tight to try eating anything now. "Everyone has begun harvest and will be busy until winter. Once the snows come, neighbors visit less. There's nothing to be concerned about until spring, and by then you'll be gone. No one will ever know you were here."

Andrew shook his head. "And what of the man

who just left? Daniel. A fine, Old Testament name. He seem none too pleased. Is there any danger from him?"

"He'd never do anything to risk our safety, even if he doesn't like the arrangements." She sighed as she walked to the fireplace. *Oh, Daniel.* Now that she thought about it, he'd shown jealousy toward Jarrett, also. "I don't know if he's more upset because you're British or because you're a man."

A puzzled expression shadowed Andrew's eyes. "Forgive me, but I am most truly confused. Why would this man, Daniel, be jealous of me if..." He paused, his brow furrowed like a newly planted field. "What of your husband?"

Rachel froze, half-crouched, the blackened cakes still on the floor at her feet. "My husband?"

"Yes, Joseph...your husband."

She stared at him. "My husband?" She bit her lips together to hinder the laugh rising. Even her hand cupped over her mouth could not stop the laughter from bubbling up. She straightened. "I forgot I'd let you believe that. But Joseph's my brother. I'm unmarried."

~*~

"Your brother?" He hadn't even considered that relationship, but it made perfect sense. The friendly aloofness with no sign of deeper affection. It wasn't a marriage of necessity after all—it wasn't even a marriage. Siblings. "That definitely clarifies a few things. To be honest I was beginning to wonder about you colonists. Seeing you go into the same bedroom...I hadn't—"

"This isn't England, or even Boston. Out here

whole families often share one room simply because there is only one room. When my family first settled here, Joseph and Pa built a room in the loft of the barn so he'd have a space of his own, but since we brought you here, he didn't feel right about leaving me alone in the house. It wouldn't have been proper."

Proper? Andrew cringed at the word. A young, unattached woman had been dressing him, tending his wound, and even disposing of his waste. How could that be considered proper? Heat singed his face, no doubt turning it a ghastly shade of scarlet. One thing for certain—she wasn't coming anywhere near him again. At least, not in the capacity of his nurse.

15

Andrew's heart thudded as Rachel stepped from the bedroom.

Her lips pursed with the hint of a smile as her dark eyes fell on him.

Their gazes met.

"What do you want help with today, Joseph?" She turned to her brother and moved to the table. As she walked, Rachel pulled loose tresses over her shoulder, running a brush through them, but with little effect on the ripples. Probably the result of always wearing her hair in a braid. What a pity she didn't leave it as a silky shawl over her shoulders as it lay now.

"I need to turn the wheat so it can finish drying," Joseph said from where he crouched at the fireplace. "I could use your help with that later." He fed the flames with logs he'd just brought in.

Hopefully, they would put out the fire as soon as breakfast was prepared. It already felt much too warm in the confines of the cabin. Or was Andrew the only one overheated? Perhaps. But the humidity, no one could ignore. To some extent it was likely responsible for the fullness of Rachel's honey waves.

And she was unmarried. Unattached. Unspoken for. Only her youth could be responsible for that. It would not be long before a man came along with the remedy. A man like Mr. Daniel Reid.

Andrew relaxed into the pillow and crossed his arms.

Rachel set the brush aside and took the large skillet from its hook, trading place with Joseph. "How do eggs sound to everyone?"

Her brother murmured a "good" as he took up the milk pail and moved out the door.

Andrew managed a nod, though unsure he could swallow anything. Strange how one day ago he had been completely fine with her married status, and now the thought of another man making advances to her proved enough to sour his stomach.

"I'll put on the kettle, as well." Rachel cracked one egg after another against the edge of the pan and dropped them in. She deposited the shells into a small pail at her feet. "I should change your bandage this morning."

Andrew shifted on the cot, his body stiffening. How would he explain himself to her without causing offense?

~*~

Rachel blew out her breath. This was ridiculous. "That bandage has been on for over a day. We need a new one before your wound festers again."

Andrew shook his head. "Maybe so, but you shall not be the one to freshen it."

Hot water caught the hem of her dress as she dropped the basin to the floor beside the cot. She jumped back, giving her skirt a shake to release her frustration. "I have been the one dressing your wounds since that first night. You didn't put up this much of a fuss the other times. Why now?" She folded her arms and tipped her head.

He looked straight up, but the hardness in his expression wavered. "Circumstances have changed."

"Nothing has changed in the last day. Unless you mean it's different now you know we hope for your recovery. But how does that affect these circumstances?"

"It is not that." His gaze darted to her, and then away. "There are certain situations that should be avoided if at all possible. Propriety and morality dictate what is appropriate, and though I recognize in the past there were necessary allowances and—"

"I still have no idea what you are talking about." Rachel gathered the cloths she'd set on the table. "So let me clean your wound before it festers again."

"But it is not proper."

She whirled, bringing her hand to her hip. "Why? Why was it acceptable a day ago, but not now?"

"Because you are unmarried." Andrew shifted, color curling over his ears and across his face.

Rachel stifled a laugh at his embarrassment, and then her own cheeks heated. She set her hands on the table. He was too correct. It had been different before, an aloofness of patient and nurse. Distance between them that was swiftly crumbling. "What do you propose we do then? That bandage still needs to be changed."

Silence. It was hardly fair for him to create a dilemma and not supply a cure.

"We can't wait for Joseph." She grabbed the cloths and returned without looking at him. "So either you come up with a plan, or we continue the way we have to this point, and you simply ignore the fact I'm a woman."

Angela K. Couch

His usual baritone deepened to a rumbling base. "Indeed, that would prove very difficult."

Rachel dropped one of the cloths into the basin and laid the others over his covered legs. Acknowledging his meaning would hardly move them in the right direction. "Difficult to come up with a plan?"

"A plan, I already have."

She met his gaze—drawn into his eyes and everything that lay hidden within his soul. Goodness. Gentleness. And something more...

"The fact that you are a woman, however, I shall never be able to put from my mind."

For an endless moment Rachel couldn't move, couldn't look away. A strange sensation spread through her. She tried to swallow.

"I must apologize." His voice stroked her ears. "I have made you uncomfortable. That was not my intention."

She stepped back. "No, it wasn't that." Rachel forced a smile, but avoided his eyes. "What is your proposal—your plan, I mean?"

He cleared his throat. "Bring a chair over, and place the basin and everything where I can reach it. I shall do it myself."

"Are you sure you'd be able to? You may find it quite painful to wash it well, and you would have to sit up enough to see clearly what you are doing."

"I shall manage."

Rachel dragged two chairs over. She refilled the basin and set it on one chair for cleaning the wound, and across the other she laid the fresh bandaging with a thick layer of salve already applied. "Make sure you set the salve directly over the open area, and please, if

112

it is at all hot or festered, let me know so we can try a warm bread-and-milk poultice again."

He answered with a nod.

"I'll check back in a little while."

Rachel took a deep breath as she closed the door. Nice, fresh air was what she needed. Now, to get some work done.

Joseph could probably use help starting on the wheat, but as she stepped into the barn her gaze wandered to where the ax hung. She grabbed it and moved toward the stump in the garden. The tilled earth was still mud, but not as soppy as it had been the day before. Even so, it clung to her boots, weighing them down. Rachel sank the ax into the top of the stump and then used the spade to clean her soles.

As she again changed tools, she eyed the six-inch root she'd already cleared dirt from. Tears stung her eyes. Blinking them back, she swung the thick blade downwards. More welled in their place and spilled over. Moisture streaked her face.

Her father had been able to make short work with even roots this large. He and Joseph had cleared hundreds of trees the first two years in the valley. And he'd always removed the stumps. It was a matter of pride with him. He wouldn't have his land marred with half rotted remains, waiting for nature to take its course as some farmers did.

Oh, Papa.

How happy those years had been as their family set their roots deep in this land, breaking soil, planting, and building their home. They'd worked together, the future clear in their minds. Then Mama had fallen ill and left them. Now Pa was gone. Rachel paused to wipe a sleeve across her eyes. How were they supposed to survive this wilderness?

~*~

Andrew finished securing the bandage and dropped back onto his pillow. He yanked the blanket over his leg, and then tucked his hands under his arms. They trembled but he was done now.

Thank you, Lord.

With head throbbing and body drained of strength, he closed his eyes to be met by Rachel's image. The fact that she was unmarried and completely free from attachment still ignited sparks within his brain. How could he not smile?

16

Four days later, Rachel shook out the breeches and draped them over the clothesline. Her efforts to remove the stain had not been completely successful. She reached for one of her dresses to hang and realized that she'd been humming.

From all that dwell below the skies, let the Creator's praise arise.

The song had been one of her mother's favorites, though she had loved all of Isaac Watts's hymns. How many times had they washed clothes, or gardened, or worked at any other task singing together?

Let the Redeemer's name be sung though every land, by every tongue.

The first words of the last verse sounded in her mind, something cold and hard settling in her chest.

Eternal are thy mercies, Lord.

Perhaps it was so. Everything would be touched by His love. Everything would be made right. But eternity was too distant—The Lord was too distant.

She grabbed up the basket and hurried to the cabin, no longer wanting to be alone. As she pushed open the door, a moan met her ears. The basket dropped as she rushed across the room.

Andrew clung to the side of the cot, one knee on the floor.

"What are you doing? How did you fall off?"

He released a low grunt. "I did not fall—not exactly."

Rachel reached for his arms.

He held up a hand, halting her, and then rested his forehead on the cot as he drew a breath.

She placed her hands on her hips. "What exactly did happen?"

"I was trying to move."

"Are you insane? Surely you remember where that got you not a week ago."

"I was only trying to get to the rocking chair. A mere three feet. Not exactly a case of insanity."

"Then you can explain your present predicament?"

Andrew tweaked a smile. "I would rather not."

"I'll lift under your arms and get you back onto the bed."

"Please, no," he moaned.

She paused, her hand brushing across the breadth of his shoulders. "I would think you'd want to lie back down after this."

"I would prefer never to have the need to lie down again so long as I live. Every inch of my body screams from being stuck on that plank. I fear my..." He glanced at her. "I fear there are parts of my body which must be permanently bruised."

"This is hardly a plank, as you call it. I even freshened the straw in the mattress, what, a month ago—shortly before we found you." She gripped his upper arms, her fingers hardly making it half way around the thick muscles. Rachel took a deep breath, steadying herself. "What do you propose?"

His jaw stiffened. "Will you help me over to the chair?" There was an edge to his voice. How much it must cost him to have to ask for everything he needed. There he was, a man in his prime, a gentleman of no small means—judging from his speech and mannerisms—and yet almost completely dependent on her.

"I'm sorry." She tightened her grip on him. "Tell me when."

"Now."

Rachel positioned more to his left, sliding her hand under his arm and across his chest. The other hooked upward toward his right shoulder, and she waited while he slipped his second knee to the floor.

Andrew's body flinched with pain, but not a sound escaped him.

"Push with your hands and I'll guide you up."

Sweat beaded on his temple. His hair brushed against her cheek.

She breathed him in. "Whenever you're ready."

He moved, rising several inches before she remembered to assist. Her body pulled tight against his as he gained his feet. His chest expanded under her arm, reminding her to breathe.

"I need to get in front of you," she said with a glance at the rocker. "We're almost there. Maybe lift your arm, so I don't have to let go."

He did so with no other comment.

The linen shirt did little to hide the firmness of his chest and back as she slid her hands across them. Warmth crawled up her spine, but she didn't dare let go.

He balanced completely on one leg, which trembled. His breath caressed her face, and she stole a glance at his—so close, only an inch or two away. His mouth was at eye level. It had a nice form to it.

Then he dropped back, lowering himself, his hands clutching the arms of the chair.

Rachel stared for several seconds while her brain cleared. Blood rushed behind her ears. She stepped back. "How are you feeling?"

Andrew took slow, deep breaths, but color was slow to return to his face. "Give me a moment."

Rachel turned away. Water, that's what she needed. She poured a glass at the table, resisting the urge to splash it on her face or dump it down the back of her dress. The slight breeze from the open door did little to cool her. But at least her brain functioned again. "Do you want a drink?" she asked.

"Please." His voice betrayed a tremor.

After passing him a glass, she stood back and tried to avert her gaze—without success.

His eyes closed, and his throat trembled with each gulp.

She took the empty glass and retreated behind the table.

"Thank you," Andrew said after a while.

Rachel fidgeted with a dish towel. What was she supposed to do next? The laundry was done, the bread had another hour of rising before it would be ready to bake and it was too early to make supper.

Joseph was off to the Adlers' to use their steel for sharpening the scythe as his had rusted.

There was little for her to do in the field until he returned. Still, a hundred chores vied for her attention. The garden needed weeding, the stump remained firmly in place, Joseph had torn the sleeve of one of his shirts, and she had yet to butcher and pluck the chicken she would cook for their evening meal. She stole another glance at Andrew.

His complexion had almost returned to normal, but pain still creased his forehead. It would not be good to leave him alone until he returned to bed.

She fetched her sewing box and Joseph's shirt, and set at the table. "Do you need anything?" she asked before sitting.

Andrew shifted most of his weight on his left side. He ran the back of his hand across the stubble on his chin. "I'm fine for now. Although..."

"Yes?"

He sighed. "I am starved for conversation."

Her smile couldn't be contained. She was equally hungry to speak with him, to listen to the wonderful tones of his voice. She rotated her chair to face him. "What would you like to talk about?"

"I think it best if you choose the topic." His eyes twinkled. "If I remember correctly, the last time you put it to me, it did not end well."

"That wasn't your fault." Threading the needle took more tries than usual, but soon she had the shirt spread across her lap and began stitching. "I can't imagine what it must be like—having no memory or concept of who you are."

"I am hardly in a better position now."

"You do have your name."

"Do I?" He shook his head, scratching where his sideburn met his beard. "How am I to know that is my name? It is familiar, yes, but perhaps it is simply the name of a family member or close acquaintance."

Rachel swallowed as she lowered her hands. How could she deny him the truth? "You can rest easy. Your name is Andrew. Andrew Wyndham."

Silence filled the space between them. Then his voice pierced it. "You said you did not know."

"I didn't lie." She glanced down. "At least, not at the beginning. I found a letter in your coat that day we discussed it."

"Is that why you hurried out so suddenly? To search my coat for anything that could identify me?"

She nodded.

His frown deepened. "Why did you not tell me?"

Rachel stood, depositing the mending on her chair. Was she supposed to answer that honestly? She walked around the table and crouched by the fireplace to arrange the split logs for the evening fire—hours before needed, but at least she escaped his burning stare.

"Is it so awful that I know who I am?" His voice still reached her. As did the hurt lacing it.

"It could be." She tossed one last log into place and stood.

"Whatever my loyalties are, or have ever been, they could not diminish my gratitude for everything you and Joseph have done. You must believe that."

"I do." She turned back, immediately regretting the hurt also apparent on his face. In truth, she had no fear of the man before her, but… "But as I read that letter, I couldn't help wonder what sort of man Captain Wyndham was."

"I wonder that myself. But surely he could not have been a complete fiend."

Rachel gave him a tight smile. "An officer in King George's Armies." Who came to their land to burn their homes and slaughter all who opposed Britain's rule. A man of war. She hugged herself, chilled. It was impossible to picture the man before her as the one logic bespoke. How could a man so saturated with the Good Word be a militant?

~*~

Andrew met her steady gaze, not liking the shadow settling in her already dark eyes. He had almost forgotten they'd once been mortal enemies. Surely he had been an honorable man, even then. Though he had flashes of memories from battle, the thought of killing turned his stomach. "Can I see the letter?"

Rachel gave a hesitant nod. "Of course." She darted out and returned with the paper a few minutes later. Only a couple strands of hay graced her head this time.

"You look uncomfortable. Do you want to move back to the bed?"

Andrew shook his head as he took the letter and opened it. His hip no longer screamed at him, and the remainder of his body thanked his position in the rocker—especially his tailbone. The whiskers on his jaw were the main offenders now, but even their itch faded as he focused on the elegant scrawling across the page. He stared at the recipient's name—his name. It did feel right. He was a captain?

"Who's Stephen?" Rachel's voice pulled him from the futile search of his memory.

Andrew read down the letter. Yes. There was the name—also ringing with familiarity. Also a Wyndham. "I do not know."

"Your face is losing its color." Rachel touched his shoulder. "I think maybe it's time for you to move back to the cot."

Though the thought of laying down was again appealing, the thought of moving gave him reason to hesitate. "I suppose you are right. Only, the cot seems so far away, now."

"Oh, come along. It's still a mere three feet." She flashed a smile. "Not exactly a case of insanity."

Andrew kept his own smile subdued. He would not reward her for mocking him, though the temptation remained. This time the transition went easily. Rachel braced him upward, pivoted him on his good foot, and then began lowering him onto the cot. Abruptly she fell forward, her balance lost. She threw her hands out to catch herself before landing on him, but without complete success. The cot was still too far for her to reach. Rachel's weight against his upper body sped his descent.

"Ouch!" The shockwave tore through his hip, stealing his breath.

"I'm so sorry." She scrambled off of him.

The pain began to recede. "No. I am fine." At least, he soon would be. Enough to appreciate her nearness, if not for the torture of his leg. Of course, it would be ungentlemanly to admit as much.

"That did not go as planned." Rachel hovered, a becoming blush rising to her cheeks. "Can I help move your legs onto the cot?"

"No. I think I would prefer to remain exactly as I am for a little while."

The *clip-clop* of hooves outside the cabin spun her away. Rachel raced to the window and peered out. Her hand came to her throat as she glanced back, and then lunged for the door latch.

"What is it? Who?"

"Rodney Cowden. I've not known a man who hates the British more than him."

17

Rachel forced the tension from her face, walked out in the yard, and looked up at the middle-aged man with his heavy beard and stained leather shirt.

Rodney Cowden had lost two cousins in a skirmish with the British near Albany a year earlier, but even before that he had never hesitated to express his loathing for King George and those who pledged allegiance to him.

Rachel had agreed with him for the most part—still agreed with him—but for the man hidden behind the solid log wall of the cabin. Maybe because Andrew Wyndham no longer had loyalties to Britain…that he remembered.

"Good day, Mr. Cowden," she called out, willing her heart to beat slower. Daniel was friends with the man, but surely he wouldn't have given them away. No. Rodney Cowden would have a mob behind him if that were the case. "We haven't seen you in a while now. How is everything over at your farm?"

He swung down and swept his hat off his head. His hair, with its generous streaks of grey, lay plastered down with sweat. "Well enough, but for some neglect."

"You've been away or unwell?" His land was almost four miles from theirs.

"Away. Guess I left a day early, too." Cowden's

Angela K. Couch

hand came up to pull at his coffee-stained whiskers. "Didn't hear about that battle they fought up Oriskany way until I was on my way back last week. Feel bad about not being around to help out. They sure left their mark on the farms up near Fort Stanwix."

"Fort Schuyler," Rachel corrected. The fort had been renamed last summer.

"Yah." Cowden grunted. "That and Oriskany. Most of Tyron County seems to have had its share of trouble. I would've liked to have been here to help teach them Tories a lesson or two. Though, with all the raids north of here, I'm sure I'll still get that chance."

"I'm sure you will." She couldn't understand why anyone would be anxious to fight now that she'd personally seen and felt the aftermath.

"Listen to me, rambling on, and the ground over your Pa still fresh. I heard he was killed, and I'm mighty sad to hear it. He was a good man."

"Yes, he was." Why was Cowden even there? She could think of no business they had with him. Something about his tone felt almost disrespectful of Pa. Perhaps because there was no feeling in his words, as though he only said them because he thought they were what she wanted to hear. "I suppose you're looking for Joseph. He's out cutting our wheat. I'd be more than happy to point you in the right direction."

He slipped his hat back on his head. "Obliged. But I must say, it was a hot ride over here. Could I beg a drink from you first?"

Rachel glanced to the well. Handing him a pail would hardly be neighborly, but she couldn't very well invite him into the cabin. Any closer than he already stood was a risk. She forced a smile. "Of course. Why don't you head out into the field," she indicated the direction, past the barn and to the east, "and I'll bring you and Joseph the full pitcher. I'm sure he's also parched."

Cowden gave a nod, started away, and then turned back. "I actually only came by today 'cause I was on my way to the Reids and got to thinking about you and Daniel."

"Me and Daniel?"

"See, I've been eyeing some land farther north, up near the lakes. Been trying to convince Reid to come with me, start a new venture. Last winter he talked like it was something he wanted to do, but it seems something's got him dragging his heels now. The man's running himself ragged trying to outfit Mrs. Becker with what they need for returning to Albany."

"The Beckers are leaving?" Life was by no means easy out here, but to walk away from everything one had worked so hard for...especially from a farm as comely as the Beckers'.

"Just Mrs. Becker and the youngsters. Karl Becker never returned from that skirmish near Oriskany."

"Oh." Rachel pictured the woman, only five years her senior and already four children. Now a widow. All because the British refused to see reason and go home.

"And Daniel's set on that homestead instead of looking forward." Cowden eyed her. "You wouldn't hold him here, would you? He's too young and got too much living to do before settling down. A wife isn't for a man like him. Not yet, leastwise."

Rachel's mouth felt dry from hanging open. "I assure you, I have no designs on Daniel Reid." Perhaps she'd considered it, but calling her a Loyalist had done nothing to endear him to her. "But if he chooses to stay

in the valley, I cannot fault him for his choice of land."
With a stream running down its center and a cabin
cradled in a natural meadow, how could she?

Cowden grunted his disagreement and turned
back to his horse. "I would be obliged if you let him
know as much—about you not being interested, that is.
Either way, don't be telling him I said anything to
you." Without another word he swung back into the
saddle and rode away. So much for wanting a drink.

Their conversation leaving her unsettled, Rachel
started to the well. She would take Joseph some water
and help him for a while, then butcher a chicken for
their supper.

~*~

Rachel's gaze cut immediately to the cot as she
entered the cabin. Good.

Andrew lay where he belonged. His eyes were
closed, but the letter rested open on his chest. His hand
rose to massage his temples.

Moving to the table, she grabbed the cutting board
from its hook, and plopped the naked hen onto it. "Do
you need anything?"

Andrew replied with a shake of his head. His hand
slid over his jaw, fingers scratching through the thick
stubble. His mouth opened, its shape distorting as it
pulled to one side.

"Are you all right?"

"Fine." His hand left his face, but only for a
minute. This time his knuckles raked from one side to
the other.

"Are you sure?"

His eyes opened into narrow slits, and he folded

his arms over the letter.

Rachel bit the inside of her cheek, fighting to allow him his dignity. "You seem...disturbed by something."

"I assure you, I am fine."

She cocked an eyebrow, but said nothing.

His chin tipped to the side, brushing across his shoulder.

She smothered a giggle in her palm. When she regained control of it, she looked back. "It's your curl, isn't it?"

"Pardon me?"

"Your hair has curls, and your beard probably does, as well. You're not used to wearing it, are you?" She smiled. "Joseph and Pa never seemed to mind, but their whiskers came in straight, so they probably didn't itch like yours do."

He remained silent.

"I could find you a razor and soap if you would like."

The muscles under the stubble flexed, and then he released his breath in a gust. "Thank you. That would be most appreciated."

Rachel left the chicken and washed her hands. Rinsing the basin, she poured tepid water from the kettle and went to get Pa's shaving kit from the shelf in the bedroom. Mounted on the wall resided a decent-sized mirror, but it would be awkward to hold for him, so she opened the chest beside her bed.

Mama's silver mirror lay against the side, wrapped in soft fabric. A treasure from civilization. Rachel ran the tips of her fingers over the intricate vines carved into the handle. *I miss you so much, Mama.* She hugged it and the coarse leather of the shaving kit. "I miss you both." Blinking, she stood and closed the chest. Now was not the time for losing herself in emotion. Composure barely grasped, Rachel stepped back into Andrew's presence.

He pushed himself into a sitting position.

She dragged a chair beside the cot and set the basin on it, along with the blade, soap, and a towel. Seating herself on the rocker, she scooted forward.

Andrew scowled. "I am quite capable of shaving my own face."

"I'm sure you are, but wouldn't you like to see what you're doing?" She held up the mirror.

He glanced from her, to the object in her hand, and back again.

"You're not comfortable with me helping you with anything, are you?"

"It is not that I am unappreciative of all you have done for me, and continue to do, only...I cannot push past the feeling of what is proper and acceptable behavior."

"My behavior has been improper?"

"No, you have only been kind and generous in your actions." Andrew clasped her hand. "Please do not think my aim is to censure you. You have always performed your ministrations above reproach. It is simply hard to think of you any longer as my nurse, and I could never consider you as a servant." His gaze searched hers, and then lowered. "Forgive me. I should not have spoken. Thank you for offering your assistance."

She nodded, though he seemed unaware of it.

His fingers released hers, their absence wrapping strings around her heart and tugging.

He moved for the soap, created a lather, and spread it over his chin and around his mouth.

He was an English gentleman—since he had first opened his mouth, there had been no doubt of that. Now the reality of it seeped into her chest, making it ache. If his mind were clear, a servant, or peasant, was exactly how he would see her. Pushing the thought aside, she raised the mirror so he would have a perfect view of his face. "How's that?"

"Fine, thank you."

"Tell me if I need to move it at all."

He nodded and reached for the straight razor. It hovered for a moment.

"Are you sure you remember how?"

Andrew glared, but the right side of his mouth quirked a smile. He brought the blade downward along his jaw, leaving a clean path.

"Just wanted to be certain."

He continued, the razor cleaning both the soap and shadow from his face.

A stranger emerged from beneath. She swallowed as memories returned of the darkened battlefield and the glow of the moon illuminating the British soldier, his face twisted in agony. *Don't leave me, please.* His words echoed in her mind. *What if we had left him there?* The thought clamped her throat, as did the realization that her feelings for this man were much too strong. She didn't know him—he didn't even know himself— and he would someday leave.

~*~

It was all Andrew could do to keep a tremor from the hand maneuvering the blade. He'd not taken the time to position himself properly, and his hip had already sustained sufficient abuse for one day. He focused on the mirror and his image there. He did not want Rachel to see his discomfort, and he couldn't guarantee his eyes would keep that secret...or any of his secrets.

A knock pulled their attention to the door.

He lowered the razor as Rachel set aside the mirror.

She sent a nervous glance his direction and then to the door. "Who's there?"

"It's me, Daniel."

Her shoulders relaxed and she moved to let him in. "You're here alone?"

"Of course. But Rodney Cowden was here, wasn't he? I got the feeling he'd made a detour." Alarm widened his eyes. "Wait, he didn't see..." He motioned to Andrew.

"Of course not. I stopped him in the yard. I'm sure he doesn't suspect anything, unless you've said something."

Daniel's expression didn't show guilt, but regret was present enough. As was his attraction to Rachel. "You know I wouldn't."

"I wasn't so sure after the way you stormed out of here last time." She folded her arms and Andrew couldn't help but feel sorry for the man. He'd had his own taste of this woman's scorn. "What do you want, anyways?"

"I need to speak with you." Daniel looked to where Andrew sat, half his face still lathered with soap. The lines marking Daniel's frown deepened. "Alone, this time."

"We were in the middle of something. Why don't you go see Joseph first, and I'll come find you both when I'm done?"

His head gave a shake. "I'll wait here."

Rachel stepped back, her spine straight as she allowed him past her. "As you wish. Take a seat at the table." Her voice rose as though she were nervous. "Can I offer you some water?"

"No." Daniel's gaze remained set on Andrew. "Thank you."

"All right. We shouldn't be much longer."

Andrew shifted, releasing some of the pressure on his thigh, but none from his tailbone. He didn't want an audience. "Why not go with him now? I am sure I can manage."

She dropped into the rocker and took up the mirror.

He nodded to the other man's scowl before bringing the razor back into action. All eyes seemed intent on him, even his own, as he worked, quickening his motions as much as he dared. The shave wouldn't be perfect, but at least it would be done. So long as he could refrain from slitting his throat.

Rachel's gasp brought his gaze from the mirror, than back as he traced her stare. Blood dribbled from his chin. His reflection danced and then dropped as she released the mirror to his lap and grabbed the towel. Dipping a corner in water, she pressed it over the cut.

"Do not concern yourself." Andrew pulled the cloth away.

"You're bleeding."

"It is not more than a scratch."

Her eyes seared his.

"Let me see to this." He wiped the remaining soap from his neck. "Do not leave this man waiting. I am sure he must have something of importance to say to you."

"But..."

"Go. Please."

Without another word, Rachel stood and turned.

Daniel was already on his feet and a moment later they left.

Andrew pushed aside the pillows that propped him up, sinking onto his back. He held the mirror so he could examine the thin patch of whiskers remaining. He glowered at himself. "You really are all charm."

~*~

Rachel stared straight ahead as Daniel turned her toward the road. Though she knew Cowden wouldn't have said anything, she couldn't help but wonder if the topic of their conversation had influenced Daniel's visit. She didn't want to talk to him alone. Not when she was still angry with him.

"If you have something to say, shouldn't we find Joseph?" she asked.

"I'm not here to talk to him. Only you."

The trails marking the main route of travel this side of the river had been deepened since the last storm, but the surface crumbled to powder under their feet. Birds filled the tops of the trees, their songs uninterrupted.

If only Rachel could unwind enough to enjoy them.

At least Daniel didn't seem any more comfortable. His temples glistened with perspiration and his spine extended as though a board were attached to it.

She wouldn't shorten his torture by asking what he wanted. If he had something to say, he would have to spit it out on his own.

He rubbed his hand over his mouth and made a sound in the back of his throat. "I'm sorry, Rachel." His feet paused, but she kept walking. A moment later he again reached her side. "I'm trying to apologize."

"For what, exactly?"

"You make it sound as though I've made more than one offense."

She glanced at him and raised an eyebrow.

"The only thing I am guilty of is losing my temper—though I had reason enough for it. All the same, I'm sorry for what I said. I should have held my tongue, but sometimes you frustrate me."

"Pardon me?" Rachel stopped, turning to him. "I frustrate you?"

His brown gaze remained steadfast on her face, but flickered with uncertainty. "We used to be...friends. Now it seems as though you'd rather have nothing to do with me. Even before we got into the disagreement about the...you know." He released his breath in a gust. "I don't understand."

Sighing, she lowered her gaze. Though a bandage bulged under his sleeve, his wound no longer appeared to bother him. But how would she have felt if he, like Jarrett, hadn't survived Oriskany? "I didn't mean for you to feel that way. Please understand, my world has been turned on its head, and I'm simply trying to figure out what to do next."

"Then you're not angry at me?"

She shook her head and bit back a smile. "Not anymore."

There was a little too much relief in his eyes. Hope.

"So tell me, why is Rodney Cowden so intent on you going north with him?"

The relief fled. "What did he say to you?"

Rachel shrugged and began walking again. "Mostly that he had plans and hoped you'd come along."

Daniel grunted what sounded like disapproval. "I honestly think he just wants someone along to do the grunt work. He talks about land, but he's not a farmer. He's always off and about, making plans instead of settling in and making a life. Sometimes when he talks, I wonder what's really going on in his head."

"So you don't want to go with him?" The more she thought about it, the less it surprised her. Daniel's family was here, and there was something about the Mohawk valley, a beauty, a serenity, that held on tight to a person once it got a grip.

"Are you trying to get rid of me?"

A chuckle broke from her throat. If he had asked that an hour earlier the answer might be very different. "Of course not, Daniel. You're friendship means a lot to me. And Joseph."

"Friendship." He mumbled the word, his fist tapping against the side of his leg. Daniel glanced behind. "The...your patient seems to be recovering well."

"Yes, he is."

His mouth drew a taut line.

"But he's still quite helpless, and his memory has yet to return."

"And what will happen when it does?"

She tensed. "What do you mean, exactly?"

One look answered her clearly.

Rachel shook her head. This wasn't a discussion she wanted to have with him right now. Not after they'd just made peace. "He would never do anything

134

to hurt us. He knows he is indebted to us for his life. And I don't believe he's a violent man."

"But he is a British officer. His injuries don't change that." Daniel reached up and straightened his hat. "Sooner or later, you have to get rid of him."

Get rid of him? She closed her eyes for a moment. Andrew's face lit the shadows of her mind. Even after he left, how was she supposed to ever be rid of him? "I know."

~*~

When Rachel returned to the cabin, Andrew lay on his good side, elbow tucked up under his head. She closed the door and leaned against it, taking in the smooth line of his jaw, his features sharper than she remembered. So much more attractive. "I see you managed well enough without me after all." She smiled, but part of her wanted to cry. He needed her less and less. Soon she would be of little consequence to him.

When he didn't reply, Rachel collected the items placed neatly on the chair. The razor had been cleaned and folded into the leather sheath. She left it beside him. "You may as well keep this so you can shave as often as you like. Joseph has his own, for the little he employs it. This was my father's."

"Thank you."

Taking everything else to the table, Rachel circled to the far side and pulled a knife from the wall. With no time to cook the bird whole as she had planned, she would fry smaller pieces. Removing the first leg, she glanced to Andrew whose focus appeared to be the wall. "On what would you like to converse while I prepare supper?" She mimicked his proper English tone, exaggerating it, to lessen the tension filling the space.

He didn't even look at her. "I think I would prefer to rest, if that is all right." Though not in his voice, his mood seemed to darken the whole room.

Or perhaps that was only the shadow of her own feelings. She brought down the knife in a swift chop, shearing off the second chicken leg. "Of course it is." She continued to prepare the chicken, setting each piece in the skillet. With every inch filled, Rachel turned to set it over the fire...that she hadn't built yet. She had to get her mind focused on the tasks at hand and less on the man across the room. Even now she couldn't help stealing a glance at him and his pensive gaze.

He looked away.

Setting aside the skillet, Rachel crouched to unbury the coals from that morning. If they were still alive, she could forgo fiddling with the flint and steel.

"Dare I inquire what your friend desired to discuss with you?" A caustic edge tainted Andrew's voice.

She cracked the blackened remains of a log in half with the poker, and gently blew. A trace of red glowed in the center. Perfect.

"I am sure it is none of my affair." Irritation was no longer present in Andrew's speech.

"He wanted to apologize for his behavior the last time he was here." Rachel twisted to answer.

"Understandably."

"He's a good man."

"I do not doubt it."

She turned back toward the embers and then

looked to him again.

Andrew's eyes were closed. After everything he'd done today, it was probably best to let him rest.

18

Rachel set the basin of warm water on the chair beside the cot and stepped back. "Your whiskers barely show. You mean to shave again already?"

"After a day and a half it can hardly be shocking." Andrew worked the soap with his hands. "I used to shave every morning."

"Are you just saying that, or do you remember?"

A smile announced itself in his dimples, and then stretched across his face. "I remember." He applied the soap to his jaw. "Strange, the things that return, while other, more important memories remain hazed."

"I'm sure it's only a matter of time before you remember everything." She handed him the mirror and moved to the table. If he liked his independence so much, she would allow him what she could.

"Thank you." The rumble of his voice caressed her.

"I did very little, but I do appreciate your graciousness."

He chuckled. "In a situation such as mine, everything is of consequence and greatly appreciated. Besides, 'Sweet is the breath of vernal shower, the bee's collected treasures sweet, sweet music's melting full, but sweeter yet, the still small voice of gratitude.'"

Putting out the morning fire before it made the room too warm, Rachel rehearsed the words silently.

"It seems the Bible is not the only works you have memorized. Thomas Gray?"

The razor paused. "Yes. I'm surprised you recognized him."

"And I'm surprised you remembered him." Rachel straightened and gave a coy smile. "Why does it surprise you? He's a known poet. Is it because I live so displaced from England? Or from polite society? I told you my mother brought volumes of poetry with us."

"So you did." Andrew's gaze remained fixed on her, warming her cheeks. Then he glanced away, a more serious expression pulling at the corners of his eyes. He maneuvered the blade down his jaw without utilizing the mirror. His frown deepened as he scraped the soap from his face.

Rachel waited.

"Polite society," he finally said.

"What about it?"

"My brother." Andrew still didn't look at her. Instead, he stared at nothing, as though searching the air for the answers he sought. Clues to his past? "My brother attended Oxford...as did I. It...irritated me because he didn't study. He didn't care. He was always off to Bath or London, wherever the cream of society and his friends led him." Andrew lowered the razor to his lap and pressed his forefingers into his temples, massaging. "I remember being frustrated. He was immature and irresponsible. He held little respect for propriety, so long as everyone believed him above reproach."

"So much unlike his brother."

He glanced to her, his brow furrowed.

"His elder brother?"

Andrew made a nod. "I believe so."

"Stephen?"

"Yes." He looked down at the blade, then took it and rinsed away the soap. "Stephen."

"What else do you remember?"

"I remember..." His breath hissed through his teeth. "Envying him."

Rachel raised an eyebrow. Not quite what she expected. "Why?"

"Because he was passionate about life, and free."

"What do you mean, free?"

Andrew sank into the pillows as his hand passed over his eyes. "How am I to know? There is more clarity in the images, but they are hardly more than that. Images and feelings."

"It frustrates you, doesn't it?"

"Of course it does." His voice sharpened while increasing in volume. "My whole life dangling just out of reach, flirting with my consciousness."

"I'm sorry." Rachel tried for a contrite smile.

"No need. It is not as though you planted that stone where I fell."

"No." She allowed a slight laugh to trickle out. "The Lord is probably the One responsible for that."

"Are you suggesting this is God's plan for me?" The tension ebbed from his face as his gaze searched hers. "I..." He cleared his throat. "I suppose it would be more logical to fault myself for being there in the first place."

"I suppose." Rachel couldn't seem to look away or remove the curve from her lips. She moistened them. "It'll also be your own fault if your beard grows uneven."

He chuckled and again took up the straight blade. "I should stop allowing myself to become distracted."

"Yes."

"Meanwhile, you will remain standing there, watching me?"

Rachel grinned. "I'm testing your reserve."

"It falters with each moment."

Such sincerity marked his features. Such earnestness. No teasing. No irony. Only light shining in his eyes, and warmth spreading through her whole body. Perhaps she hadn't put out the morning fire soon enough. "I should leave you then. Joseph will be wondering what's become of me."

Andrew gave a nod, but said nothing.

If only he would say something more. She craved the sound of his voice. Rachel pinned her sunbonnet to her cap, then stepped outside and started breathing again. But where was Joseph? For some reason it didn't seem to matter, and she moved toward the garden—the stump. Instead of locating the ax or even fetching the spade, Rachel climbed onto the wide center and tucked her feet up under her. "Oh, Papa, what am I to do?"

"Rachel?" The wagon creaked as it jostled its way from the barn to the garden. Joseph brought it alongside the tilled ground and dragged the horses to a stop. "What are you doing sitting there?"

"Nothing." She looked down at the mess of dirt and splintered wood. "Just considering how I'll get at the lowest roots. They'll be hard to reach."

"And at least one probably taps straight down. It'll be a bear to get at." He shrugged and motioned to the wagon. "But we're wasting time talking. We can deal with this after the crops are in and everything else is done. Come on."

Rachel jumped from the stump and climbed onto

the seat beside him. She glanced back only once as they drove out to the field.

~*~

Andrew wiped the towel across his face, drying it. Pain pulsated against his skull as he tried to focus on his brother, linking everything he could recall into an intricate puzzle with a thousand missing pieces. The picture of Stephen became ever clearer, but their mother remained only a misty face with a disapproving stare. Their father...there was no image, only anger. Why anger?

With a groan, Andrew closed his eyes and let his thoughts wander. The tension, like a strap that had tightened across his forehead, eased. The corners of his mouth pulled up. *Rachel.* As with a soothing balm, she smoothed across his mind. He chuckled at parts of their conversation. Anything she lacked in education, she made up for with wit and God-given intelligence. "Lord, why hast Thou spared my life? Why hast Thou brought me here? Surely Thou hast a plan for me—for my life. Would it be impossible to include Rachel Garnet in that plan?"

19

Andrew glanced up from the rocking chair as the door squeaked open.

"It's really warm in here," Rachel said, pushing it wide. "The bugs aren't too bad today, why don't we leave it open for a while?"

A breeze followed her into the cabin—both were welcome. With a swing to her gait, Rachel moved to set a pail of vegetables on the table. Her lips had an upwards turn.

Andrew couldn't help but smile. Such a change from her melancholy.

She set the large pot next to the pail. "Why are you looking at me like that?"

"You seem happy today." Andrew closed the Bible. He'd spent much of his time during the past week and a half poring over the New Testament and was already to Peter's Epistles. Another day or so and he'd start the Old Testament. "I thought I heard another voice in the yard—one decidedly not Joseph's? Did someone call?"

"Fannie. Daniel's sister. There's to be a barn-raising Saturday at the Fuhrmanns'. Their barn was burned by the Briti...it burned down." Her gaze darted away. "Anyways, it'll be a wonderful time to get together with neighbors before winter."

That explained the sway in her steps. "And a

wonderful time to dance?"

A blush brought a glow to her cheeks. "There isn't much opportunity to dance out here. During the summer months, we used to hold picnics nigh every other week, but this year, what with the Briti—with so many other things to be done..."

"Indeed. Those British are quite bothersome rascals, it appears."

Rachel's face showed bemusement. Then a smile toyed with the corners of her mouth. "That they are. That they are."

Andrew feigned a cringe. "I believe that is my cue to return to reading." He reopened the book.

"Not yet, you don't." Rachel sailed to him and snatched the Bible from his hands.

"But—" His attempt to grab it back proved futile.

Her eyes sparkled. "You will sit there like a good boy and wait while I run out and fetch Joseph. We have a surprise for you."

"A what?"

She plopped the book on the cot and disappeared from the cabin. Several minutes passed, and still she did not return. Perhaps something delayed her.

What was the possibility of reaching the Bible? His leg was far from healed; however, the weeks since he had regained consciousness had brought gradual improvement. The pain was bearable with movement, but applying pressure remained out of the question. If he used his good leg to hop once, he could make it.

Slowly Andrew pushed up, balancing on his left foot. His hands gripped the arms of the rocking chair as he leaned forward. He released his right hand, and then the left. His whole right leg began to throb. This was the first time he had stood without any assistance in a long while. He wobbled, his leg weak, but he attempted to hop forward. It was too much. His knee buckled and he fell forward, his hands catching the edge of the cot. Under his weight, everything tipped toward him, threatening to dump him onto the floor. Thankfully, it dropped back into place, and he reached out for the Bible. "Thank you, Lord."

The murmur of voices neared the cabin.

Panic prickled his spine. His precarious position would make him appear ridiculous. In an attempt to salvage what little dignity he'd maintained since his injury, Andrew threw himself backward, forcing past the stab in his right leg. He caught the arms of the rocker with his hands, and lowered into it as the door opened. Stifling a groan, he forced a partial smile.

"Are you feeling all right?" Rachel immediately questioned.

"Yes, fine." Unfortunately there was no discreet way to wipe away the beads of sweat that tickled his forehead. Needing to direct their attention elsewhere, he motioned to the long, thin object Joseph held, draped with an old blanket. "Is that the rifle with which you promised to shoot my good leg?"

"I said I wouldn't shoot it until you tried to leave again. This is something to speed up the process." With a smirk, Joseph pulled away the covering.

Andrew peered at the roughhewn crutch. The pale flesh of whittled wood showed against the dark but smooth bark left untouched. "That is the finest looking branch I've ever seen—so far as my memory recollects."

"Joseph made the top so it'll fit comfortably under your arm." Rachel indicated the short length of wood wrapped in thick wool. "However, before you try it, you need to promise you'll take it easy and be careful not to cause any more damage."

He gave her a nod as Joseph handed him the crutch. Placing the wrapped woolen crosspiece under his right arm, Andrew pushed into a standing position, assisted by Rachel. Somewhat awkwardly, he put weight on the crutch and slid his left foot forward. Numb, his leg was slow to obey, but the step was successful. A grin broke across his face before he could bridle it. "I must admit, it is a lot better than the broom I borrowed."

"Yes," Rachel agreed. "And better for me, as well. You bent the bristles beyond repair."

Andrew took another step before stealing a glance at her. "I promise never to touch your broom again."

"I didn't say you couldn't use it, so long as the bristles are against the floor that you happen to be sweeping."

Joseph laughed. "A sure way to guarantee he'll never borrow it again. Well said, Rachel."

"Do not be so certain." Andrew shuffled another step. "Maybe soon I shall be of some use to you. I have so much to repay." One more step and he nodded toward the siblings. "But first if someone could assist me back to my seat...I think...I should sit for a while." His left leg burned with pain, and he struggled to catch his breath.

Rachel took his elbow, reversing his course. "How are you feeling?"

"I should be fine. After being idle for so long, my muscles seem to have mistaken themselves for fishes. Most assuredly, I am in need of practice."

Rachel took the crutch and leaned it against the wall near the cot.

"Thank you."

The ties of her dress pulled the tawny fabric tight at her waist, and then released it to cascade to her ankles. Her skirts swayed as she turned back to him. Tenderness filled her eyes as her gaze met his, and her lips gained fullness with a pleased smile. She had such a pretty mouth. Still, it was improper to stare. Andrew brought his gaze to where her brother stood.

Joseph's face bore resemblance to a mule ready to give a nasty kick. "I should get back to work," he mumbled under his breath.

"I appreciate the crutch."

Joseph glanced back, a storm rising in his eyes. "I need to see you as soon as you're done in here, Rachel."

"About what?"

"Just come out." The door remained open behind him.

"What in the world has come over him?" Rachel sighed as her hands smoothed over her skirt and straightened her apron. "Is there anything else you need before I go?"

"Do not concern yourself. It is probably best you hurry."

Rachel disappeared after Joseph.

Andrew wiped his hand across his face, his attention fixed on the place she'd stood a moment earlier.

Her brother was right to be angry.

They had saved his life and treated him with kindness, but Andrew was still the enemy. It was wrong of him to forget that. If only he could remember it. Either way, he needed to be honest with himself. She might as well be married.

~*~

Rachel picked her way across the yard, not going directly to the barn. The sun warmed her face, drawing it toward the brilliant blue sky. The world seemed quiet except the scratching and clucking of the nearby chickens. The rooster crowed his greeting.

What Joseph wanted remained a mystery, but it was Andrew who filled her thoughts. His quick smile, playful wit, willful determination when he set his mind to something, the intelligent and refined manner in which he spoke, the depth with which he knew the Bible—all combined to make him who he was. Whoever that might be.

Joseph called to her from the garner.

Rachel redirected her steps toward the tall, slender building standing behind the barn. A narrow, edged ramp came at a sharp angle from the loft of the barn, which also served as a threshing room, to the top of the smaller building.

Joseph perched on the highest rung of the ladder, checking the attachment of the chute and the height of the grain already contained in the storage.

"How's it looking?"

Joseph closed the small door. "Fine." He climbed to the ground. "When we're finished, there won't be much to spare, but we should have enough to see us through the winter and spring planting. Maybe even for those extra acres Pa and I cleared early last summer." He took her by the elbow and led her into the barn. "I need to talk to you about something."

Rachel pulled her arm away and sought something useful to do with her hands. A small, brownish chicken egg caught her eye and she plucked it from the makeshift nest at the base of the haystack. "What about?"

"That British officer in our home."

She spun to him. They had not referred to Andrew as British, or an officer, or even soldier, for some time. He had a name.

"He doesn't belong here, and he needs to leave before—"

"But he—"

"I don't mean immediately." Joseph pursed his lips, as though considering carefully what had to be said. "But sooner or later he will need to go. We'll try to give him as much time as we can, but I think it best he leave before the weather turns."

Another month. It was all Rachel could do to stand in place. "I know that. He wouldn't be safe here. I haven't forgotten who he is."

"Or what he is?"

She sighed. "Or what he is."

"Good. Because I am not completely unaware of the feelings you might develop for him. I want to make certain the wholesome compassion you have won't grow into anything more. He isn't part of our world and can't ever be. He's still a British officer, even though it's hidden."

Rachel glanced at the stack of hay where the truth lay well buried. "I know. You've been paying too much attention to Daniel. It's nothing more than his jealous nature trying to fight shadows." Rachel stilled her countenance. She couldn't let him see the turmoil wringing her insides like wet laundry. "Was there something else?"

"No...yes. Do you dislike Daniel?"

"Of course not." She turned to see if there were any more eggs hidden nearby. "Daniel Reid is a fine man. He's always been a good friend."

Joseph cleared his throat. "I'm not talking about as a friend. I know I used to tease you about him, but at the moment I am completely sincere. Could you ever see him as more?"

"I..." Rachel sucked air into her compressed lungs. Daniel Reid. Could she love him? Ever since their families met, he'd been high on her list of marriageable prospects. The only one who had rivaled him was Jarrett Adler, and now he was dead.

Once Andrew was gone, what other option would she have? Her heart felt as though it were being writhed in two as she crouched to collect more eggs. "You know I could. But why are you asking me this now?"

"I think you could do well by him. He's a hard worker and has worthy goals for the future. I want to be sure you don't take him for granted because of other distractions. Keep your mind open to possibilities." Joseph patted her shoulder before leaving the barn.

Rachel straightened, staring at the eggs in her hands. She had forgotten herself with Andrew Wyndham.

Captain Wyndham. A British officer.

Rachel dropped to her knees at the edge of the hay stack and set the eggs aside, before thrusting her hand deep to where the dirt and bloodstained coat lay hidden. She held it for a moment, numb. Her fingers brushed across the golden tassels at the shoulder and the equally elegant buttons down the front. It was the uniform of an officer loyal to the Crown of King George. It was the uniform of her enemy—the ones who had taken Pa from her. She hated the uniform and those who wore it.

She reached into a pocket for her little shears and snipped a small piece of scarlet fabric from the sleeve. It only took seconds to bury the remainder. Tucking the fabric into the collar of her dress, she held her palm over it for several minutes and forced herself to breathe. "Don't ever forget."

20

With the crutch tucked under his arm, Andrew maneuvered around the cabin. He ignored the throbbing ache and sometimes sharp stabbing pains shooting down his right leg as he worked to strengthen the other. Each day left him stronger and more restless. Especially today.

Rachel's pleasant humming came from the bedroom where she was preparing for the barn-raising. The past few days she'd talked of little else—though she really hadn't spoken much at all.

At least, not to him. The agitation that had been building over those days now worked the muscles of his jaw. He jerked his crutch forward, and then leaned into it, preparing to move his good leg.

The squeak of the bedroom door brought his head up. As Rachel emerged, Andrew's left leg seemed to lose all power. His step faltered, and he grabbed the edge of the table to steady himself. All physical discomfort faded.

Rachel's long, silvery-blue gown flowed gently with each move. Her usual braid had been wrapped around itself and pinned up on the back of her head, yet several strands the shade of morning sun escaped to grace her neck and face. Her eyes...her eyes shone, appearing lighter brown than usual, but still contrasting the tones of her hair.

Andrew straightened as he turned to face her, head inclining toward her in a bow. His gaze never wandered from hers.

Her smile had a demure quality as she dipped a slight curtsy. "It was my mother's. She had it made it in Boston years ago. It's a little worn." Rachel pulled at the skirt, twisting it so he could see the side. "Here at the hem I had a hard time matching the color of the fabric. I'm afraid the patch shows."

"Hardly noticeable." Andrew dragged a chair out and lowered into it as memories danced across his mind.

Women elegantly attired, their hair the result of hours of preparation, fine oddments dangling from earlobes. They moved with grace and poise and spoke with breeding and refinement. The fair and accomplished ladies of England.

And yet, as he watched Rachel's every move, it became clear that he had never beheld anyone as beautiful. "You look lovely."

Rachel met his eyes for a brief moment before she hurried to the fireplace. Her cheeks wore more color than a minute earlier. "I'll put this stew over the flame to heat for your dinner and supper. You can have it with those biscuits left over from breakfast."

"That will be fine, thank you." He shifted on the hard chair. "I hope you have a delightful time."

"I'm sure we will." Rachel looked back to him, her expression soft. "I wish you could come." As soon as the words left her mouth, a hand slipped to her collar. A strained smile formed on her lips, and the tone of her voice sharpened. "I'm sure you would have enjoyed how we Continentals throw a ball."

"I do not doubt it." Andrew forced a lighthearted

smile, though it was far from what he felt. "You colonists never cease to amaze me."

Rachel's gaze stayed. She opened her mouth as though to speak.

He waited.

The door opened and Joseph called for her, announcing it was time to leave.

She hurried to where her shawl hung, and then back to the table for the Dutch oven containing the cake she'd baked for the event. "Have a good day," she said as she trailed after her brother.

The door again closed, leaving Andrew alone. Pushing to his feet, he hobbled to the fireplace to pull the pan of thick stew from the heat. He slid it onto the table and stared at it. Without any feeling left in his stomach, Andrew maneuvered away, pacing the boundaries of his prison until his legs threatened to give out. He seated himself on his cot—the one that had held him captive for so long.

Releasing a cry, he bashed his crutch against the wall with all his might. The crutch remained strong, and his frustration increased. He struck it again, over and over, each time with less strength until finally it dropped to the floor, unmarred.

~*~

The evening air had a chill to it, testifying that summer was spent. In the movement and excitement of the event, no one seemed to mind except the older folks who sat against the wall of Fuhrmanns' newly constructed barn, looking on.

As the lively music came to an end, Rachel thanked her partner, Mr. Fuhrmann, a widower with five half-grown children, and moved to where Joseph stood in discussion with Matthias Adler about the harvest they were bringing in. She was grateful their community was small, not allowing for language and culture to separate them. They needed each other, depended on each other.

"What are you doing standing here when I know of several young women hoping you'll dance with them?" she reprimanded Joseph, not bothering to suppress the smile on her face. She had made up her mind to enjoy the party. No thoughts about the war with the British, or British people at all, not a single one. She'd felt enough pain this summer. Rachel paused for a moment to catch both her breath and composure.

"Ja, Joseph, listen to your sister." The older man chuckled. "Especially the oldest Reid girl. I do believe she has been vatching you all evening."

Joseph scowled. "It's not like that. She's just a kid."

"She's only a little younger than I," Rachel protested.

"My point exactly." He bumped her arm with his elbow. "I mean, she's still running around with her braids down and—"

"Maybe you haven't had a good look at her lately."

Even Matthias nodded toward the person in question. He gave Joseph a pat on the back and wandered to where his wife sat.

Crossing his arms, Joseph scanned the area cleared for dancing.

Fannie stood with her mother and younger sisters. Her hair formed elegant black ringlets that fell gently about her shoulders. A creamy yellow dress accented her womanly form.

As though sensing his gaze, Fannie glanced at him. Her dark lashes lowered as a blush rose to her cheeks.

Rachel was about to give her brother a push in the right direction when a hand warmed her arm. She turned. Daniel.

"Would you dance the next with me?"

"All right."

He led her to where other couples gathered.

The man with the violin pulled the bow across the strings, announcing that the music was to start. As they formed a line, she bit back a smile.

Joseph had invited Fannie and moved to join them.

The tune played merrily and the couples were soon breathless.

Daniel took Rachel's arm at the end and led her from the other dancers. "Would you like to sit out for the next one?"

"I think I am due for a rest," she panted.

"Perhaps you'd accompany me on a short walk to the stream." His head ducked as he cleared his throat. "It's lovely with the moon so full."

Rachel hesitated before supplying him with another nod. His sudden uncertainty did nothing for her own, but she placed her hand on his arm so he could lead the way. He covered her fingers. Her heart fluttered, but not in a good way. This was all Joseph's fault. And Rodney Cowden's. If they hadn't brought up the possibility of Daniel's affection, she could have gone on pretending there was nothing more than friendship between them.

Daniel led her down the path to the babbling stream. The moon's reflection danced on the water to the strains of violin that echoed from the barn.

"It is beautiful." Some of the tension ebbed as she took in the view.

"No more than you."

So much for letting the gurgling water steal her anxiety. She liked his compliments, but wanted him to stop at the same time.

"You're beautiful." He turned to face her and one hand came up to brush a strand of hair from her face. "Right now, the moonlight makes you appear as though gold streams from your head." Daniel held her gaze. Then he turned and moved to the bank of the stream, his fingers tapping against the side of his leg. He looked back to her. Even his smile showed his unease.

Rachel's gaze drifted over the illuminated scenery as she searched to lighten the air between them. "It has been a fine evening. Everyone seems to be enjoying themselves."

"That they do."

"We haven't had much opportunity for gatherings this summer."

He grunted. "It's probably been for the best. What with...it's easier to keep secrets this way."

She set her hand over the taut muscles of Daniel's forearm, ridged under the fabric. "Let's not talk about him—or that—right now."

"Of course not. This is hardly the place. And even if it were..." He crossed the back of his hand over his brow. "Rachel, I've been meaning to speak with you of something for a while now, but with...it has never been the right time."

She kept her gaze lowered.

"With your Pa gone, I felt it proper to speak with Joseph first. I finally did about a week ago." He paused to clear his throat. "I wish to call on you, Rachel—to court you, proper like."

Words caught in her throat as she looked at him.

Concern touched his brow, forming a new dimension of shadows. "What are your thoughts?"

Rachel ran the tip of her tongue discreetly over her lips. Almost twenty years of age, skirting around an attachment was gone if she didn't want to end up an old maid. She'd be foolish to turn away his affection. He was a good man, and she admired the determined strength in his jaw and the depth of his eyes. It'd be easy enough to love this man, wouldn't it? Still she wavered. She brushed her fingers over the scarlet scrap tucked in her collar.

Andrew was not a consideration here. He was leaving. He had no place in her world.

She cleared the lump from her throat. "That would be fine, Daniel."

"Truly?"

Rachel smiled, trying her best to make it real. "Yes, but I think we'd best hurry back to the clearing before tongues begin to wag."

He stared at her with marked relief a moment longer before nodding and offering his arm. "Yes, ma'am."

~*~

Andrew looked up from the book, his brain numb from reading hour after hour. But what else was there to distract his mind from thoughts of Rachel? With a sigh, he set aside the Bible. His eyes stung from the exertion of focusing on the small print in the dim light supplied by the lamp. It needed its wick trimmed for a better glow.

He covered a yawn as he gazed at the blackened window. It had been dark for a couple hours and still Rachel and Joseph hadn't returned. The evening stretched on forever as he fought the boredom, loneliness, and other feelings he wished to ignore. "I must not forget who I am."

Who am I? Unfortunately most of the answer remained obscure. Every day brought more images, but nothing concrete. "Andrew Wyndham. Captain Andrew Wyndham." Whoever that was. Whatever life he'd left behind in England, or duties that may have been his.

A strange sensation passed through him like lightning. Duty. Clouded faces from veiled memories pressed upon his mind, begging to be understood and revived. After several minutes they faded into the dark abyss of his past. Andrew maneuvered back to the cot and dropped to his left side, letting the frustration bleed away as weariness took him. As he relaxed, the images again rose from the mists of his mind.

"What of your duty to your family? You are the eldest. Our future rests in your hands. Will you lead us to ruin?" The voice he knew and the face he had often seen. His mother, her auburn hair piled high on her head, and her face staunch.

"What of my duty to God?" he had wondered.

But she hadn't heard him. She never did.

"The church is a worthy profession, but it is not for you. I will not see my eldest son give himself to some country parish when his family is in need. You father has

159

Angela K. Couch

not placed you in the position to waste yourself. His debts have left us with almost nothing. So it is decided. Politics is the only profession that can rightfully restore us."

"Mother, we have spoken of this before. You know I do not wish to join Parliament. Even the thought I find detestable."

A smile slid across her face. "Then perhaps you should find more occasion to dance, Andrew."

"Dance?"

"Yes. I have noted Miss Grenville is very fond of dancing. The invitation Baron Glastonbury extended you and your brother shall give you ample opportunity to secure her affections. A fortnight in Derbyshire is just what is required."

"Miss Grenville and her ten-thousand-a-year, is that what this is about?"

Footsteps across the plank floor pulled Andrew awake. His head seemed swollen, yet the memory remained, and it was indeed that—a memory.

"Sorry if I awakened you." The glow of the tiny flame touched Rachel's face as she took the lamp in her hands. "How was your day?"

"Fine." He rolled onto his back, his gaze never leaving her. Why did she have to look so hauntingly beautiful? "And yours?"

"It was good." She smiled, but only with her mouth. She turned with the lamp toward the bedroom where Joseph had already retreated.

Andrew clamped his eyes shut. Miss Grenville was as much a mystery as any of his past, but there was no doubt in his mind that he had never felt anything this strong for her.

160

21

Rachel stole a glance across the table at Andrew. He'd been quiet this morning and was hardly putting a dent in his noonday meal. Not that she fared much better at clearing her plate—nor had she given him much opportunity for conversation. It was easier to simply avoid him. The coarse swatch of his uniform was not proving as effective as she'd hoped. She stood and moved to where the empty pails waited near the door. "I need to get some fresh water for the dishes."

"Don't be long," Joseph called after her.

It was a Sunday afternoon. Everything that absolutely had to be taken care of had been finished before they'd sat down to eat. They wouldn't be harvesting today, so why would she need to hurry? Not bothering to ask, Rachel stepped into the sunshine. Unfortunately it did little to penetrate the shadow that embraced her as she walked to the well.

After drawing water, she remained perched on the wooden base, staring into the deep hole. Its bottom glistened. With two fingers she slipped the red scrap of cloth from her collar and sighed. She could never regret bringing Andrew from the battle field that night, or that he recovered...but why did he have to be so good, so genuine? Why did his eyes have to captivate her, or his voice penetrate her? Why did she have to fall in love?

She loved him.

The realization swelled within her eyes. How was she to give her life to Daniel, or any other man, when the British captain already possessed her heart? What an impossible situation. She had to fight it—to not feel anything.

"Rachel?" Joseph hollered from the cabin.

She fortified herself with a deep breath and then slipped the snippet of red out of sight. Hefting the pails of water, Rachel carried them inside. She stopped short.

Joseph sat with the Bible open on the table.

Andrew pushed himself to his feet, a gesture he was making a habit of.

Her attempts to dissuade him seemed to fall on deaf ears, so she didn't bother saying anything. Still, it would be better for his thigh if he put etiquette aside until he got back to England.

Her brother glanced up. "I've been doing some thinking. It's well past time we had a Sabbath meeting. The way we used to."

Rachel released the pails near the fireplace, the contents sloshing over the brim. It was too soon. "Let's wait until the snow falls. I have so much that needs doing. I mean...what with..."

Joseph held her gaze, a look of fascination and disbelief forming a furrow on his brow. Could he so easily see through her?

"Fine." She slumped in a chair across from him.

With a "good," Joseph motioned toward their British captain. "I already invited Andrew to join us."

Rachel glanced at his pleasant smile and attempted a civil one.

The devotional began with a short prayer, offered

by Joseph, and then he turned to the Bible. "I'm afraid I don't know quite where to begin," he confessed to Andrew. "Before our Ma died, we read daily. Pa was a little busier, but would see to it that every Sabbath we set time apart for discussion and study. I don't even remember where we left off."

"There should be a marker." Rachel fiddled with an inch-long tear in her apron. She would need to fix it before it ripped any more. "Mama's lace."

The pages rustled as they were turned. "All right—Hebrews. I'm guessing we finished chapter ten, so on to eleven. 'Now faith is the substance of things hoped for, the evidence of things not seen.'"

Rachel cringed as Joseph continued. Of all the places to start reading, it had to be the chapter on faith, the one thing she didn't want to consider right now— besides the man sitting in silence across the table.

"'Through faith we understand that the worlds were framed by the word of God...'"

Andrew's head came up. "That's interesting."

Joseph stopped. "What?"

"'Worlds were framed by the word of God.' Creation." Andrew pointed to the Bible. "But this could be understood two ways. In Genesis, we read, 'And God said,' and creation followed. All He did was speak the word. But then, in the beginning of the Gospel according to John, we read that 'In the beginning was the Word, and the Word was with God, and the Word was God.' It speaks of Christ. Of course we know from the next couple of verses in John, that 'without Him was not anything made'." Andrew paused and lowered his hand. "It is simply thought provoking, is all. I had not linked these verses before." Andrew relaxed back into his chair. "I apologize for the interruption. Please continue."

"You certainly know your Bible." Joseph scratched his beard with his knuckles. "As I mentioned, it was not as though we weren't raised without a decent amount of study, yet I feel quite ignorant at the moment. I must admit I didn't follow everything you said."

Andrew shrugged off the compliment. "The Bible has been my life for a long while." His gaze focused on the fireplace, but he didn't seem to see it. "My desire had been to take my occupation in the church. It was my intention to become a clergyman. I had even been offered a parish not far from my family's country estate." His eyes narrowed as though he were attempting to peer through the solid stones. "Though I do not think my family was in residence at the time."

Rachel couldn't remove her gaze from him, or the light dancing in his large pupils. "It certainly explains a lot." With her elbows on the table, she leaned forward. "But you never mentioned this before."

"I did not remember until last night. Unfortunately there was opposition. I had a duty to my family, but I am not sure..." He stopped, his eyes again distant.

"Was it your duty to your family that took you into the army?" Joseph asked.

The creases deepened at the corners of Andrew's eyes. "I cannot imagine how. From what I recall, my main responsibility as the eldest son—perhaps just the eldest, as I do not recall having a sister—was to restore my family's fortune and secure our place in society."

"Society," Rachel echoed. The concept seemed so out of place in this wilderness.

"Do you remember anything more?" Joseph asked.

Andrew looked to Rachel and then dropped his gaze to the table. "Shadows and fragments of this and that. There is still so much I need to piece together."

"Well, it seems that you're making progress." Rachel's chair ground against the floor as she stood.

Joseph's chuckle drew her attention. "Sorry, I was remembering how Mrs. Adler was talking last evening about how much she missed attending church like they did back east, and how much she hoped that someday we'd have our own preacher." He grinned. "If only they knew we had one right under our very own roof."

"Very funny, Joseph. Just don't forget what they would do if they found out we had him right under our very own roof."

"I wasn't serious. It's simply an amusing thought."

"Yes. And to think you first wanted him dead." Her face burned as she glanced to Andrew.

His brow lowered, shadowing his eyes.

"I'm sorry, but Joseph seems to forget himself. I mean nothing against you." And hurting him had not been her intension.

Joseph snapped the Bible closed. "What has gotten you so worked up all of the sudden?"

"Nothing at all. But I still have plenty I need to get done today before Daniel comes." She smoothed her skirts. "I told you he aims to call tonight."

"That's fine, as long as you don't mind the rector and I having a bit more of a discussion." He looked to Andrew. "There have always been a few things in the Bible that stump me. Perhaps you'll be able to shed some light on them."

The creases in Andrew's cheeks deepened as he moved his focus to the book. "I shall do my best. I am still learning myself."

Joseph laughed. "This coming from the man who quotes the Bible like poetry and speaks Greek."

Rachel's head came up. "You speak Greek?"

"Not fluently. I prefer Latin...and French. German I struggle with." He tapped a finger on the edge of the table. "The King's English is, by far, that with which I am most comfortable."

~*~

Daniel took Rachel's arm as he opened the door. Together they vanished into the evening shadows.

Andrew pulled up to his good foot and paced the floor in a painfully ungraceful manner. There was nothing he could do for that, as pure jealousy stiffened his body.

"Is something wrong?" Joseph questioned from his seat. "You seem restless."

Andrew stumbled to a halt, but did not turn to face him. "Is it so unnatural? I have been caged within these four walls for a month. I have counted all five hundred and twenty-three knots in the rafters above my bed so many times, I am capable of doing so in my sleep."

Joseph slid his chair back. "You know it's not safe for you to be seen."

"What if I were to wait until dusk. I would stay behind the cabin and not be gone long." Andrew sighed. "If you say I am a prisoner, I shall consign myself to this fate and be grateful for this kind prison—but if there affords some freedom, I wish to feel it. I want to breathe."

"You know you're not our prisoner." Joseph walked into the bedroom, returning a minute later with a knee length, dark brown coat and a pair of worn boots. "Take these."

Boots. That was freedom. "I no longer have to wander with nothing but long socks?"

Joseph placed the articles near the table and waited for Andrew to join him. "Being confined to the cabin isn't the only reason, is it? I'm not as blind as all that—contrary to the belief of certain young ladies." He sat down and motioned for Andrew to do the same. "Rachel is a handsome woman, but not in any extraordinary way. She might catch the attention of a man like Daniel, for example, because she's hardworking and will be an asset to any man trying to scratch out a life here. But that isn't your life. You're remembering that now."

Andrew dropped the boots to the floor and pulled the left one on. A bit of a squeeze, but hopefully the leather would stretch given time.

"You can't forget that she's American in the very essence of the word. She can't change that any more than you can change who you are, whether or not you truly know. Rachel was right—we mustn't forget how this arrangement began. Sooner or later you'll have to leave." His fingers raked through his hair. "Though, I still don't know what we'll do when the time comes."

Andrew pressed a half smile and nodded toward the rifle hanging over the door. "There is always your favorite option."

With a chuckle, Joseph shook his head. "It was never really an option. I couldn't do it that first night. Even after hours of firing my musket at every Tory and Redcoat in sight, I couldn't kill a dead man."

"I am no longer a dead man." Andrew yanked the second boot onto his other foot.

"But you also no longer wear that coat." Joseph leaned back in his chair. "Besides, I'm sure it's not a good thing to kill a clergyman."

"War is a peculiar thing, is it not? Men against men. Some protecting their land and families, others led by their duty to king and country. Yet all are men. In the end they all kill, they all bleed, and they all die— in one form or another." He rested his elbows on the table, pushing his palms into his eyes. A moaned rumbled. "I almost remember. Marching for days in the hot sun, wishing we had been wise enough to stay home. Straight lines of red-clad soldiers. I was merely one of hundreds, regardless of the fact I was an officer. It did not set me apart from my men. And then the battle...the stench of smoke as barns and homes burnt to the ground. Lifetimes of work destroyed in minutes. But what is that? Houses and barns can be rebuilt, but..." his voice cracked, "but the life of a man, created in the image of God himself...no wonder the Lord decreed 'thou shalt not kill.'"

The air fell silent as shadows grew across the room and the light from the windows faded. A lamp was lit, but did little for vision or mood as memories continued to haunt. And thoughts of Rachel. "I no longer wish to remain here," Andrew murmured.

"What do you plan to do? Where would you go?"

"Yet another thing I cannot say. I simply know I cannot remain here. Not in this house."

Joseph lit another lamp. "If it's just the cabin, there is a room in the loft you could stay in while you finish recovering. I reckon you'll need at least a few more weeks. Hopefully we'll figure out what to do by then."

"Would it not be most logical for you to take me to your army?" Andrew set the crutch under his arm and rose. "Then I would no longer be a liability."

"I'd have to lie if I said that thought hasn't continued to visit me the past couple weeks." He stood as well. "However, today I decided I could use your help. Before everything happened—the battle, our Pa's death—Rachel was a very strong believer. Not a day went by that she didn't have the Bible in hand, poring over it and preaching to me to better my ways. She used to smile a lot more, too. She used to trust in God. I thought holding our Sabbath meetings might be good, but how can I help her renew her faith, when mine's never been that strong to begin with?"

Andrew leaned heavily into the crutch. If only he could be instrumental in returning Rachel to her faith. And the one to return a smile to her face. "I doubt I would be of much assistance, but I shall do what I can." Andrew grabbed the coat and slipped it on. It fit large, but within reason. "I suppose it is dark enough for me to get some fresh air and do some thinking?"

Joseph followed him to the door and took a weathered tricorn hat from one of the pegs. "One more thing to keep in mind. Daniel Reid is a good man and has been a true friend to this family. He'll make a fine husband for Rachel." He handed Andrew the hat.

"I know." The truth of it sat heavy as Andrew covered his head. "I respect your sister and wish her the best." With a quick nod to Joseph, he maneuvered out into the crisp evening air and away from the cabin. Liberty. Independence. Was this why the colonists were pulling away from Britain?

Rachel's voice cut through his revelry. It drifted to him on the breeze, followed by Daniel's.

With effort, Andrew pushed aside the growing ache in his center. Any feelings he had for Rachel

Garnet were wrong and impossible. He needed to put them aside once and for all.

22

"Tomorrow will be a busy day." Daniel's fingers warmed hers, cradling them on his arm as he led her back to the cabin. "I should probably start for home."

Rachel withdrew her hand as they stopped at the door. "This time of year, morning always has a way of coming too soon."

His gaze dropped to linger on her lips.

Rachel slid a step back. "Goodnight, Daniel. And thank you for the walk."

He nodded, backing away, as well. "Goodnight." With a tip of his hat, he moved to where he'd tied his horse. As he faded into the darkness, she turned and reached for the latch.

"Did you have a pleasant evening, Miss Garnet?" At the soft spoken words, she jerked around.

Andrew emerged from the shadows. He removed his hat with a curt bow of his head. "I am sorry to have startled you."

"No, you didn't startle me. I'm just surprised to see you out here." Apprehension tickled her spine. Had he heard Daniel's rant...again? "How long have you been there?"

"Not long. I was in the barn looking over some things. Joseph has agreed the time has come for me to give you back the privacy of your own home. You have a decent room in your loft."

"Joseph planned it with my father when they built the barn. He wanted a place of his own. But it's been vacant this past month. It's too much of a mess to stay in now."

"I admit it could use some tidying—definitely some dusting—but I no longer wish to impose upon you."

His presence was hardly an imposition anymore, though perhaps that was the problem. With him out of the house, she would see him less. It would be easier not to think about him as constantly, and life could return to normal. However, this logic did nothing for the hollowness building in her chest. "What about the stairs? How will you manage them with your bad leg?"

"I must admit to being quite concerned when I first saw them. However, I discovered the fine art needed. As long as there is nothing I have to carry, I should manage."

Rachel wrapped one of the sharply angled corners of her shawl around her forefinger. "You've decided, then?"

His nod was almost unseen in the night. So stiff. So proper. He wore Pa's coat and old hat, but it was not difficult to picture him dressed in tailored finery, addressing his lordly associates, or genteel ladies.

"I thank you for how long you have offered your home and tended my wounds. I pray the Lord bless you for your saintly kindness."

Rachel turned back to the door, her hand reaching for the latch. "I'm sorry for what I said earlier this afternoon."

"I am not." He shuffled a step forward. "You were right. Joseph and you should not forget who I am. It would prove dangerous to do otherwise."

Rachel's grip loosened as she pivoted back to him. He was within arm's reach, and hers ached for him. Would it be so wrong, so impossible? "Andrew, I..."

He took another step, his face now only inches away, looking down at her.

Her gaze fell to his mouth as his lips parted. Soft breath caressed her face.

"Rachel..." His eyes closed and his jaw stiffened. "It is getting late. Your brother will be concerned."

"Yes." She rotated away from him and opened the door.

~*~

Andrew bowed as he took the young woman's hand. Long, dark lashes lowered over large eyes, a demure smile forming on rosy lips. She made a short curtsy as the music ended. "Thank you, Mr. Wyndham."

"The pleasure was mine." Andrew released her hand, but stepped nearer. "Allow me to return you to your friends."

She set her delicate fingers on his proffered arm. "I am glad you made it back to town in time for tonight. I have seen your brother on several occasions, but nothing of you since Derbyshire. I was beginning to wonder if you found our company unpleasant."

He led her around a group gathered in conversation. One of the men wore regimentals—a more and more common sight at such assemblies as tensions increased with the American colonies. One last fling in society before being shipped to another continent. "I assure you, that is far from the truth," he said, putting the war from his mind. It had little bearing on his life or plans. This woman and the next few minutes held all sway. "I had business to complete at

Oxford."

"Are you finished your studies there?"

"I am."

"And what is next for you, Mr. Wyndham?"

Instead of directing her back to where her party waited, he took a turn toward the veranda. "I have been offered a parish at Newbury."

"You mean to take your occupation in the church, then?" A crease appeared on her otherwise smooth forehead.

"I do."

"But surely there are much grander offices for a man such as yourself?"

They stepped into the warm night air, and Andrew turned to face her. "My mother would agree with you, but the church is where my heart is." He forced a smile. "Newbury is an enviable parish, and, located between London and Bath, it is by no means isolated from society. My family's country estate is near there."

Her face remained unreadable for a minute, and then she tipped her head coyly to one side. A dark ringlet danced beside her ear. "Are you seeking my approval for your chosen profession, Mr. Wyndham?"

He held her gaze, painfully aware of the moisture gathering on the back of his neck. Maybe the air was too warm. "I am."

"And what purpose would my good opinion prove to you?"

Andrew glanced back at the assembly.

A couple lingered near the door, but not close enough to overhear.

"I would seek your hand in marriage, Miss Grenville."

Andrew's eyes opened to the darkness. His heart was the only sound, each pound breaking the silence. He pressed his thumbs into his temples, massaging them. It was more than just a dream. The images had been too clear—too precise. And now, instead of fading as dreams did, the scene gained depth and clarity.

Staring into the night, Andrew replayed the memory, more faces merging from the haze. His mother had been there. She'd nodded him toward the veranda. He was returning with Miss Grenville when a group of young gentlemen in regimentals had moved past. His brother, Stephen, had been one of them.

"What is this?"

Stephen had jerked away, looking smug as usual. "I was bored."

"You were bored?" Andrew wanted to shake his smirk away. "What about Mother? You know what this will do to her?" She adored her youngest son.

"Not here."

"Then we shall go someplace else."

"Please!" Stephen groaned. "Cannot your lectures wait until tomorrow? Come, brother, stop making a scene in front of this lovely creature." He'd turned all his charm toward the lady on Andrew's arm. "Miss Grenville." He bowed. "Perhaps I should rescue you from this boorish brother of mine. Would you dance this next one with me?"

They made their way to the middle of the floor as the other officers laughed and moved on. There had to be a way to change it—a way to get him out of the army.

Andrew had found his mother's face among the crowd. Never had he seen such emotion in her face. *Do you have any realization of what you have done, little brother?*

The cabin was almost pitch-black save a soft glow

of moonlight stealing through the small windows. Andrew buried his face in his elbow. He had withdrawn from the ministry and his dreams. Two days before his regiment left England, he'd received news that the parish he had hoped for was given to a Mr. Arthur Wilhurst, an acquaintance from his time spent at Oxford.

His mother never said anything to him about his sacrifice, only of her gratitude.

But where was his brother now?

"The fool." Andrew pushed himself into a sitting position, reaching for the letter he'd tucked away. The words were undistinguishable in the darkness, but his mind reviewed them nonetheless.

The request for Lieutenant Stephen Wyndham's transfer to the eighth regiment has been approved.

His regiment. Andrew had wanted him close and had acquired the commissions needed. His family's position. His education. Money. It made it easier to keep his promise. He set the letter aside and grasped his crutch. Balanced on his good leg, he hesitated. Joseph's mild snore and a cricket were the only sounds. He maneuvered toward the small bedroom and paused at the doorway, steadying his weight against the frame.

In the smaller room, there was even less light, making it barely possible to discern the beds or the sleeping forms upon them.

An increasingly familiar ache rose within. His past was returning, stripping away any fantasy or hope of remaining in this valley...with Rachel.

As soon as he was able, he would leave and find his brother. Then they would return together to England where Andrew would fulfill his duty to his fiancée.

23

Andrew sat on a handcrafted chair near a makeshift table constructed from a tall length of stump with a thinner slab of wood laid on top. He propped his crutch against the wall of the small room.

Rachel finished sweeping the dust and a trail of straw from the floor.

"Thank you, Miss Garnet."

Rachel set aside the broom to spread two blankets across the bed. "All I ask is that you remember to give your leg time to heal." She smoothed the last patchwork quilt out before glancing over her shoulder. "I still have misgivings about you being out here all by yourself. I saw how you climbed those stairs, and it scared me to death. If you ever lost your balance..." Her eyes closed as she shook her head.

"I appreciate your concern." If that was truly concern. Understanding what she felt or thought about him was becoming increasingly difficult. Not that it mattered. "I shall avoid plummeting to my death."

"Is that statement supposed to improve my confidence in this arrangement?"

Who could be sure what would satisfy her? No. That wasn't fair. Of course she wanted him to finish healing...so she would finally be rid of him. Her courtship with Mr. Reid would proceed much smoother with him gone. They would be married before Christmas.

Andrew swallowed back the bitterness in his mouth and the jealousy that seemed to taint his every thought. He reached out for the Bible Rachel had placed on the table. Joseph's concern for her was understandable and he had promised to assist. "Wouldn't you rather keep this in the house where you can read it?"

"I think not. You seem to put it to much greater use than I have in a long time."

"Do you not miss it?" Andrew tried to keep his voice light. He needed to proceed gently.

Rachel remained silent for a moment. She straightened, but avoided his eyes. "I don't have time—I need to get dinner ready." She started for the door.

"What are you running from?"

"I'm not running from anything, I simply have a lot I need to attend to."

"I think you are running—running from yourself, from your belief in God, and perhaps even God Himself."

"He abandoned me first." Rachel raised her gaze, her eyes ice and her face rigid. "Don't presume you know me or my life."

"My apologies, Miss Garnet, but I know God does not abandon His children, especially in their sufferings. We abandon Him—usually when we need Him the most. The Savior gave the invitation when He said, 'Come unto Me all ye that labor and are heavy laden, and I will give you rest.' And again as is stated by John in his epistle: 'Herein is love, not that we loved God, but that He loved us, and sent His Son to be the propitiation for our sins.'"

A mix of emotions played across her face and she turned away. "I don't need you preaching to me, Captain Wyndham."

As her footsteps echoed her retreat down the stairs, he glanced about the room, surrounding him like a cage. He couldn't bear it. Grabbing the crutch, he made his way through the main area of the loft over a layer of chaff and around piles of freshly threshed wheat. The large doors hung open, and he sat on the ledge, ten to twelve feet above the ground.

The road was only partly visible, mostly hidden behind a line of trees. The front of the cabin peeked from the corner, and a clearing, some of it tilled, stretched around it. Mounds and rows of green latticed the black earth of a garden, but he had never paid enough attention to discern which were potato plants or some other vegetable. Not that it concerned him.

Rachel breached the border, an ax in hand, moving toward a huge stump. She raised the ax above her head and sank it past the dark soil into the roots. She must have cleared the area earlier. But where was Joseph? This surely was labor for a man and not a young woman, even in this wilderness. She'd never be able to remove that monstrosity by herself and really, how many times could her slender arms possibly heft the large ax over her pretty head?

Far more times than he'd imagined. The fervency and power in her swing was admirable...and strange. The women with whom Andrew had been acquainted in England became distraught at lifting more than a cup of tea. Women of sophistication and elegance, they trained themselves to be proficient in language, the arts and music—not digging in the earth and milking cows. Rachel Garnet was so very displaced from what he had ever considered accomplished, or even acceptable. She was a peasant. A farmer's daughter. Common by everything he knew by which to judge...and yet, hardly common at all.

In England, if he had seen her, she would have never touched his mind, her station so far below what his had been. But given time to know her, he could not help but admire her. She was intelligent, and kind, and beautiful, and perhaps a superior creature to the ladies of his past acquaintance. She was genuine.

Andrew chuckled as the crack of an ax against a solid root met his ears. "And very determined." If only he were not attached. If only he were free to act with little thought of duty or obligation. Desire clamped a vise across his chest. *If only I were American.*

~*~

Rachel cleared the supper dishes from the table. Her gaze wandered to the chair Andrew usually took. It remained empty. "Why don't you take some roast up to him?" She tried to maintain a look of disinterest.

"I told you already, when I invited him down for supper, he said he wasn't hungry tonight, and to not bother bringing him any," Joseph stated.

"But he hasn't eaten anything today, has he? He wasn't hungry for breakfast either, and hasn't been in since first thing this morning." Water splashed as she plunked the plates into the basin. "Maybe he's ill."

Joseph leaned back. "He was up and about a couple of hours ago trying to help me in the barn. He looked fine."

Rachel drummed her fingers against the table. "Maybe he's changed his mind."

"If he changes his mind, he's capable of coming down and getting something."

She picked up the dishcloth and wrapped it around her hand, fiddling with a loose thread at the corner. "Maybe his leg is bothering him more than he wants to let on. As you said, he's been on his feet a lot today. He won't be up to coming in even if he changes his mind." Rachel tossed the cloth into the basin and moved for her shawl with the plate she'd already fixed for him. "I'll take him something anyway. He can always eat it later."

"Rachel." She was half way to the door when Joseph's voice stopped her.

"What?"

"Nothing."

A minute later she scurried through the barn. What would she say to ease the tension? Andrew was probably avoiding her after their exchange of words that morning. "Well, I will not sit back and let him starve to death while he wallows in his stubborn pride."

Andrew's voice carried from the room above. The words deepened with passion. A prayer—a very personal, soul wrenching prayer.

The pleading resonance of his voice held her in place.

"What am I to do, Lord? Almost no choice remains to be made. I must find him, but how do I know he is not already dead?"

A drawn-out pause draped its way around her heart.

"Do not let it be so, Lord," Andrew continued. "He is still young. He should not have been here in the first place. Neither of us should be. I should be back in

England serving Thy purposes, and Stephen should be attending to his studies. Yet here we are...only Thou knoweth exactly where. What am I to do, Lord? I need a miracle if I am to ever find him. For that purpose I come before Thee with my humble fast. Thou hast the power. I know this. Help me trust in Thy wisdom and accept Thy will." His words faded.

Rachel turned back to the stairs.

"Oh, God, help me accept Thy will...and my fate. I cannot...I cannot allow myself feel. Or hope. God, give me strength," Andrew's voice was soft and sincere.

A black creature flew down from the rafters, the wind from its wings brushing her face. A scream squeaked out as the plate dropped. The stoneware shattered on the floor, the crash sending an echo through the loft.

Andrew emerged, silhouetted by the lamp on the table behind him. He leaned heavily on his crutch. The light reflected moisture in his eyes. Had he been weeping? Despite this, he was far from sorrowful. Instead his expression seemed livid. "Why are you here?" A deep cleft appeared between his eyes.

"I'm sorry. I was bringing you some supper—a bat startled me. I'm so sorry. I—"

"I told Joseph I did not want any," Andrew said.

"I'm sorry."

"How long were you there?" When she did not answer, his frown deepened. "It must seem quite humorous to you, I suppose, listening to a grown man pour his soul out to God. There, you have witnessed it. You may leave."

Rachel couldn't move, the sharp tone of his voice cutting her, paralyzing her.

Andrew's breath was heavy and jagged as he

stared her down. "What do you want from me? You have seen me in every humiliating way possible. You have watched me beg for my life, lie as helpless as an infant. You have seen me literally crawl on my hands and knees. Yes, I am your enemy. Yes, I fought against your people—against your own father and brother. Well, here I am. Do what you like, but leave me some dignity. That is all I ask. Let me be a man, whether you see me as one, or not." He turned in haste to retreat. His crutch caught on a protruding plank and he staggered. He cried out as he tried to catch himself with his bad leg. He stumbled to the floor with a loud moan, and then a yell of frustration.

Rachel rushed to him and grabbed his arm to help, her heart aching. She'd never intended him to feel less than he was, and he was very much a man. "Are you all right?"

"Leave me alone." He jerked away. "I do not require your assistance any longer."

He might as well have slapped her. "I'm sorry. I only wanted to help."

"You have helped enough." Andrew pulled to his feet and hobbled back into his room, limping badly. "I want to be left alone." The thin plank door slammed.

"I'm sorry." Rachel didn't bother with the broken dish and spilled food. Once outside, she leaned against the wall and sank to the ground. She slumped forward, buried her eyes in her folded arms.

24

As always, Andrew stood, his head inclined toward Rachel as she approached. His gaze, however, hardly brushed hers anymore. For the past week he'd politely avoided her. He seemed to regret their encounter as much as she, but his distance gave her little opportunity for apology.

Silence settled into the room as she laid plates on the table.

Joseph took the soft cheese and cut it.

She did the same with a fresh loaf of bread.

Andrew poured a cup of milk, sipping it as though it were a fine wine.

After Joseph said grace, Rachel put a thick slice of cheese over her bread and took a bite, her eyes not wavering from the food in her hands.

A knock sounded on the door.

Her gaze jumped to Andrew and then to Joseph. The bread clung to her throat as she forced it down. "It must be Daniel." She smoothed her skirts as she moved around the table. Her palms moistened.

Andrew reached for his crutch.

"Let me, Rachel," Joseph said, holding up his hand. He nodded to Andrew, motioning to the bedroom as he reached for the latch. He cracked the door open a half foot.

"Rodney. Nice to see you." Joseph's voice boomed.

Rachel pressed her hands over her stomach.

"You caught us in the middle of our dinner. Can we offer you some?" Joseph asked.

Andrew was halfway across the floor.

"No, I'm fine. But I'd like a few words with you, if I might."

"Of course, of course."

Joseph stepped aside, pulling the door wide as Andrew lunged out of sight.

Rachel put a smile on her face. "Welcome, Mr. Cowden. What brings you out our way?" Surely not to question why she had allowed Daniel to court her. She motioned to a chair. Andrew's plate caught her eye.

"Thank you." He followed her gesture and sat, then looked at Joseph. "But as to why I came by today. Last Sabbath evening I'd been over to the Reids'. I was on my way home past your place when I noticed someone out behind your barn, wandering through the pasture."

"Just me checking on something," Joseph said easily.

"I figured so at first, but a few nights ago I rode by after seeing Daniel." He looked to Rachel. "Seems he's quite determined to stay put in this valley now."

Rachel fought the urge to squirm under his disapproving glare.

"Anyways, I saw what appeared to be the same man. He had something tucked under his arm, like a crutch, and seemed to have quite a limp."

Joseph leaned forward in his chair. "What are you suggesting? We have a prowler?"

"I don't know what else to think."

"Could be Benjamin Reid out with his cane for an evening walk, or hunting." Rachel struggled to keep her voice even.

"That would have been my guess as well if I hadn't just left him."

"It is mighty strange." Joseph kept his own voice remarkably relaxed. "We appreciate you coming by and letting us know. Haven't noticed anything go missing, but I'll definitely keep my eyes open from now on. I wonder who it could be."

"My query exactly." Cowden stood and pushed his hat back on his head. "But I better leave you to your meal."

"Thank you again." Rachel also rose.

"Think nothing of it. Do you have company?" His gaze was on the third plate set with food.

"We um…" Rachel couldn't finish. Another knock jerked her gaze toward the open door. All her breath escaped. "Daniel."

Joseph issued him in. "Perfect timing, my friend. Rachel already set you a plate. Rodney stopped by to warn us to watch for a prowler he thinks he's seen in the area."

"Oh?" Daniel stepped into the room, glancing about. "Might be one of the Kastner boys fooling around. They're big for their ages and wander back and forth through here all the time playing war. You know how boys are."

Cowden appeared thoughtful. "Could be, but—"

"But it pays to be wary all the same." Joseph clapped him on his buckskin clad shoulder. "We are in your debt." He followed Cowden outside. "Is there anything we can do for you?"

Their voices faded as they moved away from the cabin.

Rachel closed the door, her hands planted against

it as her pulse returned to normal. "Thank goodness, you came when you did, Daniel."

"Where is...you know who?"

She pointed toward the bedroom as she dropped into her chair, her legs grateful for the reprieve.

Daniel sat across from her and took her hand. "When will you two accept that it's not safe to have that...*man* here?"

"We've always known it's a risk." A shuffle against the floor raised her gaze to Andrew's.

He stood in the bedroom doorway, his face flint.

She untwined her fingers from Daniel's. "Let's not talk about it now."

Daniel twisted to look at Andrew. "Of course not. You wouldn't want anyone to feel unwelcome."

"Please, Daniel..." She touched his hand to get him to face her again. "Not now."

Joseph slipped in the door and released a laugh. "That was close."

Andrew leaned against the nearest wall. "I should have been more cautious. I was careless and entirely at fault."

"Maybe stick to the denser trees if you need to stretch your legs."

Daniel shook his head. "I can't believe you even let him out."

"He's not our prisoner."

"Well, maybe he should be."

"Please, can we stop talking about it and finish eating. Have you had your dinner yet, Daniel? Will you join us?" Rachel invited.

He gave a nod.

"And—Captain Wyndham, please come back to the table."

The room lapsed into silence as everyone ate.

Joseph finished first and slid the Bible onto the table.

Rachel cringed. She'd forgotten his renewed desire for Sabbath readings.

"I don't know how much time you have, Daniel," he said, "but you are more than welcome to join us for our devotions."

Daniel answered with another nod as he chewed the last of his food.

"What do you say, Andrew, will you lead us?"

"If you desire it."

Joseph passed him the Bible. "You can read from anywhere, and expound as much as you feel inclined to."

Something seemed to pass between them, some sort of understanding.

Andrew's mouth twitched as he nodded. When the dishes were cleared away, he opened with a prayer and then turned deep into the Old Testament.

~*~

"A clergyman, huh?" Daniel shook his head. "I wasn't expecting that."

"None of us were." Rachel released his arm to climb over the fence and then waited for him to join her on the other side.

"And yet, there he sat in your home giving a sermon on the three Hebrew boys thrown into a fiery furnace. What do you suppose he really meant by all that?"

Rachel sighed. She didn't want to discuss this.

Andrew intended no veiled political agenda in his

words. He'd been speaking directly to her. Trust in the Lord even in the face of death, knowing that He is able to deliver. *But if not…*still trust.

"I don't know," she mumbled. "Why don't we talk about something else? Anything not involving that man."

Daniel faced her, and cradled her shoulders. "You've always acted so protective of him. I guess I took for granted how much your charity has put you through. How exhausting it must be having one of the enemy always present. I'm sure it won't be much longer before even your conscience can rest easy at his departure."

Rachel glanced down, not wanting to risk Daniel seeing the turmoil tearing her apart, or the overwhelming sinking feeling at his words.

"I'm sorry. You ask me not to talk about him, and all I do is continue ranting." Daniel hooked her hand back onto his arm. "Let's keep walking."

~*~

Andrew cracked the loft door open to peer down at the darkened yard and the soft glow of a lamp dancing between the cabin and the forest. Daniel had left, so where was Rachel going so late in the evening alone? It couldn't be safe.

The stairs squawked under his boots as he half hopped, half bounded down them and to the main doors, slipping through.

The light flickered, disappearing and reappearing as Rachel continued between trees, deeper into the woods.

Half way across the clearing he hesitated as the

cool night seeped through his thin shirtsleeves. He'd forgotten his coat. If he turned back now, he'd never find her...and it was better she remain unaware of his presence. Ever since Andrew had doused her with his frustration that evening in the barn, he'd found it easier to keep his distance. His anger had been misdirected, but the apology she deserved proved most difficult to voice.

Tonight he only had to insure her safety. He hastened his steps. The thick foliage overhead completely blotted out the sliver of moon, plunging him into blackness as he maneuvered through the underbrush that clung to his legs and crutch. He slowed, using his free hand to shield his face and feel his way. After several more steps, he stopped. Trying to go farther without any light, or knowing the terrain was madness. He turned back.

A sob reached his ears.

Andrew followed the sound. Then the glow of Rachel's lantern led him. Hidden, he had a view of her profile.

She knelt between two graves, the lantern set aside, tears glistening as they tumbled down her cheeks. Her hands hugged her trembling shoulders. "I wish you were here, Mama. What do I know about love? I thought it would be easier than this. But I'm so miserable. I've never felt so strongly for a man. I love him."

Andrew drew back a step, seeking an escape. He shouldn't be here, lurking in the dark, watching her. Still, his feet were slow to obey. *You are engaged and she probably is, as well. Indeed, it is good that she loves him. It will make her life so much more pleasant than yours could ever be.*

He stepped from the woods. The air helped clear his mind. He pushed up his sleeves. Why did he suddenly feel so hot? He had to think rationally. He was a man, and as such he could not let himself succumb to emotion. Where would the civilized world be if men allowed feelings to rule them as women did? Utter chaos. He knew his duty, and understanding where Rachel's heart rested could only aide him in walking away when the time came.

~*~

Rachel sat back, her lower legs numb from being tucked for so long. She buried her face in her hands, and then wiped across her cheeks to brush the moisture away. If only life were not so complicated. If Daniel could be everything she loved about Andrew. Or if Andrew were in the same position as Daniel and able to stay—to love her as fully as she loved him. "I have to stop thinking. Only a few more weeks and he'll be gone. Only a few more weeks..." Fresh tears misted her vision. She blinked them back and struggled to her feet. If she stayed out here much longer, Joseph would form another search party. She wanted to be left alone.

By the time Rachel emerged into the clearing, her eyes and face had almost dried, leaving her skin stiff and chilled. Hopefully the cool air would help them gain the semblance of normal before she reached the cabin. Something rustled the branches behind her and she spun back to the woods, jerking the lantern upward.

Dark angles contrasted the light illuminating Andrew's face.

"What on earth are you doing there? You near

frightened me to death."

His eyes flickered regret and then returned to passive indifference to match his severe expression. He inclined his head in his proper bow. "I apologize, ma'am. That was not my intention."

"Indeed."

"It cannot be safe for you walking out here unaccompanied. I know this wilderness is far more secluded than the cities of my youth, but I am sure there are still many dangers."

"Did you follow me?"

Andrew's gaze momentarily evaded hers. "Please, Miss Garnet, let me return you to your home." He stepped past her, then paused and extended his arm.

Rachel hesitated, her hand hovering above his forearm. Then she lowered it into place, his skin warm under her touch. He stared at where her fingers rested, his face unarmed, a cascade of expressions warring.

"I am sorry." His arm pulled away and he worked to unroll the sleeve. "Forgive my carelessness." Andrew looked to her. "I..." His voice broke as his gaze fell to her mouth, then returned to her eyes. "Miss Garnet, I should never have—"

"No. Captain Wyndham, please. There's nothing for me to forgive." Rachel retreated a step. "I can manage fine on my own." Turning away, she raced toward the cabin, not slowing until she reached the door. She glanced back at his stationary form almost invisible against a backdrop of black. What just happened? Had he overheard her talking at her parent's graves? Did it make any difference? Or had he still not forgiven her for her intrusion a week earlier? Her mind buzzing and heart feeling as if it had been kicked by the milk cow, Rachel dove through the door and out of his sight.

25

Rachel scanned the yard for any sign of Joseph, before returning to shovel dirt from around the roots of the stump. She'd probably never hear the end of it if he caught her working on the stump while potatoes needed digging. But what he didn't know couldn't hurt her. She sank the spade deep, wedging it against yet another root, leaving no room for maneuvering. Rachel jerked up on the handle. The blade immediately shed the dirt that had clung. "Oh Papa, how did everything become so confused?" She raised her gaze to the open doors of the loft.

Andrew reclined against the side, his good leg dangling out and the Bible laid across his lap. His face and most of his body remained out of sight.

Rachel relaxed against the stump with a sigh. "I'm not ready to lose someone else, but what other option is there?"

Tapping the heel of her shoe against the cut edge of a severed root, she let her eyes close. What if Andrew did share her feelings to some extent? Could he stay? No, it wouldn't be safe. But perhaps there was somewhere they could go. To be together. Rachel ground her teeth as she skidded the spade over the root, making it visible. Such thoughts would only make it harder to say goodbye, and that was their reality. Andrew didn't belong here, and she didn't belong in England's "polite society." She glanced from the cabin to the fields, avoiding the barn.

A horse and rider raced down the road. Their shadows leapt between the trees, the colors of autumn obscuring their identities, and she spun to Andrew's perch. Already abandoned. Deep breaths slowed the rush of her blood as she climbed out of the trench and yanked up the nearest potato plant. She collected several tubers before utilizing the spade.

Daniel snatched his hat from his head as he pulled his mare to a halt at the edge of the garden. "Rachel..." He struggled to catch his breath.

"What is it? Has something happened?"

"Brant. He's raiding...five miles downriver. Where's Joseph?"

His pronouncement struck her square in the chest. "Joseph rode down to check on the cornfield."

"Where?"

Rachel ran to the horse and gripped Daniel's arm. No use trying to give him directions. No time. "Swing me up, I'll show you."

Leaning away from her, he gave her the stirrup and pulled her on behind him.

Grasping his coat, she laid her heels into the horse's sides. As the animal lurched into a gallop, clods of dirt flew from its hooves. One flipped up, striking Rachel's back. She held tighter. "Through that first wheat field." Only stubble remained. Her blood ran cold.

Joseph Brant and his raiders within five miles? If any Loyalist invoked fear in the hearts of the settlers, it was the Mohawk war chief. Rumor named him as one of the leaders during the battle of Oriskany. Had he returned?

They met Joseph at the edge of the corn, already in motion toward Hunter.

Daniel swung his leg forward over the mare's neck, and dropped to the ground, then lifted Rachel down.

Joseph redirected his course. "What's going on?"

"We're gathering men at the old fort to go after Brant. He's burning just south-east of us and working this direction," Daniel said. "We need you."

"Brant?" Joseph wiped his palm over his mouth. "I can't do it."

"What?"

He motioned to the tall green stalks and drooping tassels. The silk crowning each cob had withered to an ugly brown. "I can't wait any longer to get this corn brought in. I should have started two weeks ago. I can't risk losing my crop."

"How about your cabin and everything else? If we don't confront Brant, what's will stop him from burning this whole valley?"

Rachel stepped around Daniel. "Joseph."

"I know." He pushed his hat back to mop his brow with his sleeve. "What other choice do we have?" His breath escaped in a burst. "All right."

"I'll start the corn. Sorrowful should be able to haul a part load by himself."

He nodded and turned back to Hunter.

Daniel glanced at Rachel. "And as soon as we get back, I'll spare you a day. I can probably bring Fannie, as well."

Joseph swung into his saddle and gave a nod. "So long as we make it back." He reined Hunter toward the farm.

Daniel's hand brushed Rachel's shoulder and she

managed to mimic her brother's nod.

Joseph sprinted into the cabin as soon as they arrived. He came back out with a pistol peeking from his coat pocket and the musket in his hands. He strapped it to the saddle.

Rachel slid off Daniel's mare. "Be careful, all right."

"Don't worry." He squeezed her elbow. "I plan on finishing harvest."

You'd better.

He glanced to the garden. "Don't leave those potatoes out of the sun too long."

"Don't you worry about that."

He mounted and glanced back at Daniel. "You ready?"

Daniel's dark gaze lingered on Rachel. "I guess so."

"You both keep safe," she said to him. "You hear?"

The corners of his mouth turned upwards. "We'll be back."

Rachel stared as they disappeared down the road and behind gold-laden branches.

~*~

Andrew braced against the edge of the loft's doorframe. Below him, Rachel fought with the harness and the sorrel gelding, preparing to hitch the wagon.

Ten minutes earlier, Joseph and Daniel rode from the yard as though the devil nipped at their heels.

Andrew fumbled with the buttons of his coat, dusted it off, and then started for the stairs.

Rachel jiggled the reins, backing the sorrel to the wagon hitch. She glanced at Andrew, but said nothing.

Hardly surprising. He still hadn't found the right words to apologize for losing his temper. Unfortunately, time only deepened the chasm between them.

"May I offer my assistance?"

"I can manage."

He hooked his crutch on the side of the wagon and made his way to her. Other than for distances or on the stairs, he no longer required assistance walking. He preferred to limp. With his hand on the horse's thigh, he bent down for a loose strap. "I have no lack of faith in your ability to manage, but, alas, not what I inquired."

Her eyes narrowed but she allowed him to fasten the harness while she fussed over the other side.

"Joseph and Mr. Reid left in a hurry."

Rachel gave no reaction.

Andrew moved to the front of the horse, scratching its thickening coat. One more sign that his time here was nearly at an end. "Where are you off to?"

Her hands did not pause. "There's corn to harvest."

"Corn." He crossed in front of the horse and leaned into the animal's shoulder to take weight off his leg for a moment. "Is being well-armed required for that task?"

Rachel brushed by him as she walked around the horse. "They went after Joseph Brant and his raiders."

Andrew crossed his arms over the horse's withers. "Brant?"

"Did you know him?"

"Yes. I remember him. We met in England."

"England?" She seemed to have picked up on his

pattern of repeating one word.

"He had an audience with the king, and I met him on the docks before embarking to the Americas. We sailed together." He paused as a storm brewed behind her eyes. The next part wouldn't impress her either. "I saw him again shortly before we traveled down the Mohawk. He joined us in our siege against Fort Stanwix. His sister sent the news of the Continental force coming to meet us. You are probably aware of his role after that."

"It's called Fort Schuyler now." She tipped her head up. "After General Philip Schuyler, one of *our* congress's delegates. You can call it Fort Stanwix if the British ever win it back."

"Fair enough."

"And yes, I know Brant was at Oriskany, too."

Just as *he* had been.

She seemed fixed on putting him in his place today. Worry for her brother and Daniel likely affected her greater than she wanted to show.

Andrew steeled himself from feeding her aggression. "And now he has returned?"

The tremble of her head appeared to be a nod.

Oh, Rachel. What he wouldn't give to take all that fear away. Given a horse and a musket he would ride against Brant himself. He'd make sure Joseph...and Daniel made it back to her. But that would mean leaving her here unprotected. And no doubt their friends would question his identity. "What can I do to help with the corn?" Andrew made his way back around to her side.

"I can manage." She collected the reins and laid them over the wagon seat before climbing up. He caught her elbow to assist, and she mumbled a thank you.

The horse whinnied, and they both twisted to the road as three riders materialized from the shade.

Andrew dropped out of sight, but it was too far and open to get back through the barn doors without being seen.

"Watch yourself." The warning barely out her mouth, Rachel slapped the leather against the horse, forcing it backwards, turning the wagon at the same time.

Andrew kept one hand on the box to keep pace until the tailgate reached the barn. He lunged for cover, barely making it.

She gave the animal encouragement forward, directing the sorrel to meet the visitors.

The wagon pulled away, his crutch still hanging from the side.

~*~

Matthias Adler, Rodney Cowden, and Benjamin Reid met Rachel only a few yards from the barn. Hopefully enough distance to keep Andrew hidden—if they hadn't seen him already. They appeared upset, but had yet to rush the British officer.

Benjamin spoke first. "Has Joseph left?"

"Daniel came for him not long ago. They are probably to the old fort by now. Is there any more word on the raids?"

Cowden released a laugh laced with irritation. "Sure is. We're all racing across the countryside instead of finishing harvest while Joseph Brant probably sits comfortable at home planning his raids for next spring. Some drunk fool lit his own barn on fire."

"That's it?" Rachel wasn't sure if she could trust the rush of relief.

"Yeah. Probably left a lamp too close to his hay last night. And now the whole countryside is ablaze with fear." His mouth tightened.

Rachel let her eyes close as her breath and tension drained away. "Thank you for telling me."

"We hoped to catch them before they got any farther on this wild goose chase." Benjamin shook his head. "We will try to get to them before they reach the fort."

He nudged his mount forward, as did the Matthias, but Rodney Cowden remained in place. "Whose crutch is that?"

"Crutch?"

Andrew had not made it away clean after all.

26

Rachel's voice caught in her throat. One mistake and another spark would light up the valley. "We think you may be right about that prowler you thought you saw a couple weeks ago. Joseph found the crutch this morning on the far side of the stream by our cornfield. Though, he figures it might still be the Kastner boys playing war. Their pa had an accident with his leg a while back. It could be his, and the boys are pretending it's a musket."

"Guess that makes sense. Though I swear I saw a man, and he had a limp."

Rachel reached for the crutch and tossed it into the back of the wagon. "Joseph will take it back to the Kastners when he has some time to find out for sure."

"Why don't I take it over to the old fort now and ask around. Herbert Kastner will probably be there with the rest."

And then the whole settlement could swarm down on the Reid farm to search for the 'prowler'. She focused on keeping her expression relaxed. "No. Let us handle this. I'm sure it's nothing, and we don't want to start any more 'fires,' remember?" A chuckle. Anything to reduce their suspicion. "Not 'til after harvest. Then we can use the warmth and occupation."

The corner of Cowden's mouth turned up. "You're probably right. We'll wait. But let me know what you find out."

"Of course."

~*~

The next day, Rachel and Fannie sat together shucking corn, their brothers hauling it from the field as quickly as they could manage. Fannie sent a glance to the barn. "Does he ever come down from the loft?"

"Not often." Not since yesterday. "Sometimes for meals." Rachel pulled the last bit of dried silk from the corn cob and tossed it into the large basket. Grabbing another cob, she began the process again. "And he usually helps Joseph with chores in the barn. His leg seems be healing well now."

"It must be strange having a Briti...having someone like him around. How can you be sure he can be trusted not to do anything, like burn your house or barn while you are sleeping and make off with your horses?"

"He's not that sort of a man." Rachel focused on the work at hand. "Besides, he was practically a clergyman."

"Yes, Daniel mentioned that."

The wagon appeared around the barn and Joseph drove it to what remained of their pile of corn yet to be husked. A minute later the mound had doubled in size and continued to grow.

Fannie watched their brothers unload the corn, and lowered her voice. "Daniel's unconvinced. He fears you're playing with a snake in the grass and that sooner or later you'll be bit."

Rachel held back any comment as the men approached.

Andrew was hardly snakelike.

"This load is about ready to be hauled to the loft." She threw her last cob onto the top. They would lay them out in the threshing room until the kernels dried enough to knock off and grind for meal. She looked at the hill of corn left to be husked. The yield was excellent, but how long would this take if Daniel hadn't volunteered his and Fannie's help? Plus, it was much more pleasant with another woman to visit with.

Joseph seemed to have no objection to the young woman's presence, either. Throughout the morning they'd exchanged friendly glances and comments. Perhaps he had finally opened his eyes. "With most of the garden done and put away for winter, after today we should be about done with harvest," Joseph said as he joined them. "We were certainly blessed this year."

"You might say that." Blessed? The fact that their corn and wheat had done well did not make them blessed. "Others lost their fields and homes, we only lost our..." She couldn't say it. At least not out loud. Sarcasm stole into her voice. "But, never mind. That's not important."

"Rachel, you know I wasn't talking about Pa. But the Lord did bless us with a good harvest, and for that we should be grateful."

"We should be grateful for this day, as well." Fannie moved beside him, until her shoulder brushed against his arm. "It's often raining or threatening snow already, but that sun is as warm as ever. Which is good, seeing as hardly a person has done harvest because of how wet it was last month."

Joseph glanced up at the cloudless sky. "Well, we're ready for winter now, so we might as well enjoy the sun while it lasts."

"I agree." Daniel pivoted on the basket to face Rachel. "I was wondering if you wanted to go for a ride after dinner. Joseph already said they could manage without us for a short while."

Uncertainty fluttered within her, but she braced against it. "I suppose that would be fine, if Joseph is sure." She glanced to her brother.

Joseph nodded, his lips not keeping his desire to smile a secret.

"Good." Daniel grinned. "There's something I've been hoping to show you."

Rachel forced the corners of her mouth to turn upwards. "I should go pull the cobs away from the fire, they're probably done boiling by now." She hurried back to the house to finish preparation for dinner. Five minutes later she called everyone in for the feast.

Everyone but Andrew came, though his absence was most likely purposeful.

After she finished, Rachel fixed him a plate, and then turned to Joseph. Usually he made the deliveries between house and barn.

"Can I come with you?" Fannie was at her arm. "That's for him, isn't it?"

Rachel nodded as Joseph and Daniel headed back to the bushels of corn still waiting. "All right." She led the way, stalling just inside the barn door.

Andrew stood, keeping company with the cow, his crutch leaned nearby. He stiffened as they approached. His stoic gaze moved from Rachel to Fannie and back again. It lingered on her, his pine-needle green eyes narrowing, but not in an unpleasant way. They seemed to twinkle.

"Good day, ladies." The corners of his mouth showed amusement as he bowed. "Would you introduce us, Miss Garnet?"

"May I present Miss Fannie Reid, Mr. Reid's sister?" It was too easy to fall into his speaking patterns. She motioned to him, grateful he was watching Fannie so she could study him for this moment. Oh, how she missed him in the cabin, their conversations. "And this is Mr.—or Captain Andrew Wyndham."

Poor Fannie looked in shock. "It's a—a pleasure to make your acquaintance."

Andrew inclined his head. "The pleasure is mine." The creases in his cheeks deepened.

Rachel extended the plate. "We brought you some dinner."

"I am sorry to have inconvenienced you." Their fingers brushed as he took it.

She retreated a pace.

He looked back to Fannie. "It has become my habit to refrain from making appearances when company calls. I am afraid I can be quite unsocial. But then, that is probably for the best. Your brother, for one, hardly approves of my presence."

"You're not anything like I expected." Fannie smiled, her eyes wide.

Andrew chuckled. "I almost dread asking what it was you were anticipating. I presume that is why you followed Miss Garnet out here—to ascertain for yourself what a Redcoat is like up close. You had only to ask Miss Garnet, for she could give a very clear description, as well as many interesting details." He glanced at Rachel, and then turned completely away, leaning into the gate, staring at the cow whose only desire appeared to be a nibble of a cob of buttered corn. Andrew held it out of her reach. "My apologies, Miss

Reid, I fear I am at a lack for many of the finer social graces. I am no longer well-rehearsed at entertaining."

"No, sir. We are sorry to have disturbed you." Rachel mimicked his tone. "It is plain to see you are very busy. Perhaps we should call again at a more congenial hour." She walked to him and held out the fork. "We will leave you to your dinner. Have a good day, Captain Wyndham." She made a quick curtsy.

He took the fork. "Goodbye, Miss Garnet. Miss Reid." He looked past them as their brothers appeared in the doorway. Andrew acknowledged the newcomers, but said nothing.

Daniel barely looked at him as he extended his arm. "Are you ready, Rachel? The wagon's waiting."

With one final glance at Andrew, she moved to Daniel and allowed him to lead her from the barn.

~*~

Andrew refused to watch them walk away. Instead, he turned to Fannie and removed the edge from his voice. "I am sorry for my performance. Miss Garnet and I do not share the most affable relationship as of late, but it is better for me to not relate the circumstance. She is a fine woman. Your brother is a fortunate man."

"It is kind of you to say so." Fannie's eyes darted to Joseph, who took a step nearer.

"If you would like, we have a few bushels of corn left to husk. You could join us on this side of the cabin."

"I would be glad to give a hand." Andrew nodded to the couple as they left, and hurried with his food, more hungry for conversation. Once his plate was clean, he reached for his crutch—then paused, his hand retracting. A little independence for once. He straightened his back and strode out to join the others. He did his best to limp as little as possible, ignoring any discomfort.

Fannie studied him as he approached, her dark eyes glowing with curiosity. "I was told you were a pastor back in England."

Andrew seated himself on a chair they had brought from the cabin. "Not quite. But I had been offered a parish."

"What happened?"

He took some corn in hand and analyzed it, glancing to Fannie and Joseph for an example of how to remove its husk. As he started stripping back layers from the deep yellow kernels, he forced his face to remain passive. "I ran away to become a soldier instead. It seemed one of Britain's colonies had become revolutionary, and King George needed more soldiers to bring them back into submission." He raised a brow at the look of horror on her face.

Joseph's expression only showed amusement.

Andrew cleared his voice. "You see, in England we still have a great love for our king, whom your government has named a tyrant. Inconceivable. Can you imagine the rage we felt at such insults? I even read that Declaration of Independence, or whatever it's called—a whole list of insults and accusations against the king." Andrew paused for a moment to watch Fannie, a breath away from laughing outright. He lowered his voice to build the suspense. "I shall tell you what we resolved to do. We British told ourselves that we could either go across the ocean and put them back in their place, or—"

Joseph released a burst of laughter.

Andrew sent him a look of disapproval. "Sir, if you must remove yourself, then please do so. You are interrupting my tale. How do you expect this young lady to take me at all serious if you drown me out with that insufferable noise? You colonists can be quite barbarous." He turned back to Fannie. "As I was saying, we could either go across the ocean and put them in their place...or simply join them." He sent his best withering glance towards Joseph. "I have yet to decide which one I wish to do, but at the moment I am more inclined toward the first. There is at least one colonist in dire need of humbling."

"And you expect to accomplish that by yourself?" Joseph challenged.

"Do not underestimate me, sir."

Joseph held up his hands. "Fine. But I must say this for your story, it's more entertaining than what you told me. Now stop performing for the lady. She's already spoken for."

Fannie looked to Joseph, color touching her cheeks as pleasure filled her eyes.

He simply smiled.

She again addressed Andrew. "Did you always want to be a soldier?"

"No, I never did. It was for my brother I went—or rather, came. He was barely nineteen and my mother was concerned for his safety. He is quite a few years younger than I, and has a talent for finding trouble. She begged me to watch over him." Frustration burned in his chest. "Instead, I got myself shot, and now I have no way of knowing where he is. I can only hope he remains alive and is with our troops."

Fannie's motions relaxed as she continued with

her work. "What do you plan to do when you're well enough?"

"I must find my brother. After that..." He sighed, dropping the naked cob into a basket. He didn't want to think about after that.

27

Rachel gazed across the pleasant valley walled by rolling hills and forested areas.

Daniel pulled the wagon to a stop not far from the stream which flowed with a hushed murmur. He jumped to the ground, and then helped Rachel down. Nearby, a small cabin stood silent, neighbored by a barn and empty corrals.

"The Becker homestead."

Daniel nodded. "Mrs. Becker took her family back to Albany."

"It's a pity they had to leave. They chose a beautiful spot."

At her words, a smile brightened his face. Taking Rachel's hand, he directed her around the wagon and away from the stream. "The cabin's in fine shape for now, but in another year or so I'd like to build a house—an actual frame house." He turned back to face her. "Yes, it's mine now. I traded supplies and funds for their journey back east." Daniel's smile faded as he peered into her eyes. "You must realize though, it could never be complete without you. It could never be a home."

Her heart squeezed, and she searched for something to say.

His gaze held too much expectancy.

"Daniel, I..."

"I'm aware it might seem as if I'm rushing things, but we've known each other for more than four years now and it's been hard to take my eyes off you for the last three." He chuckled. "I don't know what more a man could want from a wife, or even a friend." His dark eyes remained locked with hers as he slipped to one knee. Daniel tightened his hold on her hand. "Rachel, I'm asking you to marry me."

The breeze against the grass and the distant song of sparrows were the only sounds as she stared at the hope and desire mingled in his expression. He was right. This felt too rushed. She wasn't ready. Rachel's lower lip gave an involuntary tremble as he regained his feet and pulled her close. His mouth moved for hers, but she turned her head away. He pressed his face against her cheek. "Rachel, you know I love you."

She nodded. There was no doubting that. "I'm not saying no, but I need time to decide."

"That is all I ask," Daniel breathed. "I will wait as long as you need."

"I'll try to answer you soon."

His arm encircled her, and she allowed hers to do the same, resting her head against his shoulder. The rise and fall of his chest marked the moment and filled her with the sudden desire to reach up and let him to kiss her. What was wrong with allowing him to love her? To show that love? She would learn to return it. He was a good man. And she liked him. Wasn't that enough for now? Slowly Rachel cocked her head back.

Daniel needed no more encouragement. He leaned down, burying her mouth with his own, his lips warm and fervent in their declaration.

Rachel's chest constricted with the thousand opposing desires. Part of her wanted to drown in his arms and forget about everything, including her own feelings. She did not love him, and it was not his face she pictured as she kissed him.

Daniel's hand swept across her collar as it encircled her neck. The course piece of wool from the scarlet coat seemed to scorch her skin. It was Andrew Wyndham she wanted. She gasped for a breath and spun from Daniel.

"Rachel? What did I...?"

She started away, not even heading in the direction of the wagon. She didn't care where she went. She just needed to walk.

"Rachel?" Daniel caught her arm, compelling her to stop. "What did I do wrong?"

"Nothing. I only...I don't know if I'm ready for this. I need time to think."

"You're not angry with me?" The relief in his voice tore at her conscience.

"No, I'm not angry. Why would I be?"

"I love you, Rachel."

"Then give me time." Her fingers pressed against her collar and the swatch of cloth over her heart. "A little more time."

~*~

Rachel rolled onto her side. She'd stuffed the mattress with fresh straw, and yet every lump pressed against her weary body. She shifted onto her stomach and buried her head in the pillow. Sleep evaded her. Returning to her back, Rachel stared at the dim shadows of the rafters.

Dawn would arrive, and with it a thousand things requiring her attention: meals to prepare, animals to feed, food to preserve.

Joseph planned to butcher one of the hogs and would need her help. Then all the meat would have to be cut, salted, and hung in the smokehouse. The other cow still had its calf on, but required milking to help with a touch of mastitis.

And Daniel would be stopping by sometime in the morning. Would she have an answer to his proposal? How could she even consider it with Andrew still here? Maybe after he left, given time...

Rachel needed sleep, but notwithstanding the work that waited, she wanted dawn. She shot a glance at Joseph's sleeping form, jealous of his soft snore. She pushed the blankets aside and got up. Pulling her shawl from the bedpost she tiptoed to the pitcher of water on the table. She poured some into a cup, but the lukewarm liquid did little to calm her mind.

Moonlight shone in the windows with silent invitation. Slipping on her shoes, Rachel escaped into the yard. She wandered through the fields, her thoughts abstract. Still, green eyes and a warm smile made her insides ache. A hundred if-onlys played a mournful song on her heartstrings.

The barn door made a soft creak as it opened. The milk cow looked at her. Rachel made her way to the steep stairs leading to the loft. They sang baritone with each step, as though telling her to turn back. All was silent in the small room and she moved across the floor to sink into the chair opposite the bed.

Andrew slept, his breathing heavy.

The sound washed her with nostalgia. How many nights had she sat listening? It filled her with comfort. He was here, alive and well. What else mattered? Leaning back, Rachel never took her eyes from his shadowed form. "I never meant to hurt you that day," she whispered. "I've never thought of you as anything less than a man. A man any woman would dream of calling her own." Out of habit one hand stole up to the collar of her nightgown, yet the small piece of scarlet fabric was no longer there. How could it be? It was already in her hand.

~*~

Something beyond his memories and the dreams. Andrew's mind reached for consciousness. He opened his eyes to the dark and shivered. The temperature continued to drop a little more each night. He would need another quilt tomorrow. Or to leave. He rolled onto his side, and began rearranging the blankets to better ward off the chill. His motions froze. Across from him sat Rachel, her arms hugging a shawl, her head flopped back against the wall.

"Why have you come?"

She remained asleep.

Perhaps he needed to pinch himself. He must still be dreaming. No. This was something his fantasies had never considered. He had never let them...could not let them. He wanted too dearly for her to care and to be free to care in return. Could that be the reason she had come? Surely there was some other explanation.

Pushing all hope and desire from his mind, Andrew rose to his feet. He wrapped the quilts around her shoulders and tucked them up around her neck. His fingers brushed her chin. And lingered. He moistened his lips. They felt dry and chapped. Then, ever so slowly, Andrew bent down and pressed his mouth to her hairline.

Rachel stirred, but remained asleep.

Andrew heaved a breath. He could not drag his gaze from her, the pain in his center almost surpassing anything his hip had known. *What now? I cannot stay here any longer and feel this way. I love her, Lord. Thou knowest how hard I have tried not to.*

Not bothering with his crutch, Andrew went down the stairs. He found his way to the large stack of hay and dropped to his knees beside it, digging deep before he grasped the thick fabric and pulled the coat free. He struggled to his feet, staring at his past.

How could I let myself forget? Andrew slipped his arms into the sleeves and pulled it on. It fit perfectly. It knew its owner. He brushed the crimson cloth, smoothing its wrinkles and dusting away the dried grass.

Duty.

He moved to the door only to collapse against the wall beside it. His vision blurred. How could he have forgotten the image so very clear to him now? The first day he had donned his regimentals. He had gone directly to Miss Grenville. "You need not wait for me," he had told her, releasing her from their engagement.

"I am not a capricious female, Mr. Wyndham. I have given you my word to become your wife."

"It could be years." Andrew had shaken his head, not wanting her to waste her youth. "Suppose I am unable to return?"

Her delicate chin rose in defiance. "I refuse to consider that eventuality, so you simply must return."

~*~

Rachel opened her eyes to the soft lowing of a cow

and the gentle rhythm of milk striking the sides of a pail. She jerked to her feet, ingesting the rude surroundings. The cot across the small room was abandoned, its blankets now draped across her shoulder. "Oh, my!" She gripped her shawl, the quilts shedding to the floor as she scrambled through the door. Her feet faltered at the top of the stairs.

Andrew sat beside the milk cow on a small stool, his hands somewhat clumsily at work. He didn't turn to her, but it was impossible that he was unaware of her presence.

With face flaming, she bolted down the steps and out the door, headlong into Joseph.

He caught her shoulders. "Careful." His gaze dropped to her attire, or lack thereof. "What are you doing out here in your nightclothes?"

"Nothing." Rachel writhed away from him, racing to the protection of the cabin's walls. She fell into her bed, breathing hard. What had she done?

Andrew was probably furious—though he had draped his blankets over her. But that was probably because he was a good man.

What a fool she'd made of herself. How could she face either him or Joseph again?

The door to the cabin slapped closed, and Rachel moaned. Her brother would not let this go. Taking deliberate breaths, she rolled to her feet and began to dress.

Joseph passed in front of the fireplace, his footsteps sounding out his path.

The size of the bedroom window was unfortunate—there was no way out except past him.

As soon as she opened the door, their gazes met.

His face was rigid, expressionless.

Rachel cleared her voice. "I told you, Joseph. I wasn't doing anything out there, but getting some air. Last night I couldn't sleep. I thought maybe if I walked for a few minutes..." She moved to the table to pour a drink. "I ended up in the barn and fell asleep there."

"Where exactly?"

Her hands hovered over the pitcher. "I won't lie to you. I was sitting on that chair you put in the room."

"You were what? It's been weeks since he's needed someone to watch over him while he slept. What possessed you? What were you thinking?"

"I don't know." Rachel turned away and crumpled into a chair. "I don't know."

"Maybe we did this all wrong." Joseph paced. "It's past time for him to leave."

"No. You won't send him away. Not yet. And, for goodness sake, not because of me!" She looked up, her eyes burning. Now wasn't the time to cry. "Daniel proposed marriage to me yesterday. That's what you wanted, isn't it?"

He stopped and faced her. "Yes. Because I thought it would make you happy."

"It doesn't. It makes me confused."

"What is there to be confused about? He's a good man."

"Yes. A good man, a handsome man, a man well set for the future and even the present." Her voice broke. "What more could I desire?"

"Rachel, you must—"

"Not right now, Joseph. I know what you would say. I know what I need to understand. I know it just as well as you, if not better. I simply don't want to force love. I don't want to become a wife, for that purpose alone. Why must that be so wrong?" She drew her hands across her eyes, clearing them. "I'll be well enough. But I need time to think."

"Rachel..."

The room lapsed into silence.

Then Joseph's hard soles announced his departure. The door closed.

With a deep breath, Rachel stood and straightened her skirts. There was work to do and breakfast to prepare.

28

"Good morning." Andrew found his place at the table.

Their eyes met and her cheeks flamed. What must he think of her? She dropped her gaze to the steaming corn biscuits she was conveying to a plate. "Morning." It clung to the back of her throat. How was she supposed to sit across from him, or Joseph, and still stomach any breakfast? Maybe she could tell them she was feeling unwell and excuse herself. No. Too obvious.

The door creaked open again and Joseph moved to them, dropping into his chair.

Rachel passed him a plate. *I'll just focus on him and keep the conversation going.* She kept her eyes from Andrew, but with him in her thoughts, there seemed little to converse about.

Joseph was still out of sorts. Within minutes, the room again conceded to uncomfortable, apprehensive silence.

Finally, the men left and her muscles began to relax. Her back ached after half the night spent in a hard chair. Despite the list of things she had to accomplish, Rachel left the dishes on the table and started for the door. She needed to clear her mind and stretch her spine. It was time to do some more damage on the stump. She slipped behind the house, but the ax wasn't near the woodpile, and she couldn't find it in the barn.

Was Joseph using it for something, or had she forgotten it in the garden? She took the spade. There was always more dirt to clear away.

The echo of the ax cracked against wood. A tall form stood near the stump, the ax brought high over his head. Daniel? No, he would have come to the cabin first, and his build was a little heavier, taller.

Andrew.

Though not visible from the road, how dare he risk it?

Besides, she hadn't asked for help. And she didn't need it. That was her stump. Bracing herself, Rachel shouldered the spade and jogged across the yard. She only made it half way before she slowed.

Andrew's reddish-brown waves were tied at the nape of his neck. His homespun shirt waved in the breeze, already beginning to show signs of perspiration. With his right leg in the hole, and the other braced against the stump—probably to release the pressure on the first—he brought the ax down. The crack was followed by the muffling of dirt. He'd broken through the root. Andrew shifted and took aim at the same root, several feet from the base. He was hardly the half-dead captain they'd brought home. In the past almost two months he'd gained back most of his weight and, though his complexion was still fair, it was not the ashy-white it had once been. He was vibrant, and alive, and sweaty....

And everything she wanted. Oh, how she wanted him.

He took several swings before moving for a different angle. His sleeve wiped across his brow, and he stretched his back. Then he halted, his gaze on her. "How long have you been there?"

"Not long." Rachel came within several feet, and then pushed the spade into the dark soil. "I'm sorry if I startled you."

"I had been keeping a close eye on the road for any more guests, but I am afraid I became a little lost in thought." He snatched his coat from the stump and thrust his arm into it. "I am surprised I did not see you there, or hear you."

"Out here it's not necessary to be seen in a coat. Sometimes it's not very practical."

His second arm slid into place and he smoothed the front, but left it hanging open. "I suppose you are correct, yet my upbringing remains deeply engrained."

She cleared her throat, the awkwardness building as she motioned to the stump. "You don't have to do this."

"I felt I should do something to repay you before I left. You should not have to do it by yourself." He glanced at the ax, taking it up again. "Why has Joseph not helped?"

"How are you so certain he hasn't?"

Andrew's lips pressed into a smile as he motioned to the loft door. "I have been watching."

Warmth touched Rachel's face. "Joseph doesn't have time for this. My pa was going to remove it, but he's not here anymore. So I'm doing it myself."

His eyes were soft and deep as his fingers brushed her sleeve. "That is no longer necessary. Let me help while I can."

A deep crater and severed roots marked the hours she had slaved and wept here. She'd made it her task, but now she didn't want it—not without him. "All right."

A wry smile played on Andrew's mouth as he turned back to the root and raised the ax. "Did you sleep well last night?"

Rachel fiddled with the edge her apron. "I wanted...I wanted to apologize for intruding. I'd been out walking and...and I..." What could she say? *I'm in love with you, and the thought of marrying another man is driving me insane. I miss watching you sleep.*

"You don't owe me an explanation." He brought the ax down, and she jumped back. "I suppose you were simply concerned I might attempt to burn your house down and make off with the horses while you slept."

"You heard that?"

He nodded.

"I'd be more ashamed if you believed that than the true reason. But if you heard Fannie, then you must have also heard my reply. I would trust you with my life."

His face remained passive. "Are you certain?"

She nodded.

"Then why were you there?"

This time Rachel did not look away from his intense gaze. "I wanted to apologize."

"For what wrong?"

"For the evening I stood on the stairs, listening as a man poured out his soul to his God."

Andrew turned away.

She grabbed his arm. "I've been haunted these past weeks by the words you spoke that night. I don't want you to hate me any longer. I don't want you to think of me in that way. That was never my intention. I didn't mean to intrude or offend you."

"I know. It is I who should apologize. Besides, you have reason for any judgment against me."

"This?" Rachel withdrew the bit of red fabric from her pocket and held it out.

"What is this?" He took it.

"It's from your uniform. I've carried it with me as a constant reminder of who you are."

Andrew's gaze moved from the scrap of scarlet to her eyes, his own hardening. "I see. But was it really needed? I mean, how did you put it before? You have the way I speak—my wonderfully English accent—to remind you of exactly who I am. Was the pile of hay in the barn too far away for the color of my uniform to reside? Did you ever truly risk forgetting who I am?"

"You don't...I didn't..." Rachel shook her head, tangled in a disjointed knot of thoughts—and feelings. "I mean, I don't see you like that."

"But it is what I am, is it not? Even I remember that well enough now. I am a captain in His Majesty's armies, sent to squelch a rebellion. I was there to fight against your neighbors and even your brother and father." His lips thinned. "I fought against that man you love so well."

"What man?"

His brows rose as did a chuckle in his throat, the swatch from his coat still clenched in his hand. His knuckles showed white.

"Daniel Reid?"

Andrew laughed out loud, bitterness making it sharp. "Have you not made plans to marry him?"

Her heart leapt with understanding. "You jealous fool."

Andrew's face flushed either out of embarrassment or anger, but he held her gaze, his jaw working. He shoved the red fabric back in her hand and lifted the ax. More of a confession than a denial.

"You are jealous, aren't you?"

"Why would I be jealous?" He raised the ax to swing into the root, but then twisted, planting the blade deep into the top of the stump. Andrew released the handle. "But what if I am?"

29

Rachel forgot to breathe.

Andrew's back straightened. He turned to face her. "What if I think you are the most beautiful creature of my acquaintance? What if I miss being in the cabin with you—to hear the sound of your voice in the morning, or the tapping of your feet as music rehearses in your mind? What if..." He let the sentence die.

"What if what?"

Andrew shook his head. "I need to go. I must not delay any longer."

"But..."

He started toward the barn, but seemed to limp more than usual.

Rachel ran after him, seizing his arm. "Wait. What about my what-ifs?"

"What?"

Rachel swallowed back all uncertainty. "Exactly. What if I love the way your cheek creases when you smile and sometimes when you speak?" She ran her thumb along his face. "What if I crave the sound of your voice, and your accent—and can't wait to hear what you'll say next. What if I find it amazing the way you can find traces of humor in even the most distressing of circumstances?"

The dimple in one cheek deepened as his mouth

formed a flat line. "I am not doing so well right now."

She held a finger to his lips. "You can't talk yet. I have at least one more."

"My apologies."

"What if I—make that two—what if I never want you to leave?" Rachel faltered. Dared she say everything in her heart?

Andrew pulled her hand away from his mouth, his fingers encircling hers. "What if I love you, Miss Garnet?"

A sob mingled with a laugh as she touched his face with her free hand. "Then you should stop surrendering everything to the Continentals. Colonies, countries, and war victories are fine, but don't let me go."

Andrew drew her into his arms. His heart pounded in her ear as her arms encircled his torso. The warmth of his mouth pressed against the top of her head.

Everything they'd feared, and the feelings they'd buried deep in resolve seemed to erupt, giving strength to the embrace.

"Don't ever leave me."

He only held her tighter.

"Promise me you'll never leave."

Andrew's arms seemed to weaken.

Rachel glanced at his face.

His eyes glistened. "Please believe me—I do not wish to. If I had the choice, I would stay here forever. Please believe that I would."

"If you have to go, take me with you. I'll go with you anywhere, even back to England, if that's what you want."

"If I were free, Rachel..."

"But you are free, don't you see that?"

He shook his head, gritting his teeth. "No. I am not. I have duties to my family. I must find my brother and return home. I gave my word. My family's honor and future rests upon me."

"It still doesn't answer why I can't come with you." Her eyebrows pinched together. "Is it because your family would disapprove? Because I'm only a farmer's daughter, and a colonist."

"That would mean nothing to me. Not anymore."

"Then why—?"

"I am engaged."

She stared at him, her hands pressing against his chest, hardly aware of the coolness of his damp shirt. "Engaged? To whom?"

"Miss Lillian Grenville."

Hot moisture singed the back of Rachel's eyes as it sought release. "You loved her?" She couldn't put it in present tense.

He shook his head. "No."

She wanted to throw her hands into the air. "Then why?"

"My father gambled away our fortune, and then took ill from the distresses of it all. He died when I was fifteen. It became my duty to restore our family's name and wealth. I was given the option of choosing a profession of prominence—preferably in politics—or marrying a woman of fortune." He looked into Rachel's eyes, his own pleading. "I felt myself drawn to God's labor—that was my love—and I had never met a woman whom I felt anything but indifference toward, so it seemed all I needed to do to secure my desires was to find a woman of substance and convince her the occupation of a clergy would be an acceptable one for her husband." Andrew swallowed. "I was successful."

"But if you were to join the clergy, why are you here?"

"My brother."

Every piece of his life fell into place. Everything he did was because of the obligations he felt toward others. Following his brother to a war on another continent, pursuing a woman he didn't love, and even becoming a clergy because of the duty he felt to God. "But what if you were free? What would you choose?"

"I would stay with you." The corner of his mouth twitched. "Joseph said there was no church in the area. I would build one."

Still God remained. If only He would work with her for once, and not against her. "Then stay. I love you."

~*~

Rachel's words seeped into his soul, filling it with longing. Andrew wrapped his arms around her, nestling her head under his chin. He stroked her hair. "And I you. I love you more than I ever considered possible." If he had only known such a feeling was possible. He would have never settled for a marriage of convenience, no matter how great the fortune attached, or what his mother said. How could he do so now? He couldn't.

To return to England—to spend his life with a woman he felt nothing toward? Would it be possible to pretend nothing had ever happened? Could he cherish his wife before God, and not dream about Rachel? Inconceivable.

Andrew peered down at the woman in his arms and slid a finger down her cheek, tipping her chin upwards. "You are correct. I could never leave you." His mouth lowered over hers.

"Get away from her!" Daniel's voice cut across the yard, mingled with the beating of hooves against the ground.

Andrew released Rachel and stepped back as the horse slid to a halt only feet away.

A cloud of dust drifted as Daniel vaulted from the saddle. He grabbed Rachel's arm, yanking her back. "You British dog!" He threw himself at Andrew.

Being braced for the attack was not enough. He'd not thought to position his legs with the stronger behind him, and the weight of the other man slammed him to the ground.

"Daniel!" Rachel screamed. "Leave him alone."

Her cries seemed only to aggravate the man further as he attempted to pin Andrew in place, while throwing fists in the direction of his face.

The first one met its target with a flash of light and jolt of pain under his left eye, but Andrew was not about to allow a repeat. He jerked his head out of the way, seized his assailant's arm, and rolled sideways, whipping the back of his fist across Daniel's face. The man reeled and tumbled onto his side, giving Andrew a moment to grasp Daniel's left shoulder with his left hand. He leaned his arm across Daniel's throat and thrust him onto his back. Andrew balled his other hand and cocked it by his ear. "I have no wish to fight you," he panted. "Please. End this now."

Daniel's nostrils flared as he stared up at him, rage like glowing embers in his dark eyes. Finally, he made a nod in surrender.

Andrew released his grip. When the other man did not move to attack him again, he stood, grunting as he maneuvered his right leg. Though no longer an open sore, his wound throbbed.

"What happened here?" Joseph demanded, running from the barn.

Daniel spun to him. "I accepted that you wouldn't let him die, but to allow him to touch your sister is more than I'm ready to accept. You should've turned him over to the army or shot him before this."

"What are you talking about?"

"I don't know how much you already know, or how long this has been going on, but if I had my gun, I would have shot that Redcoat pig for kissing one of our women." He turned back to Andrew and shoved him aside. "This isn't over." Daniel took the several steps to where his horse had wandered, grabbed its reins and swung into the saddle. Hooves sounded out his departure as they stirred more dust into the air.

Andrew steeled himself as he moved his gaze to Joseph's grim face.

Joseph's mouth formed a tight line. "Rachel, I want you to come to the house. And you..." He blew out his breath, shaking his head. "I suggest you pack whatever you have. I don't think it's safe here any longer."

"You don't believe Daniel would tell, do you?" Rachel's arm brushed Andrew's.

"With the whole countryside waiting for another spark to light their fear?" Joseph asked as he headed to the cabin. He halted abruptly, pausing to wait for his sister.

Rachel looked at Andrew. Her hand gripped his sleeve.

Oh, how he wanted to take her in his arms again. To kiss her. They had been so close. But maybe this was for the best. Perhaps the Lord was trying to remind him of his responsibilities elsewhere. It was time to leave.

"Rachel," Joseph called.

Andrew brushed a loose strand of honey behind her ear, and then nodded. "You should go."

~*~

As they entered the cabin, Joseph stopped by the door, not removing his coat. "What did you do, Rachel?"

"Why are you so certain anything happened?"

"Daniel said Andrew kissed you. Is that true?"

"No." She wet her lips almost tasting Andrew. "But he was about to. I wanted him to."

A shadow crossed Joseph's face as it angled away.

"And what's wrong with that?" She couldn't help but plead. "I love him."

"We're still in the middle of war," Joseph's pitch rose, "and no matter what we see him as, he is still an enemy officer and still in great danger. He's the wrong man, Rachel. It's the wrong time and the wrong place." His voice softened with a sigh.

"Everything is wrong except what I feel." Rachel looked down. She still held the small piece of red fabric. "What'll we do?"

"We have to take him somewhere safe."

"Where?"

"I don't know. Perhaps back to his army. He hopes to find his brother. With his leg not completely healed, they may send him home."

The realization struck her with a very real and powerful force. "To England?" *To Miss Grenville and her wealth?* "I'll never see him again."

"But he'll be safe." Joseph pulled his hat on and turned to the door. "I need to get some information before we decide what's best. I'll be back as soon as I can."

30

Andrew set aside the satchel Joseph had brought him and took a breath. The single change of attire had left plenty of room for food. He'd have to speak with Rachel about that.

Rachel.

His chest ached at the thought of her...of how close he had come to forgetting what duty demanded. He raked his fingers through his hair, dropping his head forward. Duty left no place for love. Not for him, anyway.

The rooster crowed, and Andrew looked out across the loft. The creak of hinges brought him to his feet. Had Joseph returned? No. His stallion usually made his presence known. Perhaps it was just the wind. Or Rachel. As Andrew reached the top of the stairs, a shadow caught his gaze and drew it toward the large haystack near the doors.

Fannie Reid crouched at the base of the hay, cramming something into an old sack. In the same motion she stood and vanished out the front.

He frowned and leaned into the railing. Though he hadn't seen what the sack contained, there was only one logical conclusion. Fire ignited the ends of his nerves. He wouldn't wait around to find out what Daniel planned to do. Andrew would give Joseph a half hour more, and then leave. He would not put them in more danger than he already had.

~*~

Rachel's pulse quickened. She stood from the rocker, fighting the urge to run to Andrew's embrace.

He slipped into the cabin, her Bible gripped in his hand. He looked nervous, but there was more than that. Deeper emotions played at the corners of his mouth and tugged his brows together. "Joseph has not returned. I must go."

Rachel sent a glance to the bag she'd packed. She couldn't let him return to a woman he didn't love. She had to convince him to let her leave with him. "Where?" Was that her voice? It sounded detached. Everything seemed disconnected, as if a dream.

Then his fingers brushed hers, wrapping around them.

She clung to his hand as though it were a thin rope saving her from a flash flood of feeling. "Where will we go?"

"I suppose I will work my way North." He jerked back an inch. "Wait. We? Rachel, I cannot let you—"

"We'll take Sorrowful. Joseph can manage without him."

Andrew shook his head. "Rachel, I could not risk your life."

"I don't care about the risk."

"Please, listen to me." His eyes shone as two dimples became ravines in the wake of a pained, yet determined smile. "This was never meant to be. But soon the Lord will wipe away all these tears and help us see His greater purposes. He remains in control."

"It seems to me He's been detained elsewhere."

Bitterness tightened her voice. "Or perhaps He doesn't care."

Andrew's eyes darkened with sorrow. "'We are troubled on every side, yet not distressed; we are perplexed, but not in despair; Persecuted, but not forsaken; cast down, but not destroyed.'" He pressed the Bible into her hands. "That is the legacy of faith. Rachel, don't you see? That is why we're here. The Bible speaks of being proved. We are born into trials. It is how we grow to become the people the Lord desires us to become. It is because He loves us more than a moment of happiness. He's trying to build us. But it isn't all trial." Andrew encircled Rachel in his arms and leaned his forehead against hers. "The Lord gives us joy as well."

If only this moment, the feeling his embrace, would last. "For a short time—before it's again snatched away."

"I could never forget you, Rachel Garnet. And I shall always love you. You have given me a memory of joy that no one could ever steal, so long as I live. I do not care how large the next stone may be."

Her chuckle became a sob. "Why must it hurt so?"

Andrew pressed his lips into her hairline and inhaled deeply. He tipped her head back, his gaze dancing between her eyes and her lips. His breath caressed her mouth as he drew her toward his own.

The door flung open as Fannie burst into the cabin. Her hair was disheveled and her skirt torn in several places. "They're coming!" She gasped for air. "And it's all my fault."

Andrew spun. "Daniel?"

"He has your red coat. He told me he needed it to protect Rachel and Joseph. I thought he'd destroy it.

Instead he's been gathering men at the old fort. More than twenty are on the road coming from there now, with that coat as proof that you're a British spy. You must go."

As soon as Rachel's brain registered more than the words, she lunged past Fannie and grabbed the musket from over the door. She thrust it to Andrew.

"You know I cannot. I will try to slip away, but that is more for your sake than my own." He brushed a finger across her cheek, and then retreated into the yard, half running, mostly hobbling in the direction of the barn.

Rachel dropped the musket on the table.

Fannie touched her arm. "I'm praying," Fannie whispered.

But would God listen?

Rachel walked out to meet the unwanted guests. They were close now, and her blood turned cold with the realization of how many there truly were. They had come from everywhere—men, women, and even some children—and most were armed.

Daniel led them.

Rachel fought the desire to fetch the weapon out of the cabin, but Andrew was right, it would only serve to worsen an already deadly situation.

"Where's Joseph?" Fannie questioned.

"I wish I knew." Rachel felt faint at what would happen if the mob found Andrew, but how would he get away in time?

The mob swarmed the yard like wasps, their stingers primed.

Red draped down beside Daniel's leg.

"What do you want here, neighbors?" Rachel called as they began to rein their horses and pull up their wagons.

Every eye locked on her. Maybe it was good Joseph wasn't here.

She forced a smile and kept her voice friendly. "Has something happened?" Her legs wobbled.

"We've come for the man who's been hiding here." Daniel raised the scarlet coat into the air. "We've discovered he's a British spy."

Rachel felt the blood rush from her head. "My brother's away, and there's no one here besides your sister. I'm afraid I don't know what you're talking about."

"Don't play coy, Rachel. Where is that British dog?" Daniel swung from his mare.

She faced him fully, rage building within her. "There is no such man here."

A cold smile crossed his lips, and he turned back to the mob he had gathered. "Search the property. He couldn't have gotten far."

Men dashed in every direction, several pushing past Rachel and Fannie into the cabin.

The largest group raced to the barn.

Rachel held her breath. If only she trusted the Lord enough to pray.

~*~

It was Andrew's intent to pass through the barn and corrals, making his escape into the woods, but after a few yards, he remembered that the crutch remained in the loft, and the satchel. Not only were they proof of his stay there, but his hip had been strained enough today and hurt more with each step. He wouldn't make it far. Andrew returned to the barn, reaching the loft as the pounding of hooves echoed unmercifully in his ears. Trapped. There was no way to outrun them even if he had two good legs.

"Oh, God, what have I done?" He glanced to the heavy rafters above. "Do not let Rachel and her brother be punished for the kindness they have shown me. That is all I ask." A sack of grain leaned against the wall and he sat down to wait for the arrival of the mob. Footsteps on the stairs caused him to brace against the growing fear.

"'Trust in the Lord with all thy heart,'" Andrew breathed, "'and lean not unto thine own understanding. In all thy ways acknowledge Him, and he shall direct thy paths.'"

The first man appeared, searching the shadows. "I think I got him, boys!"

Andrew's legs had no strength. "I wondered when you would come." He didn't bother to mask his rich English tones as several rough hands pulled him up—Daniel would have already told them everything. "I appreciate not having to wait too dreadfully long."

"Don't worry. We know how to take care of swine like you nice and quick."

31

Rachel's heart lurched as the victory cry rose from the barn. Everyone suddenly ran in that direction, their shouts drowning out the calls of frightened animals. She grabbed Fannie's hand and pushed ahead, reaching the large entrance just as someone gave Andrew a shove down the last half of the stairs. He fell forward, unable to catch himself until he slammed against the ground, tearing the elbow of his shirt. Blood ran from his nose and more came from a cut on his lip.

"No! Leave him alone." Her cries fell on deaf ears.

Men hollered as they dragged their prize from the barn.

Daniel reached Andrew as they pushed him past Rachel. He lowered his voice as he touched the slight bruise on his jaw. "I told you this wasn't over."

She tried to grab Daniel's arm but they continued past.

In the yard they formed a tight circle around Andrew. Daniel moved into the center, his voice thundering over the crowd. "We are at war. The British have killed us, destroyed our crops, burned our houses and terrorized our families." He raised the scarlet coat above his head. "This man is a British spy and will be treated as such. What did the British do to us, our sons, and fathers? They killed them in cold blood for protecting their families. What shall we do to this spy?"

Everyone seemed to cry out at once, all calling for blood.

Rachel shoved through the mob, struggling against the mass of bodies with all her strength. Finally she broke through. "Stop this. You don't know what you're doing." Rachel clutched Daniel's sleeve. "Don't do this."

"Rachel, you are not involved in this," Daniel whispered hoarsely. "Do you know what they would do to you and Joseph if they suspected you knew who he was? You would be worse off than him. Now get out of here."

"I won't let you do this."

"Listen to him," Andrew said from beside Daniel. Fear clouded his eyes and lined his face, but his voice was firm. "Go back to the house."

"Get her out of here," Daniel yelled at someone. Several men gripped her arms, dragging her away. The remainder swarmed Andrew as though bees around a hive.

~*~

"I am not a spy," Andrew called out in weak defense. "I do not mean anyone harm."

"Not a spy?" Daniel's voice mocked. "Then what are you, a British soldier, doing in those clothes? Where's your uniform? You are a soldier, are you not? An officer?" There was a pause as he held out his burdened hand. "This is yours, isn't it?" He brought the coat down, whipping it across the side of Andrew's face then releasing it to hang limply over his shoulder, a mark of who he was. Daniel leaned close to whisper in his ear. "Tell them truthfully, priest."

Andrew gripped the scarlet coat in his hands and fingered the hole cut in the sleeve. Perhaps it was better this way. "Yes, it is mine."

Someone shoved him forward, causing him to fall to his hands and knees. Sweat dripped from his face. He remained on the ground as the mob hovered over him, spiting and shouting cruel and angry jeers.

Lord, is this Thy plan for me? Help me trust.

Pulling Andrew back to his feet, several men forced his arms into the coat. "There you have him, a British pig," one shouted.

Andrew's gaze hesitated on him, his face as familiar as his voice. Rodney Cowden. Recognition stirred deeper memories. But from where? When?

"Shall we show him British justice?"

"Let's do with him as his armies did with our sons," a woman cried out, followed by a roar of approval.

"I have a rope," a man's voice resonated

"Take him to the big oak there."

"Show him British justice!"

"Hang him!"

"They killed my boys."

"We lost everything."

"A little justice is all we want."

"Hang him!"

The voices seemed as one, yet all crying differently. Again rough hands and the barrels of guns prodded Andrew forward.

~*~

Rachel struggled to press through the crowd. Her mind spun, unable to grasp the horror of what was happening.

Andrew stared straight ahead, his face almost passive, a sheep in the midst of ravening wolves.

They would kill him.

"Wait," Rachel screamed. "You can't do this. Stop. Please." She looked up into the brilliantly blue heavens, her heart crying out despite herself. *Oh God, don't let them kill him. Have mercy, Lord.*

Rachel was again grabbed from behind and pulled back to the cabin. She fought against the arms which held her fast, but was helpless.

"Don't, Rachel." Daniel's voice touched her ear. "You can't help him now."

She swung around, a hand rising to his face with all her strength. "You dog," Rachel spat as he caught her wrist. "You've killed him. How could you do this?" She pushed away, trying to strike him with her fists. They found their mark.

Daniel was forced to step back and loosen his grip.

Rachel tore herself away and sprinted to the people she had known as friends and neighbors. They'd bound Andrew's hands behind him and were forcing him onto the back of a flat-bed wagon which had been driven directly under the largest oak. A man threw a thick rope over one of the branches and began to tie a loop at the end.

"No!"

The shouts of the mob seemed to drown out Rachel's voice.

Andrew looked up, finding her gaze. His face was marred with dirt and blood, as was the scarlet coat. Leaning heavily on his left leg, he shook his head as though warning her from taking any action to save him.

She stared, her insides in pieces. How could he be so calm? Didn't he see that they were going to kill him—that God would not save him this time? Rachel tunneled through the crowd.

Someone slipped the rope around Andrew's neck and pulled it tight.

"Wait. Wait, I tell you!"

The crowd quieted slightly.

"Please wait," Rachel begged as she reached the wagon. She glanced at Rodney Cowden who held the horses from bolting forward. "Please."

"Our minds are made up, girl."

"I know. Just give me a minute."

"I don't—"

"Another minute won't hurt nothing, Rodney." Daniel made his way to join them. "Her father was killed by them, and then he came and deceived her about who he was. Let her say her piece to him."

Cowden showed reluctance but nodded.

Rachel scrambled onto the wagon beside their prisoner.

Andrew gave her a half smile, but his eyes bore his soul. He didn't want to die any more than she wanted him to.

"Andrew."

"I am sorry to have deceived you, miss." He cocked his head to see the rope and branch above his head. "I suppose I have little choice but to promise it will not happen again."

"Don't." Reaching out, she wiped a smudge of dirt from his cheek. His face was so pale. Rachel bit her lower lip, unable to stop its trembling. Her arms flew around him, clinging to him.

"Rachel, no," Andrew pled in her ear. "Do not let them see you cry. Do not make them hate you, too."

"But I love you."

"Then walk away now. And do not hate God for this deed. For my sake—do not blame God for what men do."

"That's enough," Cowden barked from the seat of the wagon. "You've had your minute. Someone get her down."

"No." Rachel relinquished her hold but remained on the wagon. "You can't do this. Where is the law? Where's mercy? This isn't right and every one of you knows it. He's a prisoner of war, a soldier who obeyed orders, not a criminal."

"I lost both my sons to the likes of those Redcoats," a woman cried out.

Another shouted from the back. "They invaded our lands, and killed our men. Someone must be made to pay."

"I understand your anger. I also lost my father to them. But I can see that this isn't justice—it's revenge."

Very few seemed to listen to her pleadings and strong hands hauled her to the ground.

"No!"

"Careful, miss." A smile warped Cowden's face. "You might scare the horses."

Andrew was on the flatbed of the wagon, head lowered and eyes filled with peace. Closing them, his mouth moved, offering one final prayer. He still loved his God. If only God loved him in return. How could He allow this otherwise?

I don't understand, Lord...but please don't let him die like this. Rachel glanced away, not wanting to see what was about to happen.

Daniel's pistol rested in his holster.

Without another thought, she grabbed it and leveled it at the driver. "If that wagon moves, so help me, I'll shoot you dead, Rodney Cowden."

"Have you lost your mind?" Daniel moved to take the pistol back.

"Don't touch me, or I'll shoot him. And don't move that wagon."

Cowden scowled at her. "Think for a minute, girl. If you fire that pistol the horses will bolt. Either way, the Redcoat is dead."

"Yes, but you'll be dead with him."

The world paused as they glowered at each other—Cowden with the reins hovering over the backs of the excited horses, and Rachel aiming the flintlock.

Everyone waited.

Now what, Lord?

"What are you doing on my land?" Joseph's voice boomed, causing several people to startle.

Even Rachel jerked, her thumb twitching over the trigger. It was a blessing the piece wasn't sensitive.

Joseph reined Hunter in from the road.

"Glad you could join us, Garnet. We were about to practice some good old British justice. Just as they would like to see done to every last one of us 'traitors to the crown,' as they say." Sarcasm laced Cowden's words. "We know as well as they the benefit of gallows for traitors."

"Are you suggesting I'm a traitor?" Joseph stopped at the edge of the crowd.

"Yes," Cowden spat. "For harboring an enemy officer at a time of war."

"If being a Christian is treason, then you can hang

me as well. I wouldn't want to be part of this country we've been establishing. The Bible's full of examples of the Lord defending a righteous nation when they fought for their country and freedom, but let us also remember the words of Christ when He told His disciples to love their enemies and do good to them. I believe God is in support of these United States of America and our desires for freedom, but I also believe that if I had left this man to die when he was no longer a threat to our freedom or safety, the condemnation would have been upon me." Joseph glanced out across the group gathered. "I ask you to look into your own hearts and souls. Would the Lord justify you in killing this man in cold blood? Will we stain our country with the killing of men who have already surrendered to our mercy? If that is so, you may hang me, for I will not allow this." He urged Hunter forward.

Cowden gave an abrupt shout, slapping the reins against the horses' rears.

They leaped, jerking the wagon.

Andrew's feet shot out from under him, the rope cinching around his neck.

Several men standing near the horses when they bolted grabbed the harnesses and pulled them to a stop.

Andrew gagged as he attempted to regain balance on the edge of the wagon tremoring with the horses' nervousness. Then his feet slipped, swinging with his body into midair.

32

Rachel screamed. Her hands flew to her face but she was unable to block out the horrible image. Her body slumped against Daniel, unable to support itself. *No, God. No.*

Joseph yelled at Hunter. The stallion immediately reacted. People jumped out of his way to avoid being trampled. Even before Joseph reached Andrew, the knife was ready. The blade sawed through the rope. After another breathless moment, Andrew's limp body fell to the ground with a solid thud and a cloud of dust.

Rachel was hardly aware of the pistol falling as her wobbly legs carried her to him.

He gagged, gasping for breath, the rope still about his throat.

She pulled it over his head. A bright red welt marked its place. "Are you...?"

Andrew coughed. His breathing was short and sharp. His throat sounded as though it were still restricted. He struggled to move, but was unable to with his wrists bound under him. Rachel fumbled with the knots until Joseph pushed her aside and cut them loose.

Turning onto his stomach, Andrew's hands rose to his throat and face. Ever so slowly his breathing steadied and deepened. He pushed onto his hands and knees.

She held his trembling shoulders, finding it hard to catch her own breath. Eyes closed, she buried her face in his hair. Andrew was alive...For this moment, that was enough.

"It's all right," he whispered, his voice shaky and hoarse. "The Lord is watching over us."

"He's only ever failed me."

Andrew coughed again, trying to clear his voice. It did little to help as he attempted a few more words. "No. He heard you today."

"But—"

Joseph pulled her up, tearing her away from Andrew. Strong arms wrapped her in place despite her struggles.

Andrew's eyes rolled back in his head, his body losing strength as two men dragged him to his feet. The mob seemed oblivious to the fact that their prisoner had lost consciousness. They continued to aim their weapons while arguing over what was to be done.

"Hold on!" Benjamin Reid made his way through the crowd, using his cane to push aside anyone who stood in his way. Fannie followed in his wake. As they broke free of the mob, she hurried to Joseph's side.

"Listen up." Benjamin waved the cane above his head as he moved in front of the British captain. He soon had everyone's attention. "This man a prisoner of war. We will take him to Fort Schuyler where Colonel Gansevoort can decide what's to be done. Now who has a horse we can take him on?"

Joseph released Rachel. "I'll accompany you with my wagon. He isn't in any condition to ride."

Rachel looked back to him, in his red coat and homespun breeches. His eyes were again focusing, but he still leaned heavily on the men holding him. *Oh, Andrew.*

"Then I suggest everyone else go home," Benjamin shouted. "The excitement's over."

While several grumbled, most appeared eager to get back to their own farms and chores before evening. The mob dispersed—Rodney Cowden and Daniel among the first. By the time Joseph returned with both horses hitched to the wagon, only a few men remained.

Fannie stayed with Rachel, clinging to her arm as they waited. When Joseph pulled the wagon to a halt, the younger woman let go and hurried to him. She gripped his leg. "Are you sure it's safe for you to go?"

Joseph leaned over and brushed his hand down her face to tuck a lose curl out of the way. "It'll be fine." His face, however, was stone and his brow lowered with concern. "I haven't done anything wrong."

Fannie pushed up on the side of the wagon and planted a firm kiss on his cheek.

He looked down in surprise, then pleasure as she withdrew to where Rachel stood. A wide grin flashed across his face. It vanished just as quick. Joseph turned back to the other men who forced Andrew into the back of the wagon. "Watch that right leg of his."

A groan escaped Andrew. His brow furrowed and his eyes closed. "Could I have some water?"

The men appeared to ignore him.

Rachel came to life. She raced to the house for a cup. She also grabbed a quilt, stuffing it under one arm. "Wait," she called. She climbed into the back of the wagon.

"Get out of there, girl," one of the men shouted at her.

She shook her head. "I'm going, too."

Joseph pivoted in his seat and pointed a finger. "No. Give him a drink, and then get out of this wagon."

"Please let me go, Joseph. I can't—"

"No. That's final. You stay here and take care of things 'til I get back. You hear me?"

"But..." There was nothing left to say.

By the expression on his face, he wouldn't give in. "Hurry."

Rachel glared at her brother before helping Andrew drink. With trembling hands she wrapped the quilt around his shoulders.

His fingers found hers, squeezing them. "Thank you." Andrew's hand withdrew. His face turned away. He was letting her go. He wanted her to go.

Somehow finding strength, she crawled to the tailgate and slipped to the ground.

"I'll try to be back by tomorrow night," Joseph said, pulling her gaze from the man she loved. "If something happens and...if for some reason I'm detained, I'll send word."

She nodded, but dread welled. "Be careful."

Benjamin scaled onto the seat beside Joseph and three other men mounted. The group directed their horses to the road.

The two women watched as their silhouettes, outlined in the lowering sun, disappeared from sight.

"Will you pray with me?" Fannie whispered.

Rachel continued to stare at the last spot she'd seen the riders. She would never see Andrew Wyndham again. But at least he was alive. "Pray?" she echoed. "Yes."

~*~

The temperature continued to plummet. Rachel pulled the rocking chair near the fireplace, and sat with her feet curled under. Tightening the blanket's grip around her shoulders, she rocked back and forth, willing the movement to calm the anxiety which had been growing within her throughout the day. "Where are you, Joseph?" she questioned into the heavy silence. "What's keeping you?"

Her attention returned to the dance of orange and red flames over the charcoaled logs. It'd been over twenty-four hours since the men left for the fort. Every minute making up those hours brimmed with worry for both Joseph and Andrew. Now, as night came and the sun faded from sight, her hope of Joseph's safe return sank as well.

No longer able to hold still, Rachel surveyed the room. Her mother's Bible sat on the edge of the table, untouched since Andrew brought it back. She brushed her hand over the cover, her heart yearning for comfort. She melted into a nearby chair and pulled a lamp closer, turning through the pages, her thoughts far away.

This had been Andrew's love. He'd made the Bible a part of who he was. So many recollections of him involved this book as he read out loud, discussed and quoted it—spouting the Word.

The Bible was all she had left of him except...a hand stole to her pocket and her fingers closed around the small scrap of wool. She studied the fabric, remembering the scarlet coat as it was forced onto him, as he was led to the wagon, as he hung from that horrid rope. The memory strangled her. *What if Joseph hadn't come in time? What if...I love you.* Rachel closed her hand around the swatch, and her gaze moved to the words on the page. The Book of Psalms, fortieth chapter. She submitted and began to read.

I waited patiently for the Lord; and He inclined unto me, and heard my cry.

Rachel hadn't waited with any sort of patience for the Lord. At her first true trial of faith, she had faltered—avoided Him, instead of calling upon Him for support and comfort. No wonder everything continued to fall away from her.

He brought me up also out of an horrible pit, out of the miry clay, and set my feet upon a rock and established my doings. And He hath put a new song in my mouth, even praise unto our God: many shall see it, and fear, and shall trust in the Lord. Blessed is the man that maketh the Lord his trust.

Trust. The thing that held her from her God. Rachel had always believed in His existence, but had she ever truly trusted Him? There had never been much of a need before. Her life had been simple and happy. She'd taken for granted that it would not change. But with the death of her father, while still recovering from the loss of her mother, everything had changed. She couldn't help but blame God. How could she trust Someone Who would cause her such pain?

Don't hate God for this deed. For my sake, don't blame God for what men do.

"But God could've stopped them," Rachel whispered. "Doesn't He have the power to stop men from doing evil? If God created the world and everything on it, why couldn't He have saved Papa? Why couldn't He have protected Andrew..." And now Joseph?

A trial of faith. Isn't that what Andrew was trying to tell me? Men were born to be tried. But why?

Her head snapped up as the explosions of muskets firing split the night and shattered the silence. Rachel tore to the small window near the door. Just as she lowered her head to peer into the darkened yard, one of the logs in the fireplace sparked loudly, pitch igniting. She jerked, glancing over her shoulder at the flames. Even as she ascertained it was not a danger, glass sprayed in all directions, the windowpane bursting. Something heavy crashed to the floor.

Her shaking hands brushed the sharp splinters from her shoulder as she stared at the large stone.

Shouts of men sounded through the broken window, angry and most almost incoherent— intoxicated.

"Come out, you traitors!"

33

Andrew placed one foot in front of another, limping badly. He was fortunate to be able to walk at all, and even more so to be alive.

The guard, however, was impatient and gave a shove forward. "Hurry along."

"If you desired your prisoners to move faster, it would do you well to not shoot them in the legs during battle."

"I agree," the guard answered with another push. "If we shot them in the head, it would speed things along nicely."

"Always trust a colonist to lighten a conversation."

The guard grunted and moved to un-plank a solid wood door. "In here."

Andrew stepped past, pausing as the door sealed. He blinked his eyes to adjust to the dim light of a lamp on a table near the far wall. Men sat, laid, or paced the large room. Most wore the familiar regimentals—though many of the scarlet coats hid under woolen blankets to ward off the chill bite in the evening air that seeped through the cracks of the ill-fitting log walls.

"Bless me, I swear I am seeing a ghost," one man exclaimed, coming to his feet. He wore a thick beard and was dirty and tattered. He reached out to touch Andrew's arm. "My eyes swear that you are none other than Captain Wyndham, our God-praising clergy, but I know I saw the same man fall in battle two months ago."

The man had been another of the seventy British reinforcements St. Leger had sent the Tories and Iroquois at Oriskany. "Surely you did not expect me to allow a little musket ball to send me to the next life, Derek O'Conner."

"I should have guessed. But tell us, Captain, where have you been keeping yourself all these weeks if you never made it back here before General St. Leger broke siege? They have not returned, have they?"

"No. As far as I have heard, they are long gone from the area."

"Yes, our guards have been pleased enough to inform us of all their victories." His friend looked at him, a question marked his brow. "But you have yet to answer me, Captain. Where have you been keeping yourself, and how did you ever survive? And your regimentals—you seem to have lost all but your coat."

Andrew glanced down at the clothes the Garnets had given him—another reminder of what he left behind. He forced his mind from Rachel. There would be plenty of hours with her memory in the days to come. "First, what do you know of my brother? Did you see what happened? Was he still with the general when they retreated?"

The man shook his head. "I am afraid not."

His stomach clenched. "He...he is dead, then?" Andrew wiped a hand across his face, feeling numb and exhausted. He'd lost everything. He almost didn't catch what his friend was saying.

"Course' not." Derek motioned to where a soldier pulled to his feet, staring wide-eyed at the newcomer. His reddish beard was wispy and short, his face marked with dirt, but his green-brown eyes twinkled.

With a flood of relief almost stealing his strength, Andrew staggered across the distance between them. He wrapped his arms around Stephen, his fingers gripping the woolen fabric of his brother's coat.

"We thought you were dead." Stephen clapped him on the back.

"No deader than you." Andrew released his hold.

"But when they came back from Oriskany, they said—"

"They were mistaken. I was wounded, but a Christian family took me in and brought me back to life. The Lord has been watching over both of us."

Stephen looked at him as though questioning his sanity. "We are prisoners in a rat hole. Does nothing dampen your faith?"

"I found you, and you are alive. To think I could have started north and never learned your fate." One hand came up to massage the crimson welt circling his throat. "How could my faith be dampened after the miracles I have beheld?"

"What happened to your neck?" Derek forced Andrew to face him.

"Good old British justice. I believe that is what they called it." Andrew tried to clear the rasp from his voice. "But tell me what happened after I fell. I struck my head and remember nothing more. I believe that was before you started retreating."

"I saw you go down," Derek said. "I was sure you were dead the way your head was bleeding, and your hip a bloody mess. I tried to make my way to you, but soon we started falling back. Our Iroquois warriors decided they could not stand anymore and began to retreat. There was little to be done after that. We still slaughtered those rebels though—by the hundreds."

Andrew couldn't contain a cringe. Rachel's father had been among them. "And our losses?"

"Indians, a little over sixty. Otherwise, only seven men for sure killed, though the count I heard placed about twenty wounded or missing." He gripped Andrew's shoulder. "One less, now."

Stephen grunted. "Though our casualty count is rising again. At first this hole was bearable and they fed us well enough, but the temperature is on its way down, and men are becoming ill."

"We have lost one already, and young Phillip Stuart is not too far from joining him." He pointed to a soldier lying on a pile of hay. "The winter is just beginning. One can hope they do not leave us here to freeze."

Andrew shook his head. "I overheard them saying they have plans to move us down river in the next few days. It seems I arrived in time." He glanced away, trying to keep his expression passive.

If only Rachel and Joseph had been left unaffected.

~*~

Heart hammering, Rachel grabbed for the musket she'd hung back over the door. "God, help me."

"You're not wanted here no longer!"

"Go back to Britain!"

With hands unsteady, she struggled to load. Some of the powder didn't make it in the barrel, spilling on the floor. Hopefully there was still enough. The ramrod also fought her before slipping into place, pushing the ball and packing the powder. Gun ready, Rachel pressed against the door.

The shouts and curses still assaulted her, but they seemed to have moved past the house.

Rachel pulled the door open.

Men with torches stood near the barn.

The bellowing of cattle and frightened cries of the animals sounded as they erupted from the large doors and raced into the night. She held her breath in horror at the sight of their stock escaping in all directions. Moments later, brilliant flames leapt from the barn walls and a nearby stack of hay.

"Stop!" Rachel raised the musket barrel into the air and squeezed the trigger. The explosion deafened her, its force pushing her back inside the cabin. Without pause, she grabbed another cartridge to reload.

The ramrod was still in the barrel when some of the men charged the front of the cabin.

She tried to shove the door closed with her shoulder, but a sudden thrust threw her backward. The musket was ripped from her grip by a large man as he barreled in.

She tried to grab it. "Leave me alone, Cowden."

He pushed her back with a chuckle as he tossed the gun aside, and then lunged for her.

Rachel darted to where a cast-iron skillet hung near the fireplace. Dodging behind the table, she wrapped her hand around the skillet's handle, gripping it tight.

Dancing flames highlighted his face. Cowden appeared possessed as he neared, seemingly unaware of her newfound weapon. He moved to trap her, the stench of alcohol foul on his breath. His hand grasped her free arm.

Rachel cracked the skillet across his head.

Cowden stumbled back, dazed.

She raced for the musket near the door, just as another man appeared in the opening. Rachel threw herself forward to grab the barrel. Slamming against the floor, she rolled onto her back and swung the butt of the gun toward the second attacker.

He caught it with his arm, grunting with pain, but somehow holding it fast.

For the second time the gun was wrenched from her hands. Rachel cursed her long skirts as she attempted to stand. A foot tangled and she dropped to her knees. Sharp pain shot up both legs.

Cowden, recovered from the strike, grabbed Rachel's arms from behind, yanking her to her feet.

She attempted to jerk away. "Why are you doing this?"

"We don't take kindly to Loyalists," he growled. He pulled her around to face him. "We came for your brother, too. Where is he?"

Rachel yelped in pain as the second man grabbed her hair, yanking her head around. "He's got to be here somewhere, and you'll make it a lot easier on yourself if you tell us."

"No."

He brought his knuckles across her face.

Rachel's mind reeled and tiny white sparks appeared behind her right eye. She closed it against the pain.

"We don't want to hurt you, girl. Just tell us what we want to know," Cowden insisted.

"What good will it do you? He's not here."

"Where is he then?"

"I don't know." Maybe it was a blessing Joseph hadn't returned home earlier, despite her prayers. Perhaps the Lord was watching out for them. An unexpected calm washed over her as though a wave over a stone. Her chin rose to meet her aggressors. "You have no business on this farm. Please release me and leave." Rachel met Cowden's hard gaze.

"You have a lot of spirit, girl, but that ain't helping you none." His hand slapped across her face.

Something popped in her jaw, ripping it with agony. Her ears rang and her stunned body slumped into Rodney Cowden's arms as the discharge of a musket reverberated through the night. She hit the floor as heavy boots pounded out a retreat to the door.

"Get off this land!" a man's voice bellowed from outside. "And don't think of coming back."

"You got a lot of gall, Dan Reid," Cowden shouted.

"You're the one who's gone too far. The Garnets are innocent. How dare you harass them? I want you and the rest of your drunken buffoons off this land immediately. Do you hear me?"

Cowden mumbled something and started toward his horse. "Come on, boys. We're done here for now."

Rachel dragged herself to the open door.

The mob pushed their horses to a gallop and vanished into the night. They were replaced as a group twice in number rode in from two directions.

"Are you all right, Rachel?" Daniel jumped from his saddle. "What did they do to you?"

"I'm fine." She cradled her jaw in her palm. "What are you and your men here for, to burn my home, too?"

"Rachel, we came to help."

"Haven't you helped enough already?" She started toward the barn, now completely consumed in flame. Rachel stared as it burned—tears cool on warm cheeks.

All the work her father and her brother, their family, had invested in that building would soon be reduced to a pile of ash.

"I'm sorry, Rachel. I didn't mean for it to go this far."

"Did you really expect you could step in here and dispose of Andrew without affecting anything else? Did you think with him out of the way I would be more eager to love you? Well, I'll tell you this, Daniel Reid. I have never loved anyone as I do him, and taking him away didn't change that, it merely destroyed the respect and friendship I once held for you." Rachel stepped back from the heat.

The front of the structure sagged, collapsed with a groan, and a burst of sparks and flame.

"I admit I was jealous, but..." Daniel paused, his head dropping. "No, you're right. There are no excuses. I was jealous and I made a terrible mistake—no matter what my reasoning. I know you will probably never forgive me, but I want you to know that I am sorry this whole thing was started." He walked away.

She was alone. The heat from the blaze singed her face, and Rachel turned to the cabin.

Men worked to contain the fire. Others corralled the two cows, older calf and the three sows which had been in the barn. At least the horses and wagon were with Joseph.

Matthias Adler moved near and set a hand on her arm. "Benjamin told me vhat happened yesterday. And now das...perhaps you come spend the night vith us?"

Rachel managed a quick shake of her head that she immediately regretted as her neck twinged with pain. "Your offer is so kind...and tempting. But I should probably stay here."

He nodded. "I understand, though I am sure Marta will be more questioning. Vhy don't you let us keep your stock for short vhile?"

"You'd do that for us?" A sigh drained the last of the adrenaline from her veins. "I'm afraid without Joseph here I'm at a loss about what to do. I don't even know what we could trade you for feeding them."

"Not to vorry about that. Our old cow has been scanty with the milk lately, and Marta is not happy. If vee keep part of your milk, it vill be fair."

"I can't thank you enough."

He tipped his hat and moved away, instructing the other men to move the animals to his farm.

Rachel slipped inside the cabin. She trekked across the floor, stumbling over the musket, seeking the lamp on the table. It had gone out. She reached for it only to jerk back in pain as a small trickle of blood ran warm down her hand. The glass chimney was broken. She found another lamp, and lit it. There was little comfort for her as the light created eerie shadows over the broken glass and overturned furniture. She took a deep breath to steady her nerves. Setting the lamp on the table, she moved to close the door.

A cool breeze continued to find its way through the small window and her gaze shot toward the offending stone.

Angrily, Rachel picked it up, opened the door, and heaved it into the night.

There was a surprised yelp as Benjamin Reid jumped out of the way. "I was planning to knock." His voice immediately became contrite. "I have some news."

"Where's Joseph?"

"He didn't come back with us."

"What? Where is he? What happened?" Alarm constricted her ribs as her heart shifted to dread.

"It seems news of what happened preceded us. Friedrich Schubert rode straight to the fort as soon as he heard there was a British spy in the area, and I'm afraid Colonel Gansevoort was not all too welcoming of Joseph. Everyone there already believed he was a Loyalist and a traitor."

34

A blanket of dark blue still covered the earth as Rachel moved to where the blackened ash and rubble marked the former barn. If only this were a bad dream—she would wake, and everything would be made right. Her swollen eye and stiff jaw were painful reminders that it wasn't a dream.

A horse's whinny brought Rachel's head up.

Joseph had taken both Hunter and Sorrowful, and he was not returning.

Fighting the temptation to look, she closed her eyes and took a deep breath. "What do you want here?"

"I know you too well to assume you won't be trying to find a way up river," Daniel said.

She took a few steps away from him. "Don't try and stop me."

"I didn't come here to stop you. I came to help." His contrite voice seemed to plead. "I brought you a mount."

Rachel locked her jaw and spun. The ache across the side of her face increased as she spoke through bared teeth. "I don't want your help."

His gaze dropped. "I accept that. I know how much you hate me, and it's warranted. All of this is my fault, but I can't change the past, or what I did. Please let me try to set it right as best I can. I'll help your brother. Pa told me you're determined to do the same. I'll lend you this horse if you allow me to escort you to Fort Schuyler in safety."

Rachel looked away. The thought of being in his company was revolting, but it could be days before she found another way to travel the twenty miles. Rachel let out her breath. "All right." She turned back to the cabin. "I'll be ready in a few minutes."

~*~

Andrew ran his thumbs over the calluses that had formed on his palms. He had never done physical labor before, but it proved invigorating and satisfying. If only he could be there to help Rachel finish getting that stump out. He would have taken a lot of pleasure in that.

"You have not said much about your recovery." Stephen dropped down on the floor beside him. "In fact, you have been quite silent today."

"I am afraid I have been somewhat preoccupied in my thoughts." Andrew folded his arms, tucking his hands out of sight.

"As have I."

Maybe it was the whiskers and the somberness in his expression, but Andrew sensed a maturity that hadn't been there before. "What about?"

Stephen scratched his fingers through his hair. "How much I have wronged you."

"It was not—"

"Please, I stated—confessed—that much, let me finish. I have had these two months to sit here and think about what I would say to you if you were still alive. It would be wrong to let all that consideration lay in waste." Their gazes met and Stephen showed a thin smile. "After all, I was the one who almost killed you."

"Stephen—"

His brother held up a hand. "Mother always indulged me in whatever I wanted, while you were given every responsibility. I never felt this unfair as you were the eldest and if Father had not wasted our wealth and land, the bulk would have been entitled upon you. It was only fitting that you bear the brunt of our misfortune."

"Nothing has changed."

"Perhaps, but it was not your duty to follow me here. You had no obligation, even as a brother. I know what you gave up for that uniform, and I want to make recompense."

Andrew shook his head. "There is nothing I need from you, but your safe return to England and—"

Stephen rode over him. "You never wanted to marry Miss Grenville. I am not blind...though I wonder if she may be."

Ah, bitter truth. Something, perhaps that truth, felt wedged in his throat. "What does that have to do with anything? I have already given my word to the lady."

"But, if you were given the option of withdrawal?"

Images of Rachel, her scent, her hair in the first rays of dawn, the taste of her breath as he leaned down to kiss her, assaulted him with overwhelming force. The muscles in his jaw tightened, making it hard to answer. "I suppose I could get myself killed."

His brother chuckled. "Nothing quite that desperate, Andrew."

He let a laugh rise, but it exited with the sound of a grunt. "What did you have in mind?"

"Miss Grenville is a becoming creature, and her

wealth only enhances that beauty. I shall marry her myself."

Andrew's head snapped toward Stephen. "You?"

"Why not? I thought we made quite a connection during our stay in Derbyshire. I imagine the only reason she accepted your proposal in the first place was due to my neglect." He winked. "Trust me, Andrew. Everyone will be happier this way."

Especially me. And Rachel.

"You are more affected by this than I imagined."

Andrew hardly heard him. He had to think of a way to remain here. A way to make Rachel Garnet his wife.

"Is there someone else?"

"Yes," he said without thought.

"Who?"

His brother sat in an officer's uniform. Even with the grunge that surrounded them now, Stephen would never understand the quality of Rachel Garnet.

Neither would Andrew have, if not for the untainted vision the Lord had blessed him with at their first acquaintance. To see her as an equal—as she deserved to been seen. Instead of offering his memory of her to his brother's mocking, Andrew protected her by saying nothing. He smiled. God willing, he would find a way to be with her. *Please let it be within Thy will, Lord.*

The heavy door to their prison creaked on its large hinges, and Andrew was dragged back to the present.

"Everyone up!" a guard shouted.

Several more stepped past him, encouraging the men to their feet.

"Where are you taking us?" Derek pushed to the front of the pathetic column forming.

Andrew and Stephen joined him.

"Albany," the guard mumbled as he shoved them out of the door where more Continental soldiers waited. "Your General Burgoyne has surrendered to us the whole of his army. We're sending you to join them. It's time we got you off our hands."

~*~

Rachel stared up at the tall log walls. The fortress that may have once offered safety in case of British or Indian attacks, now filled her with foreboding. "Where do we go?" she questioned as they passed into the compound.

Daniel indicated a building not far from the gate. "That's were Colonel Gansevoort has his office, but I think it would be better if I go alone to begin with."

"No."

"Rachel. Please trust me on this. We need to get a feel for the situation before we plow ahead. It's the only way to have straight furrows."

It sounded like something Joseph would say.

"Fine, but make sure you come for me as soon as you learn anything."

"I promise." Daniel dismounted and handed her his reins.

As he disappeared into the building, a silent prayer pressed from Rachel's heart toward the heavens. Her eyes rose to the unfamiliar flag hanging from a tall pole. The breeze caught it, causing the white and red stripes to dance, displaying small white stars against blue in the inside top corner.

"It is quite the sight, isn't it?"

Startled, Rachel looked back to the officer who had

spoken. He rode through the gate, flanked by another continental soldier. He reined his horse toward her.

"What flag is that?"

"Why, that's *our* flag."

"Ours?"

"These United States of America. Every country needs their own flag. There are thirteen stars to represent each state."

"And the other five flags?" They hung lower than the first.

"Those are British flags we won in our last battle here."

Rachel's gaze angled to the high flag. It waved so proudly. So freely. "There's something grand about it, isn't there?"

"The grand thing is that it's ours. And as far as I can tell, it seems to be blessed by the good Lord Himself. Why, even last week we took Saratoga and captured General Burgoyne and a large portion of his armies. This morning some of our soldiers are headed east to Albany with the prisoners we've been holding here the past few months."

Rachel's head jerked to him. "Your British prisoners?"

His eyes narrowed. "Yes."

Her heart thudded. "When do they...when do they leave?"

"They are loading onto the boats now." He watched her close. "I just returned from there."

No. She'd seen men gathered at the boats, but had been too focused on the fort and what they would do to help Joseph. She'd hoped to see Andrew again, and now it was too late.

"I'm afraid I have forgotten myself, ma'am. What's

your name?"

My name. Rachel's gaze darted to where she'd last seen Daniel. No sign of him. Or Joseph. She looked back at the officer. It was hard to take a breath. "I'm Rachel Garnet. I was told my brother is being held here."

"Ah," was all he said.

"I am here to speak with Colonel Gansevoort."

The smile pasted on the officer's mouth distorted slightly. "Why don't we go into my office, then?"

35

Andrew glanced back toward the fort. Tucked behind a row of American soldiers, he hadn't gotten a good view of the riders, but one was a woman. It had to be Rachel. If only she had arrived a half hour earlier, he could have seen her one last time. Disappointment left a sour taste in his mouth. Other than the armed escort, there was no reason not to have her in his arms right now.

"Move along." A guard prodded him with the butt of his musket.

Andrew climbed into the flat bottomed Schenectady boat. He stepped around another man to where Derek and Stephen sat.

"Get distracted?" Stephen questioned.

Andrew stole one last look at the fort, but said nothing.

Another rider approached. He slowed his horse as his face turned toward the prisoners and their guards, then redirected down the slope, laying his heels to the animal's ribs.

Andrew ducked down slightly, but didn't remove his gaze from the man. Rodney Cowden. But what was he doing here now? And where had Andrew seen him before?

"Whoa." Cowden pulled his horse up, only sending a quick glance over the prisoners. He focused on the Americans. "Where's Colonel Gansevoort? I have an urgent message for him."

"He just returned to the fort," one of the lower officers said.

Cowden's eyes again flitted over the prisoners. This time he met Andrew's gaze and the corners of his mouth tipped down. "What's their destination?"

"Down river to Albany for now."

Cowden gave a nod, and then jerked his horse's head to the side, spurring back toward the fort. Toward Rachel.

Andrew looked at Derek. "Do you know who that man was?"

Stephen motioned him to lower his voice. "Of course we do." He glanced at the guards.

Andrew blinked, everything becoming clear. *Of course*. He'd seen Cowden in their camp less than an hour before St. Leger had sent the detachment of Tories and Iroquois to intercept the American reinforcements at Oriskany. Though, Molly Brant's runners had warned St. Leger first, Cowden had brought them the news, too. He had betrayed his country and his neighbors. "But what sense does that make?"

"What?" Derek leaned near.

"He was the most intent to have me hanged. If he is spying for us, why would he want me dead?"

"Maybe he thought you would give away his secret."

Andrew blew out his breath. As the driving force behind hanging the British 'spy', Cowden would both secure his own secrets and solidify in the minds of his neighbors that he was a patriot. But what was he up to now with an important message for the Continental Army?

It had to be a trap. False information, at least. Something that would affect this valley and the Garnets. Joseph and Rachel were in the fort with that scum.

Andrew couldn't sit back and hope for the best. He couldn't risk her safety.

Their guards climbed into the two Schenectady boats. His was in the front. Perfect. He turned to Stephen. "Thank you." Andrew clasped his brother's shoulder. "I wish you and Miss Grenville every happiness, but my duty is now elsewhere. Tell mother I will send word...if I survive this." He stripped off the red coat and passed it to his brother.

"Andrew, what are you doing?" Stephen's voice became raspy as he tried to whisper.

"A distraction would be helpful."

His eyes widened. "Andrew, no."

"Please."

The boat jostled as the soldiers pushed away from the shore. Stephen jerked to his feet, half stumbling over someone as he pulled Derek after him.

"What are you doing?" the older man demanded. Others shifted, trying to get out of the way. The boat shook as Andrew plunged over the edge.

~*~

"Sir, my brother is not a Tory, and definitely no traitor."

Colonel Peter Gansevoort shook his head. He was a tall man, almost unusually so, with a commanding presence. The gentle structure of his face and kind eyes only added to his striking appearance. What was most surprising, however, was his youth. He was the commander of this fort and yet he appeared to be in his twenties. "As you have said. However, before he arrived here with the prisoner, someone had already reported that he'd been harboring a British officer. It's evident that the only reason your brother turned him over to us was the insistence of the mob. I've heard a full report." Gansevoort studied her for a moment and frowned. "It would be wise for you, Miss Garnet, not to interfere in this matter."

"But, Colonel, my brother is not a traitor. He has risked his life more than once to defend this valley. Our own father was killed by the British and the Tories." Rachel's face burned with frustration.

Daniel touched her shoulder.

She forced her voice to calm. It turned to pleading. "Colonel Gansevoort, my brother is a religious man, but a true patriot. If you will hear me, I'll tell you the whole truth of our involvement with the British captain."

"Rachel." Daniel's voice warned her not to continue.

She stepped forward, pulling away from his touch as she began to rehearse the events that had brought the British captain into their home. Who would have known how dearly she would come to care for that man.

"Joseph was of the mind to kill him then and there, but I wouldn't let him. The man couldn't hurt us now. *I* talked Joseph into taking him home to die in some form of comfort. We knew he couldn't last the night—he'd already lost too much blood. He was barely alive."

"You've had this enemy officer hidden on your farm for two months?" Gansevoort raised a brow.

"Why did you not turn him over to us when you realized he would live?"

"That was the plan, sir," Rachel admitted meekly. "But I couldn't. He didn't even remember who he was until a short time ago. Even now, he doesn't remember everything. He was no longer a soldier—no longer a threat. And now I think he's even begun to see why we're fighting for this land and our freedom."

"And so you kept him hidden away in hopes that he would want to join us?" Gansevoort finished with unmasked mockery.

Rachel folded her arms tight against her abdomen, bracing against a wave of despair. "The important thing is we never meant to harm this country. We love it with as much passion as anyone could. We've prayed long for our freedom and are grateful for each victory we've had. We'll be just as grateful as you when the British finally return to England and leave us be." The last words caught in Rachel's throat.

"I can vouch for them, Colonel Gansevoort." Daniel stepped again to her side. "I've known the Garnets for years."

Gansevoort turned away and walked to the large fireplace, holding his hands out to it as though to warm them, despite the already comfortable temperature of the room. "Miss Garnet, would you step outside for a short time?"

She glanced from the colonel to Daniel, and then left. Though she closed the door behind her, Rachel took only a few steps, before looking back. Silently she returned, and pressed her ear against the cool wood.

"Miss Garnet is an attractive girl."

"That she is," Daniel's voice answered.

"I must admit I found it hard to tell whether her

worry was more for the sake of her brother or...the British captain." A deep chuckle resonated. "You see, Reid, I am still attempting to discover your involvement in all of this. You were the one who initiated the gathering of a mob to go after the British 'spy'. Yet with the same token, here you are, defending Joseph Garnet and standing by his sister. Most peculiar."

"I was only trying to protect our interests, not cause anyone harm."

"You were trying to protect *our* interests, or yours?" A pause followed the colonel's words. "Don't be offended. I am merely musing."

Daniel started replying, but she heard no more. The plodding of hooves drowned him out and pulled Rachel's gaze back to the gate and Rodney Cowden.

He reined his horse as his gaze fell on her. His lip curled into a snarl. "Why, if it isn't Miss Garnet."

~*~

Andrew grabbed for the rock and mud, fighting the pull of the water as it worked to force his body back to the surface. He kicked his legs. The current grew stronger the farther into the river he swam. He needed the momentum.

A musket ball hissed past his ear and dug into the bottom of the river, churning up a small cloud only inches from his shoulder. A second one struck several feet to his right. He wasn't as strong a swimmer as he remembered.

As the popping of muskets continued overhead, Andrew gave up trying to keep to the bottom in exchange for putting quicker distance between him and the soldiers. His lungs already begged for air, and he didn't need a ball through the head—or any other part of him. He stayed under until his vision began to haze before breaking the surface. He gasped a lungful of air as he glanced behind.

The boats sat in the middle of the river now, men perched on the bows with weapons, searching the water.

Along the shore, more soldiers ran downstream, but still yards back, with the gap lengthening as the current sped his way.

With one last breath, Andrew dived again, just as a ball cut through the ripples at his left. He began working his way to the bank. The next time he came up for air, the boats were hardly visible behind a long curve in the river. He allowed his head to remain above water as he swam to an outcropping of rocks, the current washing him out of sight of the soldiers.

By the time he reached dry land, his hip screamed and his body shook from both cold and fatigue. Andrew staggered into the woods, the sound of the soldier's boots growing louder as they ran through the brush edging the river.

36

Rachel pushed back into the building. "I will not wait out there with that man."

Daniel spun. "What man?"

She hurried to his side, giving Cowden as much clearance as she could.

He stepped into the room and nodded to the other two men. "Fancy seeing you here, Dan. Still chasing Miss Garnet's petticoat?"

"Shut up, Rodney." Daniel's hands formed fists. "You've already caused enough trouble."

"If you don't want to hear me talking, you'd better take a step outside. I have an urgent message for Colonel Gansevoort."

The colonel stepped forward. "And what would that message be?"

"I just intercepted a friend from the Weiser settlement north-east of here. Joseph Brant is raiding the area and they beg for assistance."

The colonel sat on the edge of his table, his arms folded, his eyes thoughtful. "Where is your friend now? He didn't come with you?"

"I promised him I would come for help, and left him to return to his family. You must send men."

"Yes, I suppose I must, though right now is not the ideal time to be dispatching a force of any size as some of my men are accompanying the British prisoners. I cannot leave the fort unprotected."

"If you need men," Daniel said, straightening, "I volunteer, as I'm sure Joseph Garnet will. He's fought Brant's raiders before."

"Yes." Rachel's voice echoed in her head. If anything happened to Joseph...but what other choice was there? "Please let him prove himself."

~*~

Andrew stumbled, his foot catching on a branch. Blood rushed in his ears. He didn't have to look behind.

The soldiers were on his heels, their approach racing with his pulse.

He should have thought before jumping into the river. He wouldn't do anyone any good if he got killed. A ball whizzed over his head and he dove to the ground, the hole in his sleeve catching on a branch and ripping the length of his arm. Pressing his forehead against soft dirt, Andrew closed his eyes. "God, do not let me die out here. Not until I have warned them. Not until Rachel is safe."

He rolled over and looked through the red and gold leaves at splotches of blue sky. A breeze brushed across his face, still wet. The fort was too far away. He would never make it there without being caught, or shot, and even if he did, they would have him as soon as he reached the gate. He raised his hands to his face, wiping his palms over his eyes and back through his hair. "I surrender," he yelled out, still fighting to catch his breath. As the soldiers approached, Andrew sat up but kept his hands near his head. "I need to see your colonel. Please. I have information for him."

"To your feet," a soldier ordered. "What sort of information?"

Andrew pushed up, but took another minute to brace against his knees and breathe. "There is a man who has been selling information to us and the Loyalists. Rodney Cowden. He is even now at the fort."

"You expect us to believe you would betray your own spy?"

Andrew met his gaze. "There are people I care for in this valley. I do not want them to get hurt."

"Fine, I'll pass along your message to Colonel Gansevoort, but you are going back on that boat." He forced Andrew around so his hands could be bound. The rope bit his already bruised wrists. "Now try swimming."

"Please allow me to return with you to the fort. I do not wish to go to Albany with the others."

"That's not my problem." The soldier pushed Andrew back in the direction of the river. "We have enough to worry about besides British captains with a death wish."

~*~

Rachel rushed to Joseph as he was led into the open area of the fort. She wreathed his neck with her arms and planted her face in his chest. "I'm so sorry."

His hands braced her shoulders. His body remained tense. "What are you doing here? Rachel, this is an extremely dangerous situation."

"That's why I'm here."

"Well, you shouldn't be." Joseph's face hardened as he touched the bruised area near her eye. "What's this from?"

She winced. It was still tender. "After you left, some drunken idiots came to cause trouble."

"What? Are you all right?"

"I'm fine." Especially considering how much worse it could have been if Daniel and the others had not come. "Really, I'm fine."

"What did they do?"

The image of the ash and singed wood made her want to cry. All his hard work. It wasn't as if she could hide it from him indefinitely. "The barn. They burnt down our barn. There is nothing left of it."

Joseph stared for a moment, his face stricken. "What about the stock?"

"They're fine. The Adlers are looking after them for now. The garner was singed on the closest wall, but most of the seed should still be good."

He looked as though he'd been kicked by an ornery cow. "For eating, maybe, but not for planting. We couldn't risk it. We'll have to somehow trade for seed...and feed for the livestock." The back of his hand crossed over his mouth. "So much for an easy winter."

Rachel pulled away. "It's all my fault. If you'd brought him here as soon as his life was out of danger, everything would have been all right. We risked everything, even Andrew, because of me." She ran her teeth over her bottom lip, fighting the desire to clamp down. "I'm sorry."

Joseph gripped her arm. "We did what we thought was right. Let's not regret that."

She managed a nod, and then stepped aside.

Daniel and Colonel Gansevoort moved to them.

"You were told about the raid?" the colonel asked.

"Yes, and I willingly volunteer," Joseph said. "I

am an American and shall continue to fight for our independence."

"Well spoken, but we shall see, shan't we?" Colonel Gansevoort turned to say something to Daniel.

A shout rang out.

A small troop of soldiers entered through the main gate.

Breath caught in Rachel's throat.

Andrew was in the midst of them, favoring his right leg as he limped toward her. He resembled a cat dipped in a stream, but there had never been such a handsome one. Her father's shirt clung to his chest and his hair was partly plastered to his face, partly tousled. His mouth twitched a smile as his gaze met hers.

"Isn't this the British captain?" Gansevoort demanded. "What in the world is he doing back here, and looking like that? What happened?"

One of the soldiers stepped forward, saluting. "He tried to escape into the river and—"

"I was not trying to escape, sir. I wanted to warn you."

The colonel's eyes narrowed. "About what?"

"About him." Andrew motioned in Cowden's direction. "He's a spy for the British."

"That's peculiar, seeing that is what he was trying to convict you as."

~*~

Andrew leaned forward, working his fingers through his hair. It felt mostly dry now, a testament to the hour or so he had been sitting in this room while one of Gansevoort's men interrogated him. He had not even had a chance to talk to Rachel yet. It was she with

284

whom he needed a private interview. And perhaps Joseph as well. It only seemed proper, without her father present to grant permission.

The door creaked open, and the colonel stepped in. "The men are ready to leave. What do you make of what he's been saying?"

"I honestly don't know. He seems earnest, but it is also incredible. What if he's trying to delay us for Brant's sake?"

"And how I'd love to put him out of business." Gansevoort sighed. "Cowden hasn't flinched in his story either. The man is frantic that we hurry." He looked Andrew in the eye. "Can you tell me one thing, Captain Wyndham? Why? Why would you risk your life coming back here and then turn traitor on your army and country? Why?"

"Because there are people I care for in this valley."

"The Garnets?"

Andrew nodded. "I owe them my life."

"And that is enough reason for treason?"

No, it probably wasn't, but what was he supposed to tell him? "If you do decide to send men regardless of my warning, I want to go with them."

"Why would you want that when you believe it to be a trap?"

He raked his fingers over the stubble on his jaw. "Because I wish to remain in this valley."

"Mr. Reid wasn't fighting shadows, was he? This has everything to do with Miss Garnet?"

There was no denying it. "Yes."

"Fine. We are still sending the men, though they will be on the highest alert. You may go with them." He glanced to his man. "Find Captain Wyndham a sword—but only a sword." Gansevoort gave Andrew a thin smile. "It wouldn't do to send you into a possible battle without a weapon, and I imagine you are adept at the use of that one?"

Andrew nodded.

"But if you make one wrong move, my men will have orders to shoot you where you stand. You have your chance to prove yourself. I pray you speak the truth...and yet, if you do, my men will be marching into a trap." He shook his head. "May God help us all."

37

Rachel shook her hands, restless energy needing some form of release. At least Andrew had made it here without getting his head shot off. What had he been thinking to risk his life? She glanced to the blue heavens. *Lord, was this Your doing? Please tell me it is — that this is where he's meant to be.* A hand on her shoulder pulled her attention to her brother.

"It sounds as if we'll be leaving soon." He tightened his grip. "Stay here until we return."

"But if it is a trap set by Brant...must you go with them? You know we can't trust Rodney Cowden."

"I know."

"What I don't understand is why, if he's working for the British, he would lead the mob against our home two nights ago? Could Andrew be mistaken?"

Joseph shook his head. "No, we're already certain of who we trust. If anything, Rodney was making sure no one could doubt his loyalties. Especially if he was worried about a certain British captain saying something against him. Daniel thought it strange how set Rodney was on killing Andrew, when an hour earlier he'd been trying to convince the mob that there was no need for violence against a British soldier if he was no threat."

"So he decided Andrew was a threat because he could identify him and was..." Rachel gave a tiny smile as more than the sun's warmth touched her face, "fraternizing with the locals."

A bugle horn sounded, and Joseph's head jerked up, his hand coming to his pistol.

"What is it?"

He shook his head as his hands relaxed. "Nothing. It looks as if they're calling the soldiers to mount their horses and gather. I'm just not used to our side using a bugle. It's what the British are known for, and this is the first time I've heard the Continental troops utilize it. I don't like it."

"Though, if it works..." Rachel brushed her fingers down his sleeve.

"I should mount up, as well."

"Joseph..." *How am I supposed to let you go?* She'd already lost Pa.

He pulled her into an embrace. "You take care of yourself, all right?"

"I'm supposed to tell you that. I'm safe here, while you—" She gripped his coat, remembering the feel of Pa's arms around her just before they'd marched to Oriskany. Joseph was so much like him. She hadn't realized that until recently, watching him fill Pa's boots.

"I know." He squeezed her arms and stepped to Hunter.

"Joseph, promise me you'll come back."

He glanced at her and sighed. "You know I can't do that."

Daniel reined his horse beside Joseph's. He pulled his hat off, and looked down at it. "Rachel." He took a breath. "I wanted to say again, one last time, how sorry I am for everything. I hope someday you'll forgive me."

Her gaze darted between him and her brother. Why did everybody talk as though they wouldn't return? If they were so certain it was suicide, why would they go?

"Are your men assembled?" Colonel Gansevoort's voice spun her in that direction.

Andrew stood beside him wearing a clean brown coat and a tricorn hat. He fastened a scabbard around his waist as his gaze rested on her.

"Get Captain Wyndham a horse."

A horse? Rachel weaved her way around the gathering men and animals. "I don't understand. You're going too?"

Andrew tightened the leather tie and straightened his coat as he stepped to her. "I am."

"But you just told everyone it must be one of Brant's ruses. Why would you go?"

He glanced past her. "For the same reason Joseph is." His hand found hers.

"I still don't understand."

He slid the back of his forefinger along her jaw. "Yes, you do."

"Captain Wyndham?" A soldier approached and Andrew turned. "Your horse."

He took the bay's reins. "Thank you."

"Please be careful." Rachel's chest hurt as he gave her a half smile and moved to mount. "Andrew?"

He glanced back, his expression tender, his gaze moving from her eyes to her mouth and back again.

"Captain Wyndham."

Rachel wasn't certain who called, and it didn't matter. How could she let him go again, not knowing if she would see him again, and with his kiss—his almost kisses—burning in her mind. "Wait." Andrew looked down as she rushed to his side. Pushing his boot out of the stirrup, she replaced it with her own, grabbed the pommel and leaned into the horse to pull herself up. Half sitting in the saddle in front of him she touched his face. "I love you, Andrew Wyndham. Never doubt th..."

The warmth of his lips silenced her. She closed her eyes as the horse shifted under them. His mouth drew her in, his arm strong around her. His taste, the cascade of scents, the coarse brush of whiskers on her chin—everything intoxicating.

"I love you." Rachel sank back to the ground.

"And I you," he murmured in return, his voice a low rumble.

"Come back to me." She released his hand.

"God willing." He backed the horse several steps. "We have to trust Him." Andrew directed his horse to join the other men, an officer riding beside him.

Joseph also made his way to them.

Rodney Cowden rode near the front of the company, possibly leading them to their deaths.

Help me trust, Lord.

And yet, as the large gates of the fort closed in their wake, fear settled into Rachel's center. What if the Lord stepped aside again as He did on the day Pa was killed? Over half of the Continental force had been massacred because they had walked into an ambush.

~*~

A little over one hundred men with a half dozen of them on horses—almost twice the number Colonel Gansevoort had originally planned to send. Would it be enough?

Cowden rode at the front of the column, the lieutenant keeping pace at his side. They definitely weren't letting him out of sight.

Riding four abreast as much as the trail would allow for it, Andrew was in the second to last row, with the infantry bringing up the rear. Joseph rode on his left with Daniel, while a sergeant hugged his right. They weren't giving the British captain any room for deviance, either.

But he could hardly fault them for that. *Lord, help me prove myself.* Andrew glanced to the heavens. Everything was so close to falling into place, giving him everything he wanted. Rachel. The sensation of her lips lingered on his. No matter what the future brought, that moment would always be perfect in his mind.

"Whoa!"

Andrew's head snapped up at the cry. His horse sidestepped and came to a halt along with the others.

Cowden's mount tossed its head as it spun. One rein pulled tight as the other hung loosely in the man's hand. Broken. Cowden maneuvered the animal to the side and swung from the saddle, muttering under his breath.

The lieutenant sent a glance between Cowden and Andrew, as though questioning who to trust and what to do to expedite their mission. "Sergeant Tremain, continue on with the infantry, we'll follow."

The sergeant gave a salute and a tentative nod before twisting in his saddle to call out the command. The riders moved aside as they watched the men march past.

"What's going on, Cowden?" the lieutenant demanded, pulling his horse alongside. "We're only two miles or so from the settlement."

"This leather's old." Cowden grabbed for the bridle.

"If this is a ploy..."

"If you're so upset, why don't you find me something to fix it?" Cowden swore as he untied the short stub of leather from the bridle and tossed it aside. Then he drew a knife and began whittling away at the length of rein.

The last of the infantry passed.

The lieutenant cursed. "This is the last place we need to get separated. Madison," he barked at a lower officer. "You watch things here and catch up as soon as you can. We'll hold up on the other side of the creek if you haven't caught up to us by then." The lieutenant spurred his horse toward the troops as they vanished behind the thick brush.

The creek? Andrew swallowed, his throat dry. Hadn't he drunk enough river water today? Not sufficient to wash away the returning memories of the Continental soldiers and militia filling the bottom of a ravine with their blood as the Tories and Iroquois swarmed the ridges. It had been a successful massacre. Why wouldn't Brant repeat?

"Joseph, you have to stop them."

"Stop who?"

"The creek bed. What kind of terrain is it? Anything like Oriskany?"

All color drained from the Joseph's face. "You think...?"

"This would be the ideal place to withdraw if you knew what was coming." They all spun to Cowden as he vanished into the dense woods.

His horse stared after him.

Madison swore, firing his pistol. The shot echoed just north of them, once, then again, and again, and again, a rippling affect growing in force and volume.

It was already too late to warn the others.

38

A low rumble of thunder sounded in the north.

Rachel raised her gaze to the treed horizon and the dark haze stretching into the clear sky.

Neither were a sign of a storm—at least not a natural one. The battle had begun.

"Lord, please protect them." Rachel hugged herself, her head bowing. "Bring them home." Dread choked her. It was too much to sit here and wait, trusting everything she loved to an abstract Being. How could they expect that of her? How could she expect anything from God when He obviously put little thought into her happiness? *He loves us more than a moment of happiness. He is trying to build us. But it is not all trial.*

Wasn't it? Carving a life out of this wilderness, illness stealing Mama, the British killing Pa, their neighbors and friends destroying everything they'd worked so hard for. Would she now lose Joseph too? And Andrew...again?

The Lord gives us joy as well. Oh, the intensity and the love in his eyes as he'd said those words. And how could she argue? She had tasted joy. Moments of peace amid the storms of life. That break in reality when everything stopped for a kind word, a hearty laugh, a tender kiss...enough happiness to hold onto during the trials of faith.

God had given her that. He had brought Andrew back, and perhaps He would again.

She had to trust.

And if not?

Rachel raised her eyes to the skies, past the smoke and the fears that threatened to bury her.

~*~

Madison stared at the curve in the trail where their infantry had disappeared. Sweat beaded on his forehead as he sputtered. "We must hurry. They'll be massacred." He encouraged his horse back onto the train, his hand fumbling with his pistol.

Andrew kicked his own mount into action, cutting the officer off.

"Get out of the way." Madison jerked his reins to maneuver around him.

"If you take this road, you will ride straight into the heaviest force of Brant's men. The retreat is where they will swarm. But if we cut through the woods, we can open the gap where they are more spread out, and call our men through."

Madison hesitated, and then nodded. "All right." He raised his pistol. "Let's go."

Eleven riders remained. They crossed the road and pushed through the brush into the forest, tramping the underbrush and dodging larger branches. Maneuvering around several half rotted logs, the small band sped their horses toward the battle.

Madison fired his weapon first, and a Mohawk warrior fell from his perch on the ridge.

Several of the soldiers swung from their horses, charging the other Indians with their swords.

The battle in the creek bed remained unaffected. A glimpse through the thinning foliage revealed the infantry still on the trail, standing back to back as they fought the onslaught of both ball and arrow. Uniformed bodies already littered the ground, with more falling every second. There had to be a way to slow the attack, to confuse Joseph Brant's warriors.

Andrew twisted and thrust his hand out to the soldier with the bugle horn fastened to his saddle. "Hurry and give that to me." He motioned to the instrument. "Your turkey call was fine for the fort, but let us see what damage some good, old British fox hunt reveille will do."

The soldier had the ties barely loosened when Andrew snatched the instrument and spun his horse deeper into the woods. The landscape sloped toward a gargling stream. He sucked air into his lungs. Now charging away from the gap forming in Brant's lines, he sounded the most triumphant tune that came to mind. It had been played more than once after the British had trounced the Continental Army, and likely Brant and his men had heard it, as well.

As soon as he had reached the other side of the stream, Andrew switched tunes to one often used to signal retreat. Hopefully, they were familiar with that one. And also with the fact that the Continental Army disliked the call of the bugle horn. It was the British's instrument, and at the fort was the first time Andrew had heard the Americans employing it. Any hesitation on the part of the Mohawks could save lives.

Aware of motion to his left, Andrew directed his horse farther from the ongoing battle, never halting the call of mournful retreat. As the road came into view, he nudged the animal with his heels, racing it over the open length. A branch tore at his sleeve as he plunged back into the cover of the forest. Halfway to the other side of the stream, Andrew slowed his gait and withdrew the bugle horn from his numb lips.

The battle seemed to be shifting toward the south where the Continental soldiers had breached the lines.

The sound of the assault was still heard, but strangely detached from the calmness enveloping the immediate area. Perhaps the attack was failing after all, the Mohawk's' upper hand crumbling like the walls of Jericho to the sound of a trumpet.

Andrew glanced to the fragments of darkening blue showing through the spread of branches. The sun slipped toward the western hills. Dusk was upon them. "Lord..." The deep rumble of his voice echoed in his ears. He was alone. And yet...not alone.

An army of Mohawk Indians were hidden in this forest. They had once been his allies, but today had changed everything. He had followed his instinct—his heart—and dove into the river. What would tomorrow bring? Would it even come? It hardly seemed to matter. God was with him. Surrounding him and filling him.

A shot rang out.

He glanced to the road but saw nothing. Encouraging his horse to quicken its pace, he again began to work his way down the steep slope. The hair prickled on the back of his neck as the animal leapt through the stream. He gripped the bugle horn. If only he had a pistol instead. Was someone watching? He searched the foliage surrounding him. Nothing. Searing pain tore through his body, flinging him from the saddle. His chest seemed to explode as he struck the uneven ground and a moss covered log.

The horse bolted away and Andrew stared after it, his brain only now registering the crack of a discharging pistol. Fire ignited in his shoulder as wet warmth spread out, leaking down his chest and arm. *God, no! Not again. I have to return to Rachel. Please...do not let me die here.* He clutched the wound, trying to dam the blood stealing away with his strength.

"Why won't you just die?" Cowden stepped from behind two embracing aspens. His pistol, smoke wafting from the barrel, dropped as he drew his sword. "I knew you would ruin everything. I knew it." He circled nearer.

Andrew grabbed for his own sword, his fingers soaked in his own blood as they gripped the hilt and drew the weapon. He scrambled to stand.

Cowden lunged at him with a yell.

He blocked the first strike, but stumbled back on the log. His hand shook, the pain almost disarming him. His skill with the sword greatly exceeded the other man's, but what use was years of training and instruction when there was no strength to even hold it?

One more maneuver and Cowden flung the sword from his hand. Cowden tipped his blade, his stained teeth showing as he leered. "Now to finish off what that rope failed to accomplish."

Andrew sank to the soft ground. It was strangely warm and inviting, wrapping itself around him. Peace spread through his chest, countering the agony. Maybe death was not such a horrible thing. To return to his God. His vision blurred and darkened. A musket firing mingled with the rush of blood in his ears. A moment later someone grabbed him.

"No, God."

He knew that voice. Andrew tried to focus on the

man bracing him up. Daniel Reid? What was he doing here? Where was Cowden?

"Sit still." Daniel pressed something over the wound. "We have to get you to the Fort."

Andrew tried to nod. He had to make it back for Rachel's sake. Instead his head flopped forward, his vision fleeing with the pain.

39

The shadows lengthened across the valley and embraced the fort. Darkness.

"Miss Garnet, why don't you come inside?" Gansevoort made his way to her. "They might not make it back until tomorrow. You can't stand out here all night."

"I know." She pressed her hands over her face, covering a yawn.

"Come inside and eat something. We'll find some place for you to sleep."

"Thank you. I don't think I could eat anything. Not tonight."

He nodded and moved away.

She followed, but slower. *Lord, please keep them safe, but if not...* "God, give me strength."

Rachel sat for a long time near the fire as she prayed. Later she was led to a small room above the office with a cot piled with blankets. She buried herself under the covers to ward off the chill resonating from her center. "God, give me sufficient strength," she mumbled over and over, hour after hour. "Bring them back to me." She had finally begun to doze when a shout pulled her upright and to the tiny window.

Torches and lanterns lit the compound as men and horses seeped through the gates.

"Andrew."

Rachel ran down the stairs, her mind still fuzzy. Near the gate, she searched the ones making their way past.

Many of the soldiers carried or supported a wounded comrade. Still their numbers lacked. Hardly a horse was mounted, corpses draped over the saddles. One animal carried three of their fallen, but all wore uniforms. Where were Joseph and Andrew?

"I'm sorry, miss," an officer said as he passed by.

She spun, grabbing his sleeve. "What do you mean? Where is my brother and Captain Wyndham?"

"Rest assured your brother is fine, only winged. He wasn't far behind. And your captain..." The man glanced away, his head shaking. "He probably saved the lives of most of these men." He turned. "I have to report."

Rachel's pulse drowned out the soldiers surrounding her.

Shadows appeared as two more horses emerged through the gate. Joseph rode Hunter, swaying with each step of the animal. He clasped his left arm. Beside him, Daniel led a second animal, a body draped over its back.

"Andrew?" Dirt and blood matted his reddish-brown locks, with dark streaks trailing down his neck and face. *How could you do this to us, Lord*? Her fingers brushed his cheek as she sank to the ground. "God, give me strength..." *I can't bear this on my own*. Only his left arm dangled above his head, and she reached for his hand.

Daniel set a hand on her shoulder, his touch hesitant. "I checked him just before we came in. He's not dead. At least, not yet. I honestly don't know if he'll even make it another hour, never mind the night."

His head bowed. "I'm sorry."

Rachel stared, her mind churning as hope pressed against her chest. "But he could. If the Lord has kept him alive this long, perhaps He will give us another miracle."

Joseph came beside her. "We can only hope." He followed her gaze as it moved to his arm, wrapped in a strip of crimson saturated cloth above his elbow. "Caught a Mohawk arrow, but don't worry about it. I'm fine. We need to get Andrew inside and find a physician for him."

"I have already seen to that." Gansevoort's voice startled Rachel. He looked grim. "I gave orders for Captain Wyndham to be seen to right away. I was told what he did, and the effect it had on Brant's men. I figure we owe him now."

"Thank you," Rachel said.

What had he done?

Joseph stood beside her, holding his wounded arm as Daniel and one of the soldiers dragged Andrew from the horse. They carried him to the room the colonel had designated. Fresh scarlet showed on the wadded cloth strapped over his wound.

As soon as they laid him out on the cot, she dropped to his side, pushing his hair away from his ash-white face.

His breathing was shallow, almost undetectable.

Panic clawed at her insides. "Where is that surgeon?"

"I'm right here." A man hurried through the door, pushing past Joseph and Daniel. "We need clean bandaging and boiling water." He glanced at Rachel. "Please see to that."

"Of course." The words were scraped from her

lungs as she forced herself away from Andrew.

~*~

Hours later, seated on a low stool beside Andrew's cot, Rachel set her head on the pillow, nestling it against Andrew's head. Her hand rested over his heart, its weak, though constant beat, and the slight rise and fall of his chest making it possible for her to close her eyes and rest. "You insane, wonderful man."

She'd been told that when the Iroquois had first heard his British reveille, the assault had eased, everyone looking for a British advance. When a retreat had sounded instead, and on the other side of the creek, no less, Brant and his men faltered, giving the Continental soldiers time to retreat through the gap opening on the rise, and to form a strong offensive. With evening approaching, Brant and his warriors soon withdrew. The Continental Army had sustained a blow, with eight men killed and twenty-three wounded, but how much worse would it have been?

"Please don't leave me again. It feels as though I've lost you so many times already, I don't know how I'd survive another goodbye." She ran a finger along his hairline. "Don't worry. No matter what happens, I won't turn from God this time. I could not bear to. It would be like giving up all I have left of you." Rachel slid her hand under the blanket. His skin was warmer that it had been, but not feverish. A good sign. "I need you both so dearly." She pressed a kiss to his cheek, and then leaned back down. "I love you, Andrew Wyndham."

~*~

The darkness surrounded him, drowning him, pulling him away from the sound of her voice. Andrew fought for breath, suffocating. Why was it so painful? What had happened to him? Her words faded now, but her scent lingered. Something brushed his jaw, pressing near the corner of his mouth.

"I love you."

Rachel? Why was it so hard to focus? Why did he feel as though he were slipping away from her? Was he...? His thoughts froze on the realization. He was dying. Andrew fought the haze. He couldn't let it take him yet. *Lord, give her strength to accept Thy will. Help her stay near Thee, please. That is all I ask. I only wish I could stay here for her when she needs me most.* Focused on his breath, he deepened it despite the stabbing agony invoked. Anything to prolong his time. If only he had enough to say goodbye. *I do not want to say goodbye, Lord. Not to her—not ever again.* Were those his eyes that burned with unshed moisture? If he was capable of tears, perhaps he could force his lids open. To see her one last time. A flickering light met his attempts. He blinked back the clinging mists and willed his head to turn. Barely, but enough to make out the side of her face, so close to his own.

Her hair lay across the pillow, strands of gold and honey escaping a braid. What would it have been like to wake every morning to this vision and her nearness?

God, I do not want to die. He was forced to close his eyes, but refused to end his pleas. Not while his heart still beat. *I do not know what Thy will is for me. Perhaps it is my time to kneel before Thee, and if it be so, I shall accept that, but until I know—until Thou takest me—I plan to stay alive. I shall live each second Thou givest me for her, and to*

304

glorify Thee. Lord, give me whatever time Thou canst. Each beat of his heart, and each breath, Andrew counted, willing it to be stronger and deeper. Finally, though, what strength he had seeped away, and darkness again swept him into oblivion.

~*~

Rachel pressed her palms into her eyes, sore from days without more than an hour or two of broken sleep. She sat at Andrew's side, hour after hour without any sure sign that he would recover. His breathing deepened and his pulse seemed more regular, but she needed the confidence that he would be there, still alive, when she awoke. Leaning forward on the stool, Rachel brushed her hand over the bristly stubble on his jaw. Every day it grew longer, forming the beard he so disliked. A smile pulled at the corner of her mouth. "If you would only wake up, I would shave it for you." She pressed her lips to his forehead. "Wake up and I will do anything for you. Anything at all."

"Anything?" The hoarse rumble came from his throat.

"Andrew?"

His eyes were a dull shade of green hazel, but held a depth she'd not seen before. "You did not answer..." Andrew coughed, burying his mouth with his good arm, and wincing as he did so. When he drew it away, he attempted a smile. "My question."

She blinked, her mind refusing to focus on anything but him. "What?"

"Anything...for me?"

She bit her lips together, nodding.

"Be my wife?"

A giggle and a sob mingled. "Of course."

His eyes closed as he struggled to regulate his breath. "Good," he mumbled. "Very good."

Her heart ached to see him in so much pain again. Memories of the last time he'd balanced between life and death only made it worse. "I have a stipulation, though."

He squinted up at her. "A...stipulation?"

"Promise me you'll never get shot again."

A chuckle forced his eyes closed and deepened the lines on his face with pain. "I shall...make it a priority."

40

"What are you doing out here?" Rachel pointed back toward the cabin. "You need to be resting."

"And miss this?" Andrew raised a brow. "No, I shall be fine. Besides, if I did not evict myself from there immediately, I risked losing any sanity I am still in possession of. I am so weary of being entombed between those four walls."

Rachel shook her head at him then turned to the harnesses draped over Hunter's back. She fastened one strap before glancing at Andrew again. "Can you at least find a seat somewhere, so you aren't overexerting yourself?"

"How about on the stump? I imagine it would make for an exciting ride." He flashed her a smile that she met with a glare. "No? All right." He moved to the edge of the garden and lowered himself down on a large stone, ignoring the skiff of snow. The late October sun was quickly melting the thin white blanket they had woken to that morning.

Rachel returned her attention to the harnesses, finishing as Joseph brought Sorrowful alongside. His arm was still bandaged, but the wound hardly more than an irritant. "We really should wait until next spring," she said as he fastened the straps between the two animals. "We need to be splitting logs for the barn."

"We can do that after. This won't take long."

"Maybe, but—"

He tossed a thick coil of rope to her.

She scrambled to catch it all.

"Why don't you start securing that to the stump?"

Rachel looked to Andrew as she moved over the lumpy soil. At least he was behaving. A little over two weeks was hardly enough time to mend the hole in his shoulder or recover from the volume of blood lost. His color was starting to return, but he tired easily and was unable to hide the pain if he was up too long.

What a strange start to a marriage.

She smiled as she wrapped the rope around the base of the stump. With no clergy in the area, Colonel Gansevoort volunteered his services, and they had accepted. It was the only way Andrew would let her see to all his needs and nurse him back to health. He had no qualms with his wife seeing him in his shirtsleeves…or without them altogether.

"Are you ready there?" Joseph backed the horses toward her.

"Almost." Rachel tied the knot, and then took the loose end to her brother. "Here." Moving beside the horses' heads, she held them in place.

Joseph finished securing the rope. "All right." He stepped out of the way. "Let's move them forward."

The next hour was spent playing tug-of-war with the four inch tap root she hadn't been able to reach. Once the horses had the stump almost on its side, Joseph slipped into the hole, getting the ax under. The root snapped abruptly and the horses jerked forward, almost dragging Rachel off her feet.

"You all right?" Joseph leapt out of the hole, running to them.

"Fine," she panted. Rachel looked back at the stump and all the short appendages. It was done. It was over.

"Here." He took the horses' leads. "I'll haul this over to the edge of the woods to age."

Rachel walked to the crater. Almost three months of digging, hacking, sweating and crying, and now it was finished. *We did it, Papa. But I still wish you were here.* She closed her eyes as an arm slipped around her shoulders.

Andrew laid a kiss on her head.

"Thank you," she whispered.

"For what?"

She smiled, leaning her head into him. The list was too extensive—he had given her so much.

The whinny of a horse on the road pulled their gazes to where Daniel reined his mare into the yard. Halfway to them, he paused. Fannie slipped off from behind him, making a beeline to Joseph.

"I see you finally got that beast out," Daniel said, coming the rest of the way. He nodded toward Andrew. "I'm surprised to see you out and about."

"It was either that or take up needlework, and my arm is not quite up for that yet." His smile faded. "I have not had the opportunity to thank you for what you did. You saved my life, and I am grateful."

Daniel shrugged it off. "I figured I owed you after getting you hung."

Andrew chuckled. "There is that."

"And I'm responsible for the barn as well." Daniel looked at Rachel. "I'm sorry."

She shook her head. "Daniel—"

He held up his hand, stopping her as he dropped to the ground. "I want you to have the Becker homestead. It'll give you a place to keep your livestock this winter. I also talked to a few of the neighbors about seeing you have enough feed to last you to spring. They're already filling the loft."

Rachel stared at him, remembering his earlier excitement over the property. "You can't do that. You've spent too much time and work on owning that place. You've already done enough."

Daniel's gaze lowered to the thick leather reins laced between his fingers. "It won't do me any good now. I'm leaving the valley before winter sets in. I'm going to Albany to enlist."

"In the army?"

He nodded. "Besides, it's the least I can do for Fannie. Until the two of you are out of the way and Joseph has to fend for himself in the kitchen, she'll be waiting on that man indefinitely. This should force his hand a little."

The two in question stood with arms brushing as Joseph unfastened the rope from the stump.

"It is probably the perfect timing for that."

"Good." Daniel swung back into his saddle. "It's settled. I'll let Joseph see Fannie home. Just be sure to tell him everything first," he said with a wink, and then turned somber again, his eyes sad. "I do wish you both a very happy life."

"And you." Rachel sighed as he rode away. Hopefully someday Daniel would find every joy the Lord had given her. Someday he'd fall in love with someone else. She turned to Andrew, meeting his thoughtful gaze.

"I guess that answers that question," he stated.

"What question?"

He smiled. "Where we shall build a church, of

course."

"A church?"

"I keep hearing how much this valley needs a clergyman. That would be easy enough to remedy."

"I guess it would. And you will have everything you wanted."

"I shall. A country parish and a wife I can abide." Andrew squeezed her shoulder.

"I'm glad you can abide me, Mr. Wyndham."

He pressed his mouth to her hairline for a long moment. "As am I, my love." Andrew bent down to kiss her, but she slipped her fingers to his lips.

"Not until you are in the cabin where you belong. You've already done too much today."

He grinned, his green eyes teasing. "I thought I was just getting started."

"I'm sorry." Rachel gave him a quick kiss. "But I love you too much to allow you to hurt your shoulder any more than you already have."

Andrew wrapped her in his good arm, drawing her into him. "Then I shall have to proceed with the utmost care."

Thank you

We appreciate you reading this White Rose Publishing title. For other inspirational stories, please visit our on-line bookstore at www.pelicanbookgroup.com.

For questions or more information, contact us at customer@pelicanbookgroup.com.

White Rose Publishing
Where Faith is the Cornerstone of Love™
an imprint of Pelican Book Group
www.PelicanBookGroup.com

Connect with Us
www.facebook.com/Pelicanbookgroup
www.twitter.com/pelicanbookgrp

To receive news and specials, subscribe to our bulletin
http://pelink.us/bulletin

May God's glory shine through
this inspirational work of fiction.

AMDG

Coming Soon

Don't miss the next book in the Hearts at War series

THE PATRIOT AND THE LOYALIST
Coming April 2017

Completing his three years in the Continental Army, Daniel Reid still has no desire to return home—not after losing the woman he loves to a British Captain—so he volunteers to ride south through enemy lines and deliver a message to Colonel Francis Marion, the Swamp Fox. With his temper needing a release and a dark haired beauty finding her way into his broken heart, Daniel decides to join the Swamp Fox's efforts against the British. Little does he know the British still have the upper hand.

Lydia Reynolds has learned that love comes at a price, and she refuses to pay. Better to close her heart to everything and everyone. When her brother-in-law won't grant her passage to England, where she hopes to hide from her pain, New Englander, Daniel Reid, becomes her only hope—if she can induce him to give her information about the notorious Swamp Fox and his troops. When the British grow impatient and Daniel evades her questions, Lydia must decide how far to take her charade. The poor man, already gutted by love, hasn't grown as wise as she. Or so she supposes…

Until the truth is known, the muskets are loaded…and it is time to decide where true loyalties lie.

God Can Help!

Are you in need? The Almighty can do great things for you. Holy is His Name! He has mercy in every generation. He can lift up the lowly and accomplish all things. Reach out today.

Do not fear: I am with you; do not be anxious: I am your God. I will strengthen you, I will help you, I will uphold you with My victorious right hand.
~Isaiah 41:10 (NAB)

We pray daily, and we especially pray for everyone connected to Pelican Book Group—that includes you! If you have a specific need, we welcome the opportunity to pray for you. Share your needs or praise reports at http://pelink.us/pray4us